Copyright © 2025 Philip Parrish

All rights reserved

The characters and events portrayed in this book are fictitious. Any similarity to real persons, living or dead, is coincidental and not intended by the author.

No part of this book may be reproduced, or stored in a retrieval system, or transmitted in any form or by any means, electronic, mechanical, photocopying, recording, or otherwise, without express permission of the publisher.

ISBN: 9798282370553
Independently published

Cover design: Ian Feeney
Cover image: Login / Shutterstock

philip-parrish.com

By the same author

Game of Life
The Bleeding Horizon

Exiles Incorporated

Twelve stories by

Philip Parrish

*To my wife Hollie, for all those sacred spaces
we've shared on our journey through life*

We shall not cease from exploration
And the end of all our exploring
Will be to arrive where we started
And know the place for the first time.

TS Eliot, *Little Gidding*

Contents

Uluru	1
Athena	18
Nazca	42
Joyeuse	61
Amrita	82
Rumi	103
Janeiro	117
Genjo	137
Attu	159
Loki	177
Angelo	201
Mundi	227
Acknowledgments	259

Uluru

"Don't leave me, mama."

Spirit burrowed deeper into her guardian's bosom. She craved closeness, but Air, Wind, Fire and Mother Earth wanted to bury her in the wilderness. She was only a shared dream to them. An unfathomable weight slowing their advance. *Let the ground swallow her*.

"I'm scared, mama," she shivered. "Scared I won't find my way back..."

Home. A realm of dark fog. She didn't know what she was or where she came from. Only that she'd woken misshapen in the four elements' minds. She'd not arrived alone. Voices followed. Rattling cries underground only she could hear. *Let me out. Let me out. Let me out.*

Air, Wind, Fire and Mother Earth accelerated into the void. The golden orb above had summoned the four elements to carve a new world with their thoughts. This was dreamtime, explained Mother Earth. First to flow from their minds was a dry, blood-orange plain. The second, a suffocating roof of endless blue. Why the elements created was a mystery to them.

Spirit was a mystery too. Too inanimate to challenge; too unsettling to ignore. A lone thing lodged in their consciousness. When the time was right, they would feed her to the parched plains. Until then, Mother Earth absorbed the gentle questions dripping from the child's mind.

"What am I mama?"

"I'm not sure, little one. We don't know yet."

"When will we know?"

"Soon. Our dreams will tell us where you belong."

"What's a dream, mama?"

"It's what brings this world into existence."

"Will I ever dream?"

"We don't know. Just be still, little one. Just be still."

Spirit watched as Air, Wind, Fire and Mother Earth spawned the landscape, slowing to stillness then sleep. In dreams they convulsed and contracted, bleeding together. Fusion culminated in a splintering screech and the grinding of invisible jaws. *Krrrraccck. Chuggachug. Krrrraccck. Chuggachug. Krrrraccck. Chuggachug.* Spirit thought space itself would shatter.

Each time one element was most powerful, their primacy signalled by a spasm of colour. Air's white vapour. Fire's reddish smoke. Water's blue swirls. Mother Earth's hazy green. Ripples of energy surged and subsided with a boom and a crackle. Droplets of light spurted upwards then softly descended.

There were two kinds of droplets. Sleepers and dreamers. Sleepers hovered with uncertainty, then evaporated. *Pfffffftishhh. Pfffffftishhh. Pfffffftishhh.* Dreamers flourished, swelling into material form, flecking the void with silver-grey streaks, brownish-green smears and fluffy patches of white ascending to blue. *Plink. Plink. Plink.* Rivers. Trees. Plants. Rocks. Jagged, beautiful, solitary rocks. Spirit loved those most. She did not change, so was neither sleeper nor dreamer. Not real or unreal. Somewhere in between.

While Air, Wind, Fire and Mother Earth woke from dreamtime and sped into the dark, Spirit drew patterns between the rocks in their wake. The fragments changed colour in the sunlight, from orange to red to pink to brown to amber to yellow. *Plink. Plink. Plink.* Once part of something, now alone. Spirit wished a huge rock would reunite them all one day.

Rumbling persisted. *Let me out. Let me out. Let me out.* Sleepers, perhaps. Neglected droplets existing briefly in showers of light before dissolving. Soon Spirit would join them in the ground, wherever the four elements chose to bury her. Their only passenger, abandoned to drown in the dusty sea.

In quieter moments, Spirit looked to the light in the sky to discern a grander purpose. When the sun's sparkles hung in black, its orb displaced by a ghostly grey disc, she pictured its rays streaming somewhere faraway. Where someone like her was buried in the wilderness, drawing comfort from shattered patterns of discarded matter. *Let me out. Let me out. Let me out.*

"There's something underneath, mama."

"What do you mean?"

"Something crying."

"What does it say?"

"Let me out."

"Just be still, little one. Just be still."

Spirit couldn't move, anyway. She was an ungainly lump of heaviness. *You're beautiful*, Mother Earth once whispered. Perhaps mama was talking about the inside, not the outside. Spirit noticed the difference. During the day, the elements hurtled forwards. In the stagnant dark, their inner worlds moved even faster, expressed in hurried gasps. *No. No. No. No. No.* They feared what lay ahead, no matter the flurry of wonder they created. Soon they would be gone. Every time they dreamt something, the paler they grew.

Air was a blanched mass of heaving and blasting. His swirls and surges cleaved the canvas into which the other three elements flowed. Words broke in frenetic gusts, hinting at something momentous to come. Air's dreamers were visible only in traces and trails of chaotic patterns. He spread everywhere, neither beginning nor ending.

Water was stranger. Soothing and gentle, dead-eyed and dank. A fluidity that rushed from whisper to roar. Her dreamers brooded on the ground, coalescing into patches of grey liquid from which brownish-green tentacles wafted in the residual breeze of Air's demented charge.

Fire raged at the light in the sky, his surly red eyes downcast to the desert, angered by how far they'd come and how far they'd left to go. He threatened to scorch the world, until an encircling Water quietened him to a simmer. His dreamers were embers of gold, spewing and singeing.

None of the quartet were affectionate for what they created. They were passive portals through which nascent land passed like rays of light. Except for mama. She was Mother Earth who birthed the rocks. The only element Spirit could taste. Their shared secret was the sweetness of her nectar, trickling into Spirit while the world was smothered in black.

"Where did we come from mama?"

"We came from darkness into light."

"Can we go back and see, mama?"

"No, there is no going back. Only forward."

"Where are we going?"

"We'll see."

"Why are we here?"

"I've told you. We're here to dream the world into being."

"What does the world mean, mama?"

"I don't know. We're here to begin something we can never understand."

"What do I look like mama?"

Mother Earth paused.

"Like nothing I've ever seen before."

"Is that why you're burying me?"

"It's for the best. We must prepare for the parting."

"What's the parting?"

"It's what happens when we finish dreaming life into the new world."

"Will we part too?"

"Yes. One moment we will be here. The next we won't. Only the light in the sky will decide that. Just be still, little one. Just be still."

"No mama. Will *you and I* be parted?"

"Yes. We cannot change what we're made to be."

"I don't want to part from you. I want to follow you everywhere."

Mama breathed slow and deep. Spirit rose and fell with her. Everything broke apart, it seemed. Sky and ground. Night and day. Dreamers and sleepers. Mother and child.

"Just be still. You'll be safe in the ground. I can feel it. You were born to be something else. In a new place where you can start new dreams. New stories."

"What's a story mama?"

"A story is something that brings people together. That has a beginning and an end. Except the world is different by the time you reach the end."

The next morning, Fire wailed into the depths of space. His yellow form turned sickly pale with impatience; the heat which once warmed Spirit's core drifted over her in a feeble chill.

"This has gone too far," said Fire. "We must bury her. I want her out of my mind. She is too much for us all. This is slowing us down."

"No, we're not ready yet," said Mother Earth.

"We cannot carry her much longer," spat Fire. "No dreams. She must be a sleeper that's stuck. We bury her. Now. She's the reason we're fading."

"A sleeper?" said Air. "Or a different power. Something deeper and older."

"She hears voices below," said Mother Earth.

"Then she belongs in the ground," snapped Water. "If she is something different, she will rise. For us, this stops now. She is too heavy."

"I will not do it yet," said Mother Earth.

"She does not belong with us," pressed Fire. "She doesn't move. She doesn't dream."

"No, we must wait," said Air. "Not everything is a dreamer or a sleeper."

Dreamers and sleepers. The chosen and the abandoned. The real and the unreal. Spirit wondered what happened if you were neither. The voices in the ground were like that. Sleepers buried too quickly; their screams alternating from diffident whispers to seething tumults of pain.

Let me out. Let me out. Let me out.

That night Spirit dreamt for the first time. Borne on Mother Earth's shoulders, she travelled the new world dropping rocks from her hand. *Plink, plink, plink.* Orange, red, pink, brown, amber and yellow nuggets of dust, the sun blessing her trail with a kaleidoscope of warming shades.

Something followed. A living thing, unlike anything Spirit had seen. A beautiful creature with deep brown skin. Another lady, like Mother Earth. She was alone. Light, thin and steady, floating freely across the plains. Her elegant shape swung softly. Ribbons of black hair flailed from the head. The sun's rays glistened on her round face. Within was the lightness of Air, the depths of Water, the fury of Fire, the tenderness of Mother Earth. A special sweetness that nourished the ground wherever she walked.

Spirit journeyed deeper into the dream. Far ahead, a monumental rock rose towards the sky, defying the stale flatness. *Her rock.* A sacred place to unite the smaller stones. The rock's splendour even seduced the sun, whose streaks of light danced across the undulating surface, transforming its hue. Orange again, then red, pink, brown, amber and yellow.

When Spirit woke, tiny multi-coloured rocks clustered in her outstretched hand, powdery and warm to the touch. She tried to crush them, but their jaggedness resisted.

Pangs of pleasure rippled through her. On the ground was another, then another, snaking off into the new land left behind. Spirit searched to no avail for the beautiful creature with dark skin. She would never forget that wandering figure.

"How much do you love me mama?"

Mother Earth had not been asked a question like that before.

"Love?"

"Yes, you know what I mean."

Mother Earth softened.

"This much."

"How much?"

"This much," she said, rolling her eyes across the land and sky.

"Even though you're not my real mama."

"Even though I'm not."

"But I can dream you're my mama. So you may as well be."

"Yes. Dream whatever you like. Dreams tell you where you belong."

"What if I dream we never part?"

"Then maybe we won't."

"What if I dream I belong with – "

A screaming scorched through the ground. *Krrrraccck. Chuggachug. Krrrraccck. Chuggachug. Krrrraccck. Chuggachug.* A chorus of wails quaked from the belly of the world. *Let me out. Let me out. Let me –*

In the distance, a lump appeared on the horizon line.

"What's that mama?"

"What's what?"

"That."

Air, Water and Fire trembled. They could not see anything in the void.

"Visions," roared Fire. "She dreams."

"This is the time," hissed Water.

"What are you seeing child?" said Air.

Spirit remembered the tiny rocks slipping from her hand. One day they would not be alone. All would find their way to the mother rock.

"Home," she said. "My home."

"Your dreams have spoken," Mother Earth said. "You're about to transform. This is the parting."

"Set her down," said Air, nervously.

"No, not here," said Spirit. "Over there. I'll tell you when to stop."

A hush fell over the elements. Their shapes contracted, their depths shallowed. The quartet moved meekly in concert towards the invisible target.

"Go quickly," said Spirit. "Your dreamtime is done."

As they drew closer to the dream rock, Spirit marvelled at the gigantic orange phantom, part-apparition and part-reality. To the elements, the place was nothingness. To Spirit, it was everything.

"Here," said Spirit. "Bury me here."

Mother Earth placed Spirit down and kissed her. Amber warmth flowed into the deepest places.

"Don't leave me, mama," Spirit said. "We can still be together."

"I'll always be with you, little one. Right underneath you."

Mother Earth's tear swept sideways and downwards through space, flooding Spirit with alien tranquillity. With that, Air, Fire, Water and Mother Earth dissolved into space, leaving behind the lonely landscape they'd bleached themselves out creating.

"Don't... leave," moaned Spirit.

She longed for the beautiful deep brown creature which moved upright. The hunger within that body; a space desperate to be filled. One day, the creature would visit the dream rock carrying something special within. Like Mother Earth did. Summoning time past and time future.

"I will show you how much I love you, mama."

Deep below, the sleepers awakened. A roiling mass of energy quivered and quaked. Dust flew up. *Whuuuck. Whuuucck. Whuuucck.* Cracked ground vibrated. *Drruuthick. Drruuthick. Drruuthick.* Spirit breathed. The world breathed too, blasting fine grains of rock around her. *Thwack. Thwack. Thwack.* The air moistened. The soil swelled. The sleepers' song sounded. *Let me out. Let me out. Let me out.* All the rocks Spirit trailed in her wake rushed onto her, stinging and stabbing. Pieces of Mother Earth, hurled by Air, compacted by Fire and christened by Water amid pulsating flares of white, red, blue and green.

Space warped around the dream rock as it roared into reality. Spirit lay encased in the colossal form, its beautiful colours communing with the golden orb above. She couldn't tell where her body ended and where the formation began. The sunlight played with her. She played with the sunlight. From orange to red to pink to brown to amber to yellow. As the rock expanded, new life followed the sun's rays towards it. Plants sprouted. Animals sheltered. Birds nested. Eventually the growth stopped. *Just be still, little one. Just be still.* Spirit rested inside, breathing cool air through every pore.

You'll be safe in the ground. I can feel it. You were born to be something else. In a new place where you can start new dreams. New stories.

"Let me out."

The sun rose and fell.

"Let me out."

The land conjured more emptiness.

"Let me out."

Silence.

"Let me out."

Solitude, stretching to the end of everything.

"Let me out."

Aeons of time crept onwards.

"Let me out. Let me out. Let me –"

Closeness. The warm sweetness of someone else. Another mother. The creature with the brown skin who walked through dreamland. A lonely lady, slumbering faraway. An isolated member of a distant tribe crawling across the land. Spirit's cry rushed across the sky towards her, morphing into a dream then becoming a voice again. A kind and gentle one, melting through sun-worn flesh to nest in her soul. A dawn kiss on her soft shoulder.

"– out."

The lady slept apart from everyone else. She was a quiet soul of uncertain origin. Unable to conceive, no matter how many men tried. Squeezed to the margins for being as dry as the earth. *We cannot carry her much longer. Nothing has come from her yet.* Stringy-haired, slim-hipped, stooped of shoulder. Bedraggled. Barren. Broken by the world. Too heavy for her community.

"Who are you?"

The poking of sticks.

"What are you?"

The throwing of stones.

"You don't fit in."

The fire of tongues.

"You stick out."

The stinging of spit.

"You drag us down."

Bile, spewed by thickset angry men with furrowed brows. Encouraged by conniving women with evil eyes who plotted in shadows. She needed to create. To nurture life. To prove she could belong.

"Let me out," Spirit whispered to her.

"Who are you?" quivered the lady.

"Let me out."

"Mother?"

"Let me out."

"Mother?"

"Find me."

"Where?"

"Faraway where the sun sets. Within me are the spirits of unborn children. From there you'll become flush with life."

"They're going to leave me out here."

"Yes. They travel another way. They cannot come with you. You're on a different journey. There is something else within you."

"But this is just a dream."

"We all need dreams to awaken."

"I want to wake."

"Then wake you will. And walk. To the end of everything if you must."

"Mother? Mother?"

The lady's eyes opened. Her sleeping companions lay scattered across the plain. She wondered whether they experienced the miracle of dreams. Placing both hands on her smooth, flat belly, she imagined life growing under this thirsting flesh. A thumping heaviness soothing an aching emptiness. She left the tribe that evening, turning towards the orange sun as it bled behind the horizon.

Walk. To the end of everything if you must. Her mother's voice had travelled across this lonely territory. So could she. In the sweltering days and icy nights ahead, she pressed on, her skin soaking up the blistering heat. A slim dark figure dressed in rags with only a spear and a sack carrying water and food. She sipped and nibbled on her supplies. Richer sustenance lay ahead. Her light footsteps pattered across the plain, leaving no footprints.

She remembered as a child playing with pebbles in the dirt, throwing them in the air to see if they landed in patterns. Her last memory of mama. Still, lying on her back. Not breathing. Not moving. She clambered on her chest and pushed her fingers between the cold, closed lips. Only the rising and falling of the sun offered companionship, until a wandering member of another tribe brought her into the fold. Neither fully accepted nor fully apart. A life of fragments.

She walked and walked. To preserve water and food, she sucked pebbles to stave off growling appetite. *Don't leave me*, she whispered to the earth every night. She said it during daylight too, when the sun's rays threatened to peel the flesh from her body. *Let me out*, said a voice. *Let me out. Let me out. Let me out.* A trail of rocks stretched across the baking furnace. Through the stinging tears and desperate breaths. Orange to red to pink to brown to amber to yellow. Each one a restorative drop of fluid guiding her beyond the blurring heatwaves. *Plink. Plink. Plink.*

After countless sunsets, the rock rose into view. A speck. A lump. A hill. A mountain. A gigantic swelling in the ground. *The spirit of unborn children. Flush with spirit. Flush with life.* She quickened her pace. Her footsteps began to thud. The ground crunched. Closer, closer, closer. Days and nights passed, the rock purring out to her across land. Head lifted, tears rolling and arms spreading, she ran. Dust flew. Running turned to dancing, dancing to delirium: a decompressed speck of movement in a landscape of shrivelled static.

Let me out. Let me out. Let me out. Le –

She slammed her body into the rock's surface. *Ppphhhwwwuuyyyyyackhhh*. Pushing her breasts and hips into the stone, she let the rock's warmth radiate her bones. She wanted to curl her soul around its circumference. With enough pressure, her love would wear the colossus away and ignite the dormant voices inside.

"Don't leave me this time, mama. Don't leave me."

As the sun set, she ran her hands across the stone like a greedy lover, skipping round its edges in search of an opening. A passage or cave from where the spirit of her unborn child would flow into her. Incarcerated voices reverberated. Whether they came from the rock, her heart or another place, she could not fathom. All she knew is they were growing stronger.

"Let me out," she screamed, thumping her fist against the rock until bruises rose on the edges of her hands. "Let me out. Let me out. Let me out. Let me out."

Night fell. She collapsed to her knees and rolled onto her back, one hand pressed against the rock for solace. As her fingers slid down the surface, she drifted into thick sleep. In her dreamworld, she passed into the rock, walking barefoot through a universe of black. Singing stirred. An indecipherable chanting high and low. Above, where the sun used to be, a crack of light sent shafts of blinding whiteness into the dead space. Through it leaked multi-coloured droplets of stone, floating down like teardrops. *Plink. Plink. Plink.* Delicately they soaked into her body and flooded her womb, where they swelled in chorus.

Let me out. Let me out. Let me out.

When she woke, the real world hadn't changed. The sun's ferocity remained, as did the maddening quiet. The rock's vast shadow protected her from hungry birds swarming the sky. She circulated the shape, stroking the rock with one hand and recalling her mother's stiffening flesh. The other rested on her belly.

Floating across the outback, she returned to what once was home. The breeze swished her hair; the ground's warmth buoyed her tired feet. Many moonrises later, she found the disconnected band of wanderers which used to be family. Equanimity radiated from her eyes. Men lost their composure in the gaze. Women feared her cruising stillness and the shimmering of her deep brown skin in the sunlight. Without word or hesitation, she guided the leader to a secluded spot. The last man she took, his roughness smoothed into the supplest of clays.

In the days that followed, the leader could not detach himself from his new mate. Squatting at his feet, she was lover, guardian and gatekeeper. He wilted like a parched flower in her presence. The other men and women looked on dumbstruck as a child formed in her womb. During evening feasts around firelight, the new mother told them about the magical rock faraway where she'd danced with Spirit in the wilderness, all the earth's colours twirling in her eyes. During pregnancy, the tribe kept her apart in reverence. She was an isolated figure again, swelling in the sterile landscape.

"Do not touch her," commanded the leader. "She is too sacred."

Soon the parting came. The sun blanketed the wilderness in vicious white heat. The new mother lay unsheltered on her back. Her skin was swathed with sweat and her voice broke like a dying beast's. Labour pulverised her insides, draining the colour from her dark skin. Elders of the tribe crouched around in a circle. Together they chanted, arms locked and feet stamping.

A darkness fell across the new mother's mind. She could no longer feel parts of herself. In the delirium came Earth, Air, Wind and Fire. Droplets of light exploded before her eyes. Some fading, some growing. Blood trickled, flowed, then gushed. Her flesh surrendered. She was going to another place. Neither solely apart nor solely alone. Somewhere in between.

"Dance," she cried. "Dance. To the end of everything if you must."

In an explosion of pain, new life emerged between her legs. A baby girl one moment. A rock the next. Changing shape and colour in the searing light. The elders held it aloft towards the sun, howling in triumph. A tender squeal underneath the din. A child. A face she would never see. A voice she would never hear again.

"Don't leave me, mama. Don't leave."

In her dying breath the new mother uttered her final word. The sound faded as it flowed through her mouth, like Air, Wind, Fire and Mother Earth had once turned ghostly pale with exhaustion.

"Uluru."

The leader fell to his knees and screamed. He scratched the soil with his fingernails and rammed his head into the ground, demanding answers from the unforgiving rock.

"Don't leave me, please don't leave me," he wailed, wishing the sun would boil everything in its destructive light. The only reciprocal noise was the meekest of moans, brewing somewhere faraway in the deep.

The community burned the new mother's body to dust, watching her corpse's smoke race into the clouds. Her essence had already departed, floating to the magical rock above the indifference of the desert.

"Dance," the leader declared. "To the end of everything if we must."

The next day, they packed their belongings. A gruelling trek of many sunsets followed, breaking the strongest of bodies and elevating the lightest of souls. Joy erupted when they saw the speck on the horizon. A mound. A hill. A mountain. Named in honour of the spirited human who first touched its surface.

Uluru.

Upon reaching the mother rock, many wept. Their new home. A place rendered sacred by story. The tale of how the spirit of an unborn child trapped within the rock had possessed the new mother. A dream turning a rock into a child into a woman into a family into a people.

The community venerated the new mother's baby, the first in a long line of dazzling jewels. In womanhood, she circulated Uluru, retracing the steps of her mother. Later her children danced its circumference, a playful procession to coax other unborn spirits out of darkness into light. From their hands dropped painted stones, each one representing a new life to come. *Plink. Plink. Plink.* No descendants would feel like outsiders. All would be at one with the ground beneath their feet.

Generation after generation nestled in Uluru's bosom, bewitched by the monolith's undulations and colours. Eventually nobody remembered where the name came from. Some believed Uluru meant Crying. Others that it was Big Rock. A few said it was the name of a place. Nothing more, nothing less. Briefly it was called Ayer's Rock. In a vast island christened Australia. A country alone but belonging to a grander whole. All part of Mother Earth.

I will show you how much I love you, mama. I will show you.

For the rest of Earth's time, Spirit lay within Uluru, waiting and absorbing. The people of the outback brightened, faded, and dissolved. New dreamers. New sleepers. Some lived a long time, others disappeared quickly. *Pffffffftishhh. Pffffffftishhh. Pffffffftishhh.* Minor compounds drifting like sand in the breeze or flickering like flames in the fragile dark. Scattered lonely souls on desert treks searching for companionship's warmth. Arriving at Uluru to be still. To know themselves. To wonder what was happening inside.

Spirit was the one who slowed them. Who laid a guiding trail. Who gave meaning to the wilderness. Who wanted to be close. To be held. To stir all the sleeping children within and inspire them to dream. *Let me out,* came their voices. *Let me out. Let me out. Let me out.*

High above, the golden orb in the sky listened to each soul awaken. Air, Wind, Fire and Mother Earth lowered their selves in reverence, as each new spirit formed its natural shape to journey through life's brevity. Slowly the elements embraced these earthly powers with the gentleness of a mother's love, until all four danced in harmony to the rising rhythms of the mysterious songs within.

Athena

Christos bounded through the door of his aunt's home onto the twilight street. Swishing an olive branch into the frigid air, the man of the house decapitated one, two, three Medusas with his sword of fire. Tonight, his quest for wisdom would begin. Athens would conceive a new hero from its infected slums, while nobility shrank indoors bolting the locks in their minds.

The boy twirled through the darkening labyrinth, skirting round snoring and spluttering vagrants. The late afternoon sun no longer sparkled on the luscious crop of blond hair curling around Christos's shoulders. *The most handsome eight-year-old in Athens*, his mother said before she fell ill. *Definitely the tallest. Blessed by Apollo himself. Destined to shine like the sun over our city.*

These days Christos preferred the night-time. Sunlight exposed Athens at its worst. A mazy mess of wood and marble, smeared by neglect, war and disease. The corpses piled high in the squares and alleys; swollen faces twisted to the sky. *Our city is a beacon of civilisation*, said his father, before the plague laid waste to mind and flesh. When both he and Pericles were alive.

Scorching mythical creatures as he skipped, Christos weaved past the dying and the drunk to his new tutor's home on the city's outskirts. Chilly wind nipped his ears. He pulled the hood of his brown cloak over his head, imagining he was an incognito prince rescuing a beautiful maiden. Or Thanatos himself, stalking the neighbourhood to drag the plague's victims to the Styx. Both these fantasies he'd exchange for a decent meal. Aunt Cassie never cooked.

"Nestor's house is at the very south of the city, at a forking point between two tracks leading to the city walls," she

Exiles Incorporated

had shouted through the curtain, her sickly perfumed stench wafting through the one-storey house.

He hadn't seen Cassie's face for four days. She'd retreated to her private room behind a curtain of purple and gold, tied to a wooden post from the inside and embroidered with spindly spiderweb patterns. In the evening, while Christos played Perseus in the street, he would hear a bubbling sound and see smoke rise through the hole in the room's ceiling.

"Look for a small house set off from the others," she barked. "There is an olive tree growing around it. The branches curl into the windows, like they're about to lift the roof away. Be careful Christy. Stay away from anyone who looks like they don't know any better. When you meet Nestor, show him this."

Cassie's bony hand crept underneath the curtain hem and slid a silver tetradrachm coin across the stone floor. Her flesh was unmarked by sores; she wasn't coughing either. Christos had no idea why neither of them were sick. She wasn't *that* special. Maybe he was though.

"One day you'll be as mighty as Aries," father said during the festival of Dionysus. His hand rested on his son's shoulder, as they watched a grapple between two wrestlers big enough to swallow children whole. The same reassuring hand which eventually fell limp in Christos's own.

At the agora, Christos slayed a make-believe hydra and flew a winged horse above the bodies waiting cremation. Perhaps one was Laertes, his smelly mathematics teacher. Only two days ago, Christos saw him wandering semi-naked near the Stoa Poikile like a lost child, begging for water. His wiry body was ravaged with red swellings and white lumps. So pathetic was the sight, Christos wanted to slap his old tutor.

If he'd died since, so be it. Christos never dwelled too much on people who passed away, especially teachers. This evening, he would revive his education courtesy of his new uncle. Winding his way through more dead bodies, dead ends and double backs, Christos came to the forking point. The two roads curved away from each other, ending at city walls lined with makeshift tents for those who'd retreated inside from the Spartan invaders.

Beyond was countryside. Christos recalled playing Greeks and Trojans on unsullied pastures, overpowering weaklings from the nearby village with brute force. On his father's farm, Christos learned about the world. In the city, he learned about people. At Nestor's house, he would learn about glory.

"None of that is important as knowing thyself," echoed father's voice.

Close by, an elderly peasant scrabbled in the ground with his fingerless hands, like a dog hunting for a bone. Perhaps for a trinket, dropped by a dying stranger. Or maybe he was sifting for moisture in the dust. Further away, a lady with ragged clothes slumped against a wall under a splattered patch of darkness, nursing an empty bowl. Dried blood flecked her lips and chin. Further down, a man with a grey beard sat peacefully on a stool outside a house, breathing hoarsely, his face riddled red. Soon they would be gone. Squished one by one like ants, time forgetting who they were and why they were here.

Death. A romantic mystery to Christos, ever since the day in the orchard when father told him about the heroes who sacrificed themselves on the plains of Troy. Now death was here. Not from war, but from infection, the cause of which nobody could say. Those professing to be wise were paralysed by doubt. Everyone was waiting for Athena to purify the realm.

"Will I ever see one of the Olympians, father?" he once asked.

"No, they don't get involved in human affairs anymore."

"Except when we die."

"Yes, except when we die."

Thanatos took mother and father on the same day, in the tiny wooden hut east of the Acropolis where the family had taken refuge from marauding Spartans. Skin broken and mouths contorting, his parents burned together in bed, screaming for water. *Run to your Aunt Cassie's*, was his father's final instruction to his only child. Christos let go of his swollen hand and fled into the city's bowels, snapping off a lone olive branch from a nearby tree for protection.

In the days after, Christos wondered why he never cried when his parents died. Why he was still alive. Why he was healthier than ever. Why he was never afraid. Destiny, that's what they called it. The certainty he would set sail to an Egyptian battlefield and weave his name in history's fabric like Achilles.

All the other boys his age had either died, escaped Athens or been locked indoors. They were no longer singing as a chorus, moving across the games field in army formation, or brave enough to step outside. For Christos, a new adventure was unspooling, courtesy of a stranger at the city limits and a sparkling silver coin with a picture of Athena on one side and an owl on the other.

"You've been spared by the gods for greater deeds," Cassie said, holding his hand as the flames swallowed his parents on the pyre. She was a tall, thin woman with gaunt features and sleepy brown eyes. Curly black hair flowed like a waterfall down her back. His aunt was a strange lady; fixated on luxurious clothes, strange potions and, to Christos's surprise, her nephew's education.

"You must continue your pursuit of wisdom," she said. "There is a man I know who can help. Someone to groom you into the legendary warrior you were meant to be."

Despite her warm words, Cassie treated Christos like a slave. Every morning, he trawled the streets, exchanging his aunt's money for packages of potions from grunting voices behind shutters. *Doing business*, is what Cassie called it. To relieve the tedium, Christos fancied himself as Hermes, dispatching messages for the Olympians deciding the fates of kingdoms. As he danced the city streets with winged feet, he heard despairing adults spout their theories.

"The sickness is an evil trick by the enemy overseas."

"The Spartans had poisoned the wells."

"Our leaders provoked this through greed and vanity."

"This is the gods taking their revenge."

Christos had no sympathy for talkers. He preferred doers. Athens' food and water were running out. Dead bodies, insects, rats and shit covered the city. The doctors were dying quicker than the patients. Sometimes he pretended to be King Midas, turning everything to gold with the power of his olive branch.

At dusk, and always without a thank you, Cassie's manicured hand snaffled the packages one by one into her lair. Maybe she was trying to find a cure for the plague. Yet every time Christos asked his aunt what she was doing, she never gave straight answers. Nobody had answers in Athens. The serious men who talked in the agora were gone. Sages, apparently. Useless on the battlefield, Christos thought, because you couldn't reason with a Spartan's sword. One of them recovered from the plague, boasting he could survive anything. Then his memory went. Soon he knew neither himself nor his friends, let alone the truth of life. Just another mindless wanderer, like boggy-breathed Laertes.

"You'll find wisdom with Nestor," was Cassie's last whisper from behind the curtain. "Only if you're courageous enough to look for it."

His new uncle's home was a small one-storey abode on uneven ground, dwarfed by a huge olive tree that threatened to uproot the wood and mud building. Stomach groaning and feet aching, Christos arrived at the front door. He tucked the branch into his belt, pushed his shoulders back and thumped the warped wood. After a long wait, the door creaked open slightly.

"Good evening," he shouted. "I am Christos of Athens. My aunt Cassie sent me here to find wisdom."

A shadowed man appeared in the slit between the door and the wall, silhouetted by the yellow glow of candlelight. Christos held up the coin and pushed Athena's face into the gap.

"Not so loud," Nestor hissed.

He had tiny black eyes and ruddy skin. Breadcrumbs nested in a fuzzy grey beard. Only a few teeth remained in his mouth. His belly ballooned out his tunic. Nestor smelled worse than Cassie's potions and looked like he hadn't slept for weeks. Snatching the coin, he inspected Christos in the quivering light.

"By Zeus you *are* a pretty boy," said Nestor. "Your aunt Cassandra is good at sending me the right ones. Splendid, splendid, come through. Get out of this wretched night. We have nothing but wisdom here. Yes, yes, wisdom a-plenty here. Don't worry your pretty head. I'm not a sick man."

Christos followed Nestor inside. In the main sitting room blazed a hearth. Opposite was a small wooden table with only one chair, on which sat a mostly eaten bowl of brownish stew, the thin end of a measly loaf and a long carving knife. Nestor moved with a limp to the table, jabbing his finger at a second stool by the fireplace. Christos sat down, rested his stick on the floor and stretched his legs satisfyingly towards the flames.

"Cassiopeia was very kind to send me such a nice gift," he said, scraping and shovelling the bowl's remnants into his mouth.

"I'm happy to see a special boy who is not sick. A picture of youth. Look at you. Just look at you. Beautiful, beautiful blond hair."

In the far corner of the room was a mirror. Cassie had one of these too. Christos admired the other version of himself, and how the flames lit up his golden hair and brought out the bronze in his flesh. Curling his right bicep, Christos wondered whether his aunt's full name was Cassandra or Cassiopeia, and why Nestor didn't know either. His host belched and limped from the room, returning with two wooden cups and a jug. Hands shaking, he poured red liquid into both, passing one to Christos. The old man looked at his visitor and grinned.

"What are you seeking, boy?"

"Wisdom sir. Aunt Cassie says I need to walk the path of knowledge. She says we're in dark times. I shouldn't live in the shadow of ignorance. Not if I'm going to become the great warrior I'm destined to be."

"Many do live in that shadow," said Nestor after a long gulp, red juice dribbling into his beard. "I'm a veteran of the Battle of Marathon you know. Fought alongside Aeschylus when I was only a boy. Saved his life. Without me there would be no plays. Always knew he'd be a man of the theatre. It's how we Athenians approach the big questions. And we have many facing us. Many roles to play. What role do you play, boy?"

"Mother used to say I looked like Apollo. One day, I want to grow up and be as strong, brave and clever."

"Of course you do," laughed Nestor. "Or at least what we imagine Apollo to look like. Appearances are not always what they seem. But to conjecture about the appearance of divine powers may incur their wrath. And to aspire to the same intellect as the god of poetry is arrogant. Please now, don't disrespect Zeus and let your host drink alone."

Nestor tapped the side of his cup with his forefinger. Hesitantly, Christos tasted the wine. It was rancid, what he imagined vinegar would taste like if mixed with dog piss and left outside on a long summer's day.

"I will play the role of teacher, boy. Oh, the things I can teach you. Like how to bathe your master's feet after a long evening."

"Can I get food first?" said Christos.

"Only when invited," snapped Nestor. "Insolent child."

Soon the boy was kneeling before his tutor. He washed the crevices between his toes with warm water from a pot in the corner of the room. His mentor's skin was rough, the nails blackened. His feet smelled better than the water but worse than the wine; a dry, mouldy stench that made Christos gag.

"Not so heavy-handed boy," growled Nestor. "You're not washing pots and pans at your auntie's house."

The fire and the wine made Christos woozy. He worried he may fall asleep in Nestor's lap and his tutor would spend the night sneezing over him.

"Tell me young Apollo," Nestor whispered. "Do you know the secret to this city?"

"Wisdom sir. Of the kind Athena shows."

"Yes, but do you know where Athena comes from?"

"No sir."

"From up here," he said, tapping his right temple. "From the mind. Not from any mind. From the mind of Zeus himself."

Nestor gripped the sides of his chair and leaned his faced towards Christos's, coating him in cow-dung breath. The eyes seemed to turn inwards, like his tutor was retrieving something buried in the deepest recesses of his brain.

"It all began with lust. You know what lust is, boy?"

Christos shook his head.

"It is the desire to know another person. *To really know them.* Zeus lusted for Metis. A goddess of counsel, cunning and wisdom. Zeus chased her but Metis tried to escape, changing from hawk to fish to serpent. The king of the gods changed his form too and continued his pursuit until he overcame her. He made love to her. You know what that is, boy? To make love."

Christos shook his head again.

"The oracle of Gaia prophesied Metis's second child would be a boy that would overthrow Zeus. So the king of the gods swallowed her whole. After a time, he developed an unbearable headache. Hermes directed Hephaestus to take a wedge and split open Zeus's skull. Out of his forehead came Athena. In full armour. The goddess of wisdom and warcraft. The spirit of our city."

Christos smirked. There was something thrilling about the all-powerful Olympian having his head smashed apart by his own son.

"I like stories, uncle. But I thought I was here to learn wisdom."

"You're here to do exactly what I say boy," barked Nestor. "A story is a lie that reveals the truth, anyway. We all have Athena within us. Headaches that need release. That's the only way we can save our city. To cure the headache within."

"I want to save our city. To be a hero in our time."

"Of course you do," chuckled Nestor. "Then let us begin. Do you know why Cassie sent you? It was to find *real* wisdom. To get Athena out of me."

"How?"

"Like Zeus, Athena is living in my head," Nestor said, leaning closer. "I have a headache. I must release the wisdom."

"Me too. Not everyone in the city is as clever as they think they are."

Exiles Incorporated

Nestor roared with laughter, gusts of spit blasting Christos's cheeks.

"I like you boy," he says. "You speak well. Speaking well is the basis of democracy. And no, certainly not that clever. Everyone's a sophist these days."

Christos didn't know what that word meant. But he did know the last time mother and father developed headaches, they were dead a few days later. When Nestor's feet were dried, he gazed at his new student for a long time.

"Stand up. Turn around. Step back. Closer."

The boy obeyed, facing the hearth. He recalled how the flames had consumed his parents' bodies and the dozen stacked below them. Cassie didn't even bother to request the bones. What would those bones look –

Whhaaacccckkk. Nestor slapped Christos on the behind. A blaze of anger surged through the boy. He stifled the urge to pick up his trusty stick and take a retaliatory swing.

"Ha, ha. Apollo would have seen that coming. Now step towards the fireplace. Still. Turn slowly. Three times. Let me look at you. Yes."

Christos wanted to gnaw the edge off Nestor's table to quell his hunger.

"Go now, boy. Through the back. Be off with you. My belly is full. The wine is in my head. I tire quickly these days. Same time tomorrow. We shall see wisdom. Lift off this city's false face. Show you what is left. Give this to your aunt Cassie. Tell her it is a pleasure doing business with her."

The coin was larger than the tetradrachm. On one side was an Olympian he didn't recognise. On the other was a snake. While Nestor scuttled off into a side room, Christos shoved the leftover bread underneath his cloak.

"Farewell, young Apollo," said Nestor, handing him a torch light. "May this guide your way."

Most of the vagrants were asleep. A queer moaning came from an alleyway. Two figures were pressed against each other. A lady was backed against a wall; a man with his head lowered onto her shoulder pushed his body against her. She grabbed him by the hair, her mouth wide open as if in pain.

Christos hurried along, branch in belt, gripping the torch light with one hand and shoving bread into his mouth with the other. He disliked Nestor. But he must be wise if his aunt said so. Maybe there was some wisdom he hadn't seen. A magic trick to be summoned. Be a good guest or Zeus would be very cross indeed. Lust. Love. Athena. The city with the false face.

When he reached Cassie's home, smoke crawled through the roof above her chamber. She used to live in a much grander house until her merchant husband, father's brother, was lost at sea. All their goods went down with the ship. Yet she managed to wear pretty clothes from the city's finest tradesmen and fill the house with pretty furniture. Except in the draughty pantry, where Christos slept every night on a pile of blankets.

"Listen Christy, what's in Nestor's head is very valuable," said Cassie from behind the curtain, after he'd placed the snake coin on the step.

"I want you to do whatever he asks. And when you have the chance, bring whatever is in his head to me."

"What *is* in his head, auntie?"

"Athena, Christy. Athena herself."

Christos sloped off to his bed. Lying on his back, he stared into the pots and pans, pondering the riddles of adults. His head was hurting. To send himself to sleep, he fantasised about dragging the sun across the sky on Helios's chariot and singeing the hair from all the grown-ups so they looked bald and stupid.

The next day, Christos zig-zagged across the city, fetching bottles and packages. Tentative hands bestowed each one through wooden shutters. *Doing business.* No plague would stop that. As evening fell, he arrived exhausted at his aunt's house to find a visitor. A lanky boy with dark hair, meaty arms and a surly expression was whispering into the curtain. Christos dropped his collections and curled his hands into fists.

"I could not do it," stammered the boy. "He snatched it from me."

"Then you must go back tomorrow and try again," snapped Cassie.

"But he realises now."

"Then find another way."

"Auntie, I'm home," said Christos.

A chilly silence. Cassie dismissed the other boy with a bark. He ran out the house, shrinking from Christos's frosty glare.

"Christy, darling," said his aunt, her tone twisting into a gentle lilt. "Do you have what I needed?"

"Yes, auntie," he said, laying out his haul on the step.

"Time to visit your uncle Nestor, then. The money's in the pot on the side. Remember, I want you to be a good guest. *Do whatever he asks.*"

Night lay thick across the city when Christos arrived at the house. Despite several thumps on the door, Nestor didn't answer. Christos walked to the back yard, unkept weeds crunching beneath his feet. A rear door was left ajar: he tiptoed through with his stick raised.

"Uncle Nestor?"

Silence. Inside was even darker. A fire crackled.

"Uncle Nestor?"

A groan came from a side room, partitioned by a plain curtain.

"Where are you?"

The boy crept towards the hanging and pulled it back. Illuminated by a solitary candle on a bedside stool, Nestor lay face down on a bed, naked. His bum loomed on the bed like a huge pasty slab of dough.

"I can no longer see myself boy," Nestor said. "I can no longer see the real Athens. The real Athena. The city has lost itself in thought. This is the cause of my headache, boy. Thought. Terrible, terrible thought."

Nestor rolled onto his back, a blubbery shape with no signs of infection. He stared at Christos with a beaming smile.

"Athena is in my head," he said. "I want her out. Too much thinking will corrupt us all. We must return to a time before thought. Before the mind. We must embrace the impulses of the body without restraint. Come closer, massage my temples. Your path to wisdom."

Nestor rose and sat on the edge of his bed, stretching his legs and wiggling his toes. He straightened his spine and patted the mattress beside him. Christos sat down. The bed was moist, his uncle's body hot. Placing his fingertips either side of Nestor's head, Christos nervously pressed into the temples.

"Our city is being cursed for its pride," said Nestor, his voice slowing with the circular motions of Christos's fingertips. "For this thing called reason. The only wisdom is in the body. In the flesh. We must return to the older ways. To the instincts underneath. The pleasure of the moment. To live the last moments of life without restraint. Without reason. Shoulders."

Christos scampered to the sitting room and brought in the bowl of water and cloth. He washed Nestor's shoulders and back gently, watching the water trickle over dried skin.

"Headache," snapped Nestor.

Christos pressed the damp cloth into his temples. Right then left, left then right. *Temples*. Places to be worshipped. The mind was supposed to be the most precious thing, after all. Then Christos pictured his parents, dying in each other arms. Nestor was right. The body was the real temple. Where it began and where it would all end.

"Do you know the story of how Athens was created?"

"No, uncle."

"Hephaestus, lusting after his sister Athena, tried to make love to her but she was determined to keep her virginity. So he left his mark on her. His cream. The goddess wiped it off with a piece of wool and threw it to the ground. From this wool was born Erichthonius. He founded the city we call home."

Christos hadn't heard that story before. It was even sillier than the one about Zeus's head splitting apart.

After a chilly pause, Nestor glanced down between his legs.

"Help me, boy. I am an old man."

Christos's felt his stomach turn and his face flush.

"My sword is... weak."

Trembling, Christos lowered his right hand and closed his eyes.

"That's right. Bring Athena out of me. Cure my headache."

Nestor grabbed Christos's blond hair. Tears welled in the boy's eyes.

"Not so... aggressive," the old man snarled, digging his fingernails into Christos's scalp. "How... many... times?"

With a sudden jerk, Nestor groaned and doubled over. A whitish-grey fluid burst out, some dripping onto Christos's hand. Repulsed, the boy shoved it in the bowl of water. The mess broke apart, drifting like tadpoles.

"Good," said Nestor, curling back onto his bed, panting. "Better. Headache gone. You've done... well. Athens will thank you for it. Zeus thanks..."

Within moments, Nestor was snoring. Christos wanted to be sick. Dropping the tetradrachm on the bed, he ran into the garden to the street, hitting his head on an olive branch. He kept running until he found the agora. Sweat gathering and head pounding, Christos sat on the Stoa Poikile and sobbed.

"I am blind," wailed a beggar nearby. "Blind, blind, blind."

Christos tended the graze on his head with his fingertips, moving them up and down gently. There was no blood. Just dizziness. The massage turned to sharp tapping, then the pounding of both fists against his skull.

He had tried to be a good guest, like the older boys at the gymnasium. They often did special things for their tutors. But they were much stronger and had hair under their arms and between their legs. Christos couldn't see how that slimy white fluid would help disease go away. It all seemed pointless and dirty, like the plague. For the first time in a long time, Christos felt small. He thumped the porch's marble, wishing he was Zeus incinerating insects with thunderbolts of fire.

"Uncle Nestor is not a nice man," he said to Cassie through the curtain after telling her what happened. The graze wasn't hurting anymore, but he was still rubbing his temples. He'd developed a nasty headache.

"That's right, Alexander. He is not. His mind is not to be trusted."

"Alexander?" said Christos, eyes narrowing. "Is that the other boy?"

"I meant Christos."

"I don't want to go back to Nestor. He frightens me."

"*You will go back.* Listen to me, boy. You're in his head more than he is in yours. Charlatans like him are the real cause of this plague. They are the ones who took your parents away. You need to show me you can be a grown-up. A hero. Someone who can save this city from thinkers like him."

"I don't understand, auntie. Nestor said he thought too much. And I thought I was going there to learn from him."

"You will understand," she said. "Do you remember the tale of Perseus and Medusa?"

Christos had heard it many times before but always loved to hear it again. Especially after the disgusting story about the piece of wool.

"Yes. I love it. My favourite after the twelve labours of Heracles."

Christos reclined on the step and listened to his aunt speak softly. As Nestor said, a story is a lie that reveals the truth. By the end of the tale, the world made more sense. Adults had a strange way of doing things, but Christos knew what he had to do.

"Fly, fly, fly, my little Perseus," said Cassie. "Leap up onto Pegasus and fly, fly, fly. Be my hero. Before you turn to stone like your horrible uncle."

The next evening, Nestor was in the main room, sitting naked in front of the fire. On the table was a stinky broth and chunks of bread, with the big knife and spoon laid to one side. Christos placed his trusty stick alongside them and hovered over Nestor's shoulder.

"Bring me wine," his uncle shouted at the mirror. "Athena runs rampant today. You shall be drinking something else as well. Drinking straight from Athena's fountain."

Christos fetched the wine, filled two cups and placed one in Nestor's open palm. He drank like a thirsty dog, fluid speckling his swollen stomach.

"Drink with me you little pig. Drink. Do not insult your host."

Christos lifted his cup and pretended to sip.

"Wash me, boy. My headache is vile. Water. *Fetch water.*"

Fly, fly, fly. An inner fire roared from Christos's stomach and engulfed his body. *Fly, fly, fly.* He walked to the table, picked up the knife, crept towards Nestor and rammed the blade into the side of his throat. His tutor's arms flew upwards, fingers twitching into space, legs shaking. A squeal erupted from his mouth. Blood sprayed down his chest and onto the flames, bursting like that horrible white fluid. Grabbing Nestor's hair with his spare hand and digging the fingernails deep, Christos twisted the blade again and again, grinding his teeth as he skewered life from his uncle.

Nestor collapsed to the floor with a thud. The heat of the flames danced across Christos's flesh. Six, seven, eight times he stabbed into the neck. In each strike he could see his dying parents coiled together, their skin riddled with sores. His mother trying to speak. His father's terrified eyes.

Burn, burn, burn, he silently screamed. *Burn. Burn. Burn. I will burn the city, its people and this plague. Burn. Burn. Burn. Burn. Burn. Burn. Burn. Bu –*

When he came to, Christos was sitting calmly at the table. A pool of Nestor's blood had spread from the hearth and collected under his feet. The boy banged his forehead with his closed right fist.

Taking care not to slip, Christos rose and leered over Nestor's body. The head was severed from the neck. He held it aloft like Perseus brandishing Medusa's. Inside there was just a squidgy mess. No goddess. No Athena. Just bad stuff. He drank the rest of the wine and overturned Nestor's house until he found a sack. Dropping the head inside, Christos twisted the sack at the top, slung it over his shoulder and strolled through the murky streets towards home, munching on bread. Thanatos was nowhere to be seen.

When he returned to Cassie's house, the only light came from the dancing candlelight behind the spider-webbed curtain. Christos removed Nestor's head from the sack by its stringy hair and smeared it on the step. The dead man's eyes were still wide open. Christos turned the shocked face towards the curtain.

"Auntie."

"Jason?"

"No. Christos."

"Oh. What do you want?"

"This is my home, auntie. I have Uncle Nestor's head."

Silence. A ripple of water. Soft footsteps.

"You do? Oh yes, of course. I forgot."

The curtain twitched. A wet bony hand crept through the gap in the side making a grabbing motion. Christos picked up the head by its hair and placed it within touching distance of his aunt's fingers. She whisked it inside and gave a shriek of joy.

"Very good. Oh this is so very, very good. What did he say?"

The dumbest thing he'd heard from a grown-up, thought Christos. *And there was plenty of competition.*

"Nothing. He squealed. That was it."

"Where was his precious reason then? His fancy rhetoric. Congratulations Alexander, we'll make an intrepid Perseus of you yet."

"It's Christos. If I must do these things for you, you could at least get my name right."

"Yes, of course. Right. Now clear the kitchen, brush the front and go to bed. Oh yes, you have done well. A brilliant pupil. A scholar of the dark arts. Very, very good."

Christos ignored her demands. Trudging to the pantry, he slipped off his blood-stained tunic. In a rage, he threw a couple of pots against the wall, then fell back on his blankets and looked out the narrow window to the Milky Way. He wondered what the gods might think of what he'd done.

Mother and father. The secrets of adults. The burning injustice of this stupid city. He grabbed his crotch with one hand for comfort and clutched his olive branch with the other.

"Too many people," he muttered. "Too many people."

After a prolonged quiet, a murmur came from Cassie's chamber.

"Athena, goddess of wisdom, hear my prayers," said his aunt, a girlish excitement to her voice. "The plague has come to humble us for our arrogant ways. There is no intellect. Only the flesh. There is no wisdom. Only beauty. There is no reason. Only sacrifice."

Springing to his feet, Christos dressed in tomorrow's clothes, shoved his stick into belt and crept outside. At the side of the house was a trough filled with stagnant water. In it lay the submerged head of a dead man, kneeling with arms drooped to his sides. Christos stepped on the trough and reached up. Gripping the edge of the roof, he pulled himself upwards.

In the distance under the sparkling sky was the Acropolis. The statue of a proud Athena gleamed under torchlight. Smoke rose from the fire in Cassie's inner sanctum, passing through the opening in the ceiling and dissipating into the night. Christos crawled towards the hole and peered over the precipice. A smell of dried blood drifted up his nose.

Directly below was a huge barrel, sawed in half, and two-thirds full of steaming broth. Beside it stood Cassie, her back towards him. She wore nothing except her ornate bracelets and necklace. His aunt's skin was pale and stretched, her figure crooked rather than curved. Before her on the floor was a miniature statue of Athena, complete with helmet, staff and shield.

Cassie sunk to her knees, extended her arms forward and placed her hands at the goddess's feet. Surrounding

Athena were four wooden spikes, two on each side, planted into soiled pots like flowers. Every spike but one bore a human head. The wooden tips pierced through the top of the skulls. One of them belonged to a sage from the agora. Another's face was so bloodied and mashed it was unrecognisable. The third was Laertes. His old tutor's mouth was open, like a wild dog begging for the tiniest sip of water.

"As you emerged from Zeus's head, please accept these lesser heads as my tribute," intoned Cassie. "These heads who thought they knew more than anyone. These teachers who dared to reason away the gods. To pervert your stories for their own ends. The ones who angered you all. Who brought disease to your city."

Cassie rose and turned. She didn't have a thing between her legs like Nestor, just a triangular-shaped patch of black hair. Two fleshy sacks with shrivelled tips drooped from her chest. She sat on a stool before her dressing table, on which lay a mirror, a bowl, a spoon and Nestor's head. Cassie flipped it over and drove the spoon into its core with a squelch. Slowly she scooped out chunks of Nestor's brain matter and slapped them into the bowl. It reminded Christos of how the dead man once ate stew.

Raising the bowl aloft, Cassie carried the grey mush towards the barrel of liquid. Christos rolled away from her line of sight and looked into the night sky. *Plop, plop, plop* went Nestor's brains into the bubbling water. When Christos returned his gaze, Cassie was shoving his uncle's head onto the fourth spike with a wincing crack.

"Gracious Athena. I give you this sacrifice. With your magnanimity, I beg you grant me the gift of eternal life and beauty. Save me from this terrible disease. Protect me from encroaching death. Lead me to your realm of the immortals and the glories of Mount Olympus."

Cassie bowed then returned to the barrel. Raising her leg slowly and cocking it over the side, she lowered herself into the steaming brew. Sinking to her neck, closing her eyes and resting her head on the side of the barrel, Cassie hummed. A buzz of pure contentment purred from her lips, while vile vapours of bath and brain surged up Christos's nose. Repelled, the boy lifted his wrist to his face, scraping his elbow along the roof. A pebble rolled through the opening into the water below.

Plop.

Cassie's eyes flicked open. She stared at her nephew, face twisting from shock into undiluted rage. Her eyes swelled red, like mother's had done before she lost her voice. Christos rolled to the edge of the roof and dropped, using one hand to steady his fall. Landing in the alley and onto his back, he heard a quick succession of sounds inside. Water rippling. Curtain parting. Feet slapping.

"Wicked child," screamed his aunt. "Come back. Come back. Come back or I will haunt your mind forever!"

Christos ran. Pursuing him all the way was the stench of boiling brain and the scraping of Nestor's skull. Onwards he sped, weaving through dark streets, dying men and the drunken howls of the dejected, their despairing voices crawling over each other like vermin.

"I am on fire," one howled. "Get it off my skin. Get it off my skin."

Too many people. Too many people. Too many people. Christos never stopped, never glanced back, as if Thanatos, Cerberus and Hades were in pursuit. He knew a weak spot in the city walls, a tiny tunnel familiar to many boys his age. Crawling past the infected tents of the homeless, he burst into the undefended lands beyond. If a hundred Spartans mauled him, he would not care.

In the countryside, Christos stopped, caught his breath, snapped a branch from an olive tree and tucked it into his belt. As he looked back at the city skyline and the Acropolis, his headache returned. He hated Athens. He hated how everyone said it was a place for the wise. Most of all, he hated its myths and spells. How they got into his mind. *Democracy means everyone has a say*, his father said. But the plague was the only truly democratic thing. It got everyone in the end. And if you didn't get sick in the body, you got sick in the head.

Over the next few days, Christos ventured deeper into the countryside, sleeping in bushes and scavenging for fruit. There were no Spartans anywhere. One evening, he wandered upon an abandoned temple in the dip between two hills. Guarding it was a tall figure, looking back towards the city.

"Hey, who are you?" shouted Christos. "Turn around and show yourself."

The figure didn't move.

"Don't be a coward. Show yourself."

Christos drew closer. This wasn't a person. An Athenian. Or a goddess. This was a statue of Zeus. Father to Athena and Apollo. The great sky father. Still, stone cold and stupid as ever. In a fury, Christos lunged at the stone. There was a painful whack in his shoulder as he toppled Zeus to the ground. The idol's head cracked. The rubble of its false face scattered to mix with the dust. Inside was nothing at all. Not even grey mush. No thunder of retribution came either.

After many weeks drifting, Christos found work and board as a shepherd boy. A long time ago he dreamed of being an argonaut questing for the golden fleece. Now every morning and evening, he used his trusty stick to guide a weedy flock like they were docile children.

One morning, the farmer left to speak with the Spartans the other side of the valley. *Doing business again.* Christos considered sneaking into his bedroom to see what was behind his curtain. But he didn't want to behold any more false faces.

In a field he sat alone with the grazing sheep, twisting into the ground the point of a hunter's knife he'd stolen from the farmer's shed. A splutter, a groan, a wheezing of breath. One of the sheep seemed poorly. Alone from the flock, head drooped, its shrivelling coat had turned from fluffy white to matted grey. It was dying. Soon the others would suffer. They were all dying. Everything was dying. The plague of the city. The curse of adventure. The perils of doing business. *Burn it all. Burn, burn, burn.*

Guiding the flock into a pen, Christos closed the gate and took out the knife. One by one he twirled through the compound, slitting the animal's throats. Jabbing. Slicing. Stabbing. Thrusting. Skewering. He laughed as the sheep squealed in terror, heads wobbling and hooves jerking. Jets of blood spurted into the air and settled in specks and streaks on the white wool.

Christos liked how the chests of the animals rose and fell for the final time. Sitting cross-legged amid the puddles of blood, the boy massaged his temples. The pressing turned to tapping and then thumping. He was not a good guest. But he wasn't scared of the farmer, Cassie, the plague or Zeus.

He skipped on through Greece. On a sunny day beside a stream, he saw himself in the placid water. His blond hair had changed colour. Crowning his head was a shock of white, like the sages in the agora a long time ago.

Onwards he danced to what he thought might be Mount Olympus. To reach the summit and ask the gods directly what it all meant. Not that he was expecting much. If the stories about the Olympians were even half-true, they would mess it up like Cassie and Nestor. They probably didn't even exist.

Yet his quest for wisdom must continue. And if he reached the highest peak and only found thinning grey clouds, Christos would ram his stick into the ground and rule the world all by himself, casually flicking thunderbolts of fire at the infected creatures below.

Nazca

It was another dry morning and nothing much was happening in the sky. The community had buried its leader the night before, merrily watering the ground with fluids as his spirit soared. When dawn broke, younger folk expected to see his happy red face floating in the clouds, but the endless blue offered only wispy white. Men refused to emerge from their huts. The strongest claimed to be sick with grief. The weakest were too poorly to release anything but hot air.

Caya knew it was the shaman's broth. The demented old fool seemed distracted when mixing the snake blood into the stewing pot and incantating to the Great Being. Only men could sup the maroon drink. Only men fell sick. As the sun rose over the plain, Caya noticed how her mother exchanged a knowing smile with other women as they fluttered through their chores like fledging birds.

One day I will be like them, thought Caya as she swept outside her family's hut. She glanced down the track to see if Yavi was up, sunlight glinting on his broad shoulders. If he was curled in bed whimpering, she'd be disappointed. And angry with his parents for letting him touch the broth. He was a boy. One day he would be a man. She needed him strong, healthy and wise.

One day. When her chest was bigger, hips wider and the bleeding had begun. Caya was worryingly late. Her friend Mita became a woman last summer, welcomed into the bosom of those squawking ladies who flapped around the shaman. Caya turned the brush upside down and used the handle to draw a picture of herself and Yavi embracing. It looked silly, so she swept it away.

Last night was silly too. The broth had crippled father. Caya peered into her parents' room and saw him face down with a damp cloth on his bald head. She could smell his insides. Above the bed was the wall hanging of the Great Being, with its string of ugly heads, cavernous eyes and snake-like tongues. The colours were pretty, though. Woven into pretty patterns by pretty women's hands. The ones who cooked, cleaned and swelled with new life. The real rainmakers.

Once when she was tiny, Caya experienced sky water. Infrequent taps on the roof during a sleepless night. A child then, far away from adulthood. Now she was neither. Unready to be a rainmaker, as her father kept telling her. She must bleed first so her insides could receive the male seed. On this morning's evidence, she would be surprised if any men could summon the strength.

After finishing the cleaning, Caya walked past Yavi's hut. Her heart quickened. She lingered for a while, drawing another picture of them both in the ground with her fingertips. Nobody emerged. Bored, she wandered to Mita's hut. Her mother, a grumpy fat lady who shouted at people all day, said Mita was with the shaman learning the ways of the sky. Eventually the Great Being would flood the dry land with life. Not yet though. One day.

Drifting to the outermost huts, Caya saw the other settlement in the distance. There'd been another falling out, because they hadn't sent anyone to mourn the leader. Caya wondered if their shaman was more capable. Surely it would be better if they all prayed together, so they could take flight as one to see beyond the air.

A horn sounded. Women wittered and weaved to the centre of the settlement. Caya plodded behind them. *Always late*, her mother said. *Head and feet always moving in different directions.* In the gathering space, the shaman sat like a bony stalk on a red chair. He was a measly figure with a long nose, shifty blue eyes and spindly limbs. In late afternoons he stared sombrely into the plain, supposedly waiting for the Great Being to explain when rain would fall.

Today he was bubbling, smart enough to avoid his own concoction. His female entourage formed a semi-circle behind him. In their midst, twirling her hair, was Mita. She was broody yet light; the air seemed to lift her lovely dark hair, curves and chest above the sagging crowd. The remaining villagers, mostly women and small boys, formed an opposing pattern before the shaman. They fell silent. Caya tucked in at the end, nestling behind an elderly lady. She smelled like she'd secretly supped the broth herself.

"Our community is heavy with grief for our leader passed," said the shaman. He milked the quiet, tilting his head back and half-closing his eyes.

"The men of the tribe feel the pain the most. They're unable to undertake the sacred task which befalls us today. The condor must be completed. The voices in my head must take flight today…"

His eyes tightened, like he'd forgotten his lines.

"…or else the soul of our leader will not leave this realm. There will be no water from the heavens to bless us. To grow crops so we can live another year. We need two young women to continue the labour."

The shaman belched and rose from his chair. He was a tiny man, overshadowed by the ladies falling in line. Carrying a staff decorated with feathers and jingling stone pieces, he inspected the people before him, looking through many like they were fresh air.

"Who will complete the condor and honour our dear leader?"

Our dear leader. Everyone thought the deceased was a joke. In his last days, he barely left his hut. All the woman who lined up outside to please him would snigger at how fat he was becoming. *Women.* Sweet and submissive in male presence. Pouncing like hungry birds when alone together. Men's failings. Their bad habits. The rude manners. How tired and limp they got.

"You!"

A volley of spit struck Caya in the face. The tip of the shaman's long twig finger was an arm's length from her nose, his stare skewed towards her chin.

"We'll send you!"

Finally, proof the shaman didn't like her. Until now he'd forced a thin smile or two her way, saving the genuine ones for the prettiest girls. Caya knew everyone put on a performance, while the language of the body yielded the truth. The feet said it all. Who wanted to be here, who didn't. Which wives wanted to be with their husbands. Which ones didn't.

Stop being strange, people's bodies would say to Caya, as their eyes exuded sunshine. All because she didn't wear her hair long, hadn't grown like the other girls and didn't join the gaggling gossip. At night Caya would lie awake and rub her breasts, pleading for them to grow. Womanhood might happen when it rained, like everything else in this parched, lonely space. Love even. From someone strong, dark and muscular. Brave and romantic. Someone whose insides didn't melt after drinking too much blood.

"And this one."

The shaman had moved back to the far side of the line-up. He was pointing to an older girl with dim-witted eyes and a dumpy figure. Behind her was a fidgety lady, presumably her mother, who shoved her child towards the shaman so hard she tumbled to the ground. She rocked onto her bum, face perplexed.

Bone idle, thought Caya. *I'm going to have to shift the earth all by myself.*

The shaman raised his staff and drew pretend circles in the air. It was easy to make a scene when you didn't have to do the heavy lifting.

"You must fulfil your duty to the Great Being," he crowed. "Complete the great image. Stir the heavens to bring water. It is time for you to see…"

He pointed his staff towards the plain with a flourishing twirl.

"…the colour of the earth."

His handmaidens cooed dramatically. Two of them crept either side of Caya and placed the great shawl over her head. When younger, Caya loved to make stories about the characters on the garment. The whale. The spotted cat. The serpentine. The llamas walking the red band on the edge. Today the shawl smelled shitty, like an unwell man had farted into it too many times.

"Onwards," screeched the shaman swirling his staff. "The posts await you. The Great Being awaits us all. Rain… shall… come."

As the couple stared towards the rusty red, Mita and the sisterhood banged drums and blew panpipes. One of them, a wiry bird-like woman with a screwed-up face, slung a small spade and a sack of sweet potato onto Caya's shoulder and patted it. Caya's mother was nowhere to be seen, while her companion's guardian was anxious and ever-present.

"Go now Taru," she said. "We need you. Do not be afraid."

Taru was taller, fatter and bigger in the chest than Caya. Her feet were withdrawn and askew. Vacant eyes suggested a feeble mind, her braided hair a desire to belong. Like Caya, she too was smothered in a great shawl. Punching through the sides were flabby biceps and clunking forearms. Taru moved slowly, like she was in a very confusing daydream.

"Come on," snapped Caya. "Let's get moving. Follow me and do as I say."

Sheepishly, Taru followed.

Caya was sweating by the time they reached the plain. The final tracks to complete the condor were staked out. Six posts in total. Moving from one to the next, Caya and Taru had to scrape back the red earth until they reached grey. At the first wooden post, a piece of string was tied midway up the column, stretching off to a second post in the distance.

There were dozens and dozens of markings on the desert, some created long before Caya's time. Grey lines crisscrossing. Animals, symbols and shapes. Spider. Hummingbird. Monkey. Whale. Each sending signals to the sky. The marks in the ground would remain forever, Caya's father said, until the great flood washed everything away.

"Are you ready for this?" Caya said.

"I don't know," mumbled Taru.

"We have a big responsibility."

"Yes."

"I'll start here. You go further ahead."

"Yes."

Caya scraped back the red earth with the small spade. One, two, three. More red lay underneath. Four, five, six. This wasn't a young girl's work. Marking the land was better done by people who thumped around in search of food and hit things when they got angry.

"Have you ever seen a condor?" said Taru, watching Caya dig.

"No, I haven't."

"Is it true they live on the sun?"

"Maybe."

Caya dug further into red.

"Does the condor decide whether water comes? Or the Great Being?"

"The Great Being decides everything."

"Even what body we have?"

"Yes. Unfortunately for you. Now are you going to help or not?"

Taru trudged a few paces along the string. She kneeled, lifted her spade above her head with both hands and walloped the ground. *Crackuuth. Crackutth. Crackuuth.* Red flecks shot up around Taru, landing near Caya.

"Found it," said Taru, rubbing a pinch of light-coloured sand between her fingers and releasing it into the air.

"Your earth must be softer," said Caya.

Taru tore ahead, pausing occasionally to examine the dislodged red.

"Like people," Taru said.

"What?"

"Everyone different."

Taru grew stronger as the morning went on. A tiring Caya watched her companion work. Taru's body seemed swollen. Not with pain but with life. Flesh. Colour. Vitality. Blood. A fulsome chest and bulging leg muscles. There was something on her mind too. Not detectable in her feet, but in the glazed eyes and curvature of her wide, hungry mouth.

"What are you thinking?" said Caya.

"Rain is coming soon."

"How do you know?"

"I can tell. The sky, the wind, the heat. A change is coming soon."

"Because of what we're doing?"

"No. The rain doesn't care about what we do. The rain is just the rain."

"Then why would they send us out here."

"I don't know. What do you think?"

"Have you ever seen rain?"

"I sometimes dream about it. When I dream about something, I know it's going to happen."

"What else do you dream about?"

"Flying. One day I would like to fly away from here and never return."

With deepening breaths, Taru scraped the ground in the unforgiving sun. She reminded Caya of her father, in thrall to work and lost in his own visions. *You won't be able to stay in this home forever, little one.*

They were well over halfway when Caya began wheezing. She persuaded Taru to sit down, sip water and nibble sweet potato.

"Have you started bleeding yet?" said Caya.

Taru's eyebrows arched.

"You know. From down there. Have you bled?"

"Yes."

"What's it like?"

"It just happens. Sometimes it's painful. Difficult to clean up."

"You know I was lying earlier. I have seen a real condor."

"You have?"

"Big, strong and soaring above me. It came very close."

"Were you scared?"

"No, it was exciting," said Caya tartly. "Maybe it knew I was fertile."

"What does that mean?"

"It means you have love with you."

For the first time that day, Taru's eyes probed Caya.

"Would you like to see the world?" said Taru.

"What is out there but more desert?"

"Many things. Where do you think the llamas and wool come from?"

"I've never thought about it."

"They come from the highlands. The places of trees. Like the headdresses of the leader. It was made with the feathers of forest birds. From places faraway they don't tell us about."

"Is that where the Great Being lives? The one we see in the patterns?"

"Maybe."

"Why do you think we make these markings in the ground?"

"I don't know. The elders must have some kind of plan."

The condor was finished by noon. Taru had done most of the work and seemed untroubled by the poorer deal.

"Shall we run around its shape?" said Caya.

"No," said Taru. "Too tired."

"That's ok, I understand. Not everyone has the same energy as me. It's a shame we can't fly high and see the whole condor from above."

"Only the lights in the sky can see it. That's the way it should be. We're not meant to understand it all. Besides, whatever we draw in the ground won't match the beauty of the real thing."

"Of course," stuttered Caya. "A real condor is the most beautiful thing."

The couple fell silent for a long time, their chests rising and falling in tandem. Eyes absorbed in the horizon, Taru finally spoke.

"Do you think we're part of a bigger creature?"

"How do you mean?"

"You know, just a smaller part of a greater living thing."

Caya recalled the burial of the leader. How they wrapped his airless body in textiles and placed him sitting up surrounded by pots. Around him were decapitated trophy heads strung on a single cord. Shit was shoved in his mouth, then pinned shut with cactus needles.

"No, I'm on my own," Caya said. "We're all on our own."

"When I look up at night," said Taru. "I can feel something else. Like the sky is sending me a message. There are many worlds just like this one. Filled with people like us. Is it better to be free and lonely, or trapped and together?"

Caya gazed at Taru's figure. Her breasts, hair, eyes and soft brown skin. A beautiful girl with a beautiful mind. A fertile girl, flourishing with curiosity in the dry desert heat. A girl Yavi might like.

"What is it like to be loved, do you think?" said Caya.

"I don't know," said Taru. "I do know what it feels like to be *in* love."

"Who are you in love with?"

"I can't say."

"Who?"

"Nobody you would expect."

"Have you?"

"Have I what?"

"You know... felt his love."

"No not yet."

"Then how do you know you love him?"

"Because every time I see him my heart soars."

Caya's mother's voice, cooing in the dark. *One day your heart will soar, little one.* The clammy scent of her sweat. *And you'll feel all the love in the world.*

"Yes, I know what that feels like," Caya said. "Yavi makes me feel that way. We've kissed you know. He asked me to take my clothes off but I..."

Taru wasn't listening. She sat motionless, her breath slow and her eyes locked in a trance towards the sky.

"Look," whispered Taru.

Caya followed her stare. Directly above, a huge bird was descending quickly in circles towards them.

"What is –"

Thud. The condor landed about ten paces away. Its huge black and white body glistened in the sun. The ring of white feathers at the base of its neck expanded and retracted. The head, pink and featherless, rose to a large, dark red comb at its crown. The condor was poised, bristling with a lithe sensuality that trapped the gaze. Something grand lay within its unblinking eyes. Knowledge of lands far away. The beak was hooked and sharp. Its middle claws jutted and twitched, as if beckoning the girls.

"It's ugly," Caya said.

"No," said Taru. "It's beautiful."

The condor's eyes moved from Taru to Caya and Caya to Taru. Panic rose inside Caya. Father seemed so far away.

"Don't go near it," she whispered to Taru. "Move back. Slowly."

Caya shuffled back on her behind, grazing her buttocks.

"Taru," she hissed. "Must come now."

The condor bored its eyes into Taru. The skin of its neck flushed dull red then inflated. With a sudden flap, the bird expanded its wings, whipping the width of its majestic body into the air and lashing sound across the plain. Caya shrieked.

"Don't be afraid," said Taru gently.

The condor unfurled and closed its wings repeatedly, rolling currents of air rolled across the girls.

"It's going to hurt us," Caya whimpered.

"No, it won't," said Taru. "The Great Being has sent this. The pattern in the ground brought it to life."

"Taru, we must run."

Rising from the arid ground, Taru walked fluidly towards the unflinching condor. *How can she get so close to something so ugly?* thought Caya. *It will sink its beak into her. Spit venom from its mouth.* Her mother's voice again. *Be disciplined. Do not be tempted. You are not meant to know that yet.*

Taru slammed her hands together. *Clap.* The condor's wings twitched. *Clap.* Once more, the bird jolted. *Clap.* Taru closed in then veered to the right. The condor moved with her. *Clap.* They circled each other. Taru jerked. *Clap.* Soft motion rippled from her toes to her head like a pulse of warm air was surging up her spine. Taru's gyrations were light and ethereal, the rolling fat on her body cushioning and caressing a secret self being unveiled. *Clap.* The condor advanced each time, slowly tightening the circle.

"Show me," said Taru. Her breaths were deep and long, anchoring the quickening intensity of her dance. "I want to see it."

Clap. Clap. Clap.

The condor crept towards Taru with neck outstretched, chest inflated and tongue clicking, its black and white feathers shimmering in the noonday sun.

"We must go," said Taru. "It's calling us."

Clap.

"Taru, I'm scared."

Clap.

"Don't you see?" said Taru. "This is how we will bring the rain. We've finished the pattern. We summoned it ourselves."

Clap.

"This is what the pictures do," she continued. "They talk to the Great Being. Bring what we imagine to life."

Clap.

"Taru, don't…"

As her friend stroked the condor on its brow, the bird's wings trembled. It hissed softly, as if slipping into a dream. Taru pressed her hands either side of the condor's wrinkly face, closing its eyes. Her breasts rose in sync with the bird's growling breath. The wings flapped and stretched to their fullest, then gradually retracted. Caya kept moving. Away. Back to the post. The village. Father.

Gracefully, the condor enclosed its wings around Taru. A mesmerised Caya walked in an ever-expanding circle around the coupling. She glimpsed her friend's flushed face. Absorbed. Enraptured. At peace.

The dance exploded. A sharp, slashing sound sliced the space between them. The condor unfurled its wings and took flight. Taru crumpled to the ground on her knees, arms spread, face buried into the red earth. High above Caya's head, the condor circled.

"Taru," cried Caya. "Are you hurt?"

She reached under Taru's armpits and rolled her onto her back. Her friend was much lighter than Caya expected. Taru was not wounded but her face was strange. Spit formed at the corners of her smiling mouth. Her eyes were lost in the sky, cushioned in eerie serenity.

"We need to go back," panted Caya. "We need the shaman to –"

"No," roared Taru, rising to her feet. "It is calling us to follow him to the mountains. Upwards to the sun. *We must go.*"

Caya grabbed Taru's hands and slung her around, staring her in the eyes.

"No, you can't."

"I must go," said Taru, pulling away from her grip. "Alone if I have to."

"You have no food or water. You'll die out here."

"I want to fly. I want to fly with the sun god. I want to feel its love."

"It is not the sun god. It is just a bird. All we've done is move some earth in the ground. This doesn't mean what you think it means."

Just moved some earth. Finished a picture. Did what was asked of them. Revealed the colour below. Caya had tried to lead, like her father expected.

With a ferocious push, Taru broke free and bolted. Caya made chase and wrestled her to the ground. Face to face in the dust, Caya pressed her fingers deep into Taru's shoulders, pinning her down. Warm flesh. Soft flesh. Hungry flesh. The condor circled, neither ascending nor descending.

"I will not let you go."

Taru lunged forward, knocking Caya onto her back. Winded and dizzy, she saw the shaman's eyes in the blank blue above. His petty demeanour. The cruel ease with which he'd picked them out.

"The dream is real," barked Taru. "The picture we made has soared to the sky. Love has come to take us away."

"No Taru," stammered Caya, reaching her arms into space. "We've been sent here on purpose. This is a sacrifice. The shaman has sent us to be sacrificed."

"Caya, don't you know love *is* sacrifice?"

A swishing above. The condor peeled off from its circling and cruised in the opposite direction of the village. Taru ran in its undertow. Caya had seen people lose their minds after drinking the shaman's potions. This was deeper. Nothing was being forced upon Taru. Something was erupting within. Like she was shedding fake skin and discovering her real body.

"Taru!"

Her friend became a melee of rushing limbs, a dark splurge of movement then a feint, receding speck blurring into the horizon. There was nothing in the sky except thin spectral clouds. On the ground there was only Caya and scraped markings patterned to look like a condor. Neither would take flight anytime soon.

Heart raging, she ran back to the village. No welcoming party awaited. One of the weavers, sitting alone outside her hut, looked at her with indifference. Some men, recovered from their illnesses, shuffled about preparing for the evening feast. Caya even saw Yavi but sped straight past. She reached home, blurting her story in a rush of spit and sweat.

Mother consoled her with a hug. Father, still pale, looked suspicious. A meeting was assembled in the gathering circle, attended by all the elders. Taru's parents arrived, their desperate eyes pleading with Caya to tell another story. Her mother seemed older already, her body buckled towards the ground.

"She was different," stuttered Caya as she finished her tale. "Something took over. There was a change. It was no longer Taru."

The shaman sat pensively, inspecting Caya from head to toe with his twitching eyes. Caya recalled how his spit struck her cheek. She was about to scream into his face, when Taru's mother broke the tension.

"You shouldn't have let them go out there on their own," she roared at the shaman. "They were too young."

"The girls are nearly of age and we needed their strength," said the shaman. "They were ready for what is out there. We must make sacrifices."

"We will go out there tonight," said Taru's father. "We will not rest."

"I forbid it," snapped the shaman. "If we try to intervene, the sun god will be displeased. The land will remain dry and barren."

Caya looked at the shaman's feet. The slippery shit was making it up as he went along.

"The shaman speaks truth," interjected the leader's son, to whom everyone would soon defer. His father, a ghost from the past in control of his mind, was telling him how the world should be.

"We created the condor, and the condor came," he said. "Rain will come too. Our land will be fertile through the sacrifice of this child. We will honour her memory with full rites."

"This has not happened with any of the other patterns," said one elder, an observation ignored by everybody.

"Or maybe the Great Being is displeased in some way," said another, a taciturn man always the first to fall asleep at celebrations. "Maybe we're being taken away one by one. The leader, the poisonings, the girl. Evil is coming."

One of the other elders approached Caya. He bent towards her, so their eyes were level. Kindly eyes, accompanied by a gentle voice, warm smile and big, friendly arms.

"Are you sure this is what happened, Caya?" he said. "We've all suffered since the passing of the leader. Are you sure none of this was… imagined?"

Caya thought about yesterday's burial. The custom of handling the dead. The scouring of earth to draw big shapes in the ground. The decorations on her shawl. The talk of the Great Being. The shaman and his silly theatrics. The condor's fierce beauty. Its glistening feathers. The brooding strength that lured Taru into its embrace. Caya had never once hugged her friend. The loss felt like a scar on her heart.

"What's imagined and what's real I can no longer say," she said. "I miss my friend. That's all."

Eventually the shaman and the leader's son assembled a search party. After three days, no trace of Taru was found. The rain never fell and the entire village lapsed into a prolonged funk. Caya went about her duties: cleaning cooking, washing, serving, praying. Slowly the distance from her father dissolved. They spoke more about food, uncovering the earth, the redness below. How there was a bigger world out there she must explore. When Caya saw Yavi, she felt nothing. When she spoke to him, even less. How simple, closed and uncomprehending he seemed. He didn't imagine what lay beyond. His skin didn't glow like Taru's. And his eyes were dead holes compared to the condor's.

In quiet afternoons on rest days, Caya would exile herself to the plain and walk along the condor's beak she'd drawn with her friend. She wondered how long they would last. The scratches in the ground felt stupid, like her picture of Yavi. A useless replica of something far more mysterious. Something much more sacred. She looked skywards, wracked with dread.

One evening, Caya lay in the family hut trying to sleep. The condor dipped and dived in her mind. She felt a stirring of something below. A yearning for an unknown world. Taru had followed this urge, but Caya had hesitated. She wondered if the opportunity would ever come again, and what would happen if she left the hut now and headed to the pitch-black horizon.

Her feet decided for her. Caya dressed, crept from her home and ran onto the plain until her body begged for breath. Finding a spot to lie on her back, she dared the night sky to show its secrets. She hoped to see Taru in the stars looking down on her, enjoying the pattern they'd finished together. One day they would find each other again. A flood would be coming. Her friend would be coming. Love would be –

Silently and softly, the rain fell. A drop landed in Caya's mouth. Another on her forehead. Several more pattered her shoulders and shins. The sky was yielding. Between her legs a warm dampness came. Caya opened her mouth in a mixture of shock and delight, savouring the rain slide down her throat as the blood soiled her thighs.

Love was in her. The real world was opening its wings and taking her away. She lay there for a long time until her clothes and hair became sodden, enjoying the redness of womanhood flow from her body. As the rain beat down, Caya imagined Taru's arms curling underneath her. Together they would lift each other higher and higher, so they could be together, swooping on currents of magical air like some fantastical bird.

When the rain stopped, Caya floated home and slept at her mother's feet. At daybreak, she showed her the bloodied clothes. Mother stroked Caya's hair until she drifted to sleep. Later in the day, the entire community except for Caya danced with joy across the drenched plains. The shaman smiled through his narrow mouth to express his delight. His feet told a different story.

Over time, Caya became taller and fuller. She grew further apart from Mita. Men finally noticed her. Even Yavi. But she never found anything to talk to him about. All men proved disappointing, forever recovering from the idiocy of the night before. People lived and died. Fell ill and got better. Loved and lost. Caya remained dutiful during the day. At night she went elsewhere.

One morning a young girl in the village caught Caya's eye. A brooding creature with ravishing black hair, unblemished skin and proud hips. Zelu moved in the same way as Taru, oblivious to the forces rippling inside. Patiently and slowly, Caya circled her, until the winds of attraction whipped them together. Out on the plain, at the condor's beak, where only the sky could see them, the two tenderly explored each other until love broke forth.

On the way back they held hands, relinquishing their secret bliss at the village's outskirts. Caya danced and clapped her way home, happiness pouring down inside. *Clap. Clap. Clap. Tap. Tap. Tap.* Imaginary wings spread from her back and lifted her skywards, where she drew her lover's face so deep in the red earth time would not wear it away.

In bed, her dreams soared even higher. To a special realm in the clouds where her first love resided in the graceful arms of the sun god. But no matter how far she travelled, Caya never saw Taru again, or a condor. And for the rest of her life, in the stillest plains of her heart, Caya lamented how it never rained so heavily again.

Joyeuse

Our union began on the most joyous of days and ended on the most savage. For the power of the cross is like the power of the sword, until you can't see which is deceiving which on the descent into fire. An elite soldier should never drop his guard. On Christmas Day in Europe's holiest city, I lowered mine, letting a higher love lower its beguiling veil and thrust its lance into my heart.

My name is Benoît. I was twenty years old when I became a soldier in Charlemagne's army. A provincial boy from the green fields of the west swishing swords with the Frankish aristocracy. I was unnaturally strong and mentally agile, anticipating opponents' moves and striking at the canniest of moments. In combat I envisioned myself a snarling dragon with angelic grace. Soon a mystique swirled around me, and I was happy to wear its magic fabric.

I have always believed in miracles.

Within a year I was a member of the Scara, an honour usually reserved for the finest warriors from the wealthiest families. We protected Europe's most powerful man; his strongest, quickest and most ruthless soldiers. The most prone to adulation. The most likely to be betrayed by a kiss. An accomplished swordsman reads what isn't there and acts upon it. A doomed one reads too much and is confounded.

The omens said I would be a warrior of faith. My arrival in this world was heralded by a knight's sword driven into the door of a rural church in Aquitaine. Stirred from his crypt by the sound, Michel the priest surfaced to see my infant form mewling on the steps, steel shaft and gold hilt vibrating above my head. I was hot to the touch. A trio of ravens watched from the churchyard wall and a nearby oak tree flamed white with fire. Michel, a performer of piety who secretly loved the occult, believed I was a changeling.

"You're a gift from the shadow world," he whispered. "As bright, blinding and powerful as the sword which came with you. You have cured me of my loneliness, boy. Rescued me from this enduring chill."

Or so I was told. To me, it doesn't matter where you're from. Only what you do. Whatever happened to my birth sword, or if it even existed, I could not say. Some stories are useful, others less so. While the uncivilised villagers feared folk tales of demons and goblins, I flourished above a well of wisdom. In the crypt, I absorbed the great literature of antiquity from Suetonius to Cicero. Then I scrutinised the scriptures and pledged my sword to God.

"This is all a show," Michel warned of the Gospels. "All a show."

The Bible was his virtuous pretence, the glory of Rome his passionate vice. On winter evenings, he would light candles and tell tales of Tiberius, Caligula and Nero. I dreamed of escaping servitude's swamp to lead an army into that fabled city where Caesar was slain and Peter martyred.

I have always preferred the company of men. Those who enjoy mine rarely forget it.

Michel grew fearful of my appetites and hypnotic gaze. When I stare at someone, I see what they can become, not what they are. Imagination always usurps reality in man's mind. To instil restraint, Michel ushered me into the woods and commanded me to strip, widen my arms in imitation of the crucifixion and hold until mind or body surrendered. The more I lasted, the stronger I grew. The stiller I remained, the more I saw. The more I sensed, the wilder my visions.

One evening in my sixteenth year, I stood amid the black trees with my arms aloft, dressed only in a loin cloth and a gold chain gifted by Michel. Light waned, unseen life purred, and the shape of the saviour's face appeared on the silver moon. Bracken cracked and leaves rippled. Through the dark emerged an elderly man, cloaked in peasant greys with a gentle smile, scraggly beard and rich blue eyes. He was throned in dawn's glow. Beautiful flowers bloomed in his steps. When St Peter raised his calming hands, the moonlight revealed the marks of crucifixion. He floated forward and kissed my cheek.

"What do you see, child?"

"A holy ghost."

"Where do you walk, child?"

"Nowhere."

"Who do you walk with?"

"Nobody."

"Where have you come from?"

"I don't know."

"Do you believe in the miracle of the Lord?"

"Yes, with all my soul."

"What will you give in return for this miracle?"

"I will give…"

"Speak it, child."

"I will give…"

"Speak it, child. Believe you are a miracle of God."

"I will give…"

… everything.

There is power in cutting yourself loose from the weeds and letting fortune's currents sweep you over the precipice. Only then will you know the gravity in your soul. That evening the moon reddened and the river ran in reverse. I kissed a sleeping Michel on the forehead and rode his horse to Bordeaux so fast the lanes scorched black. Visions of a kindly St Peter held dominion over my heart the entire way.

The next day a cool-eyed aristocrat spotted me in the market and I was conscripted to Charlemagne's army. We were alien brothers: a mixture of Gallic, Slavic, Saxon and

Greek. Yet we were all violent men in our hearts. Skewering an enemy thrilled us, whether wielding our swords or preaching its high-mindedness. Together we carved out the Almighty's plan with the crunch of our boots and the tips of our steel, quelling rebellious Germanic tribes, Viking savages and Muslim marauders.

I grew fiercer with every skirmish. The pleasure of combat became carnal and holy, igniting my body and spirit. When I killed a man, I heard his soul depart. A groaning release, like something was liberated deep within. Every time you finish a man, you own his essence. Sometimes I didn't even need to kill. Summoning my love of God and staring into cowering eyes was enough to subdue my foe into surrender. The best dagger in the world can be a crucifix.

The union of faith and fire drove Charlemagne too. Swathed in veneration's smoke, he was warrior king, God's pilgrim and magic talisman. We feared his earthly power more, as did all of Europe. Our leader was conquering apostle and tempestuous force of nature, with a white beard and craggy face carved like Alpine granite. I quivered when Charlemagne passed by, absorbing the pungent mix of bloodlust and benevolence which intoxicated his army.

Dangling from his waist was Joyeuse, his personal sword. A glinting shaft of steel crowned with a gold cross guard, sheathed in a scabbard encrusted with myriad jewels that changed colour in the light. When witnessed in the sun, the transformation was awe-inspiring, like seeing dawn stream through a church window and baptise the holy cross in a divine glow. It was a pleasure and a terror to serve such a man. As a soldier, you cannot have one without the other.

Charlemagne was a wanderer like me, for there was no capital city in his domain. He was a lover of knowledge who could not read or write. Frankish bishops followed him everywhere, chanting Latin, copying codices and murmuring intrigues among themselves. The king torched Europe with sword and scripture, burning unbelievers and acquiring souls in equal measure.

I feared Charlemagne but I did not love him. I did not know what love was. Not until its smouldering irons were fired into my heart amid the freezing desolation of the Alps.

It was the Year of our Lord 800. We were marching to Rome for Charlemagne's summit with Pope Leo III. Our leader would preside over the Vatican Council to judge the lecherous old fool's alleged perjury and fornication. Statecraft and sex are lascivious bedfellows.

Accompanying our king was Fabrizio, a papal gift to lubricate diplomatic relations. A gaunt, bald man with a hooked nose and pale face, he lurked in the shadows like a dark fairy. As he walked, hands clasped in front of his belly, thin smile suspended between surprise and disgust, a *clink, clink, clink* moved with him. Fellow Scara said he was festooned with gold jewellery under his papal robes. During our trek, Fabrizio was never more than two riders away from Charlemagne. At night he divided his time between the King's tent and distant, solitary brooding, where he fiddled with his crucifix and observed men with a chilly grin.

"I see you," Fabrizio said to me while all soldiers slept, and I sat alone watching a campfire. "I see all things. And I see beauty in you."

The flames sparked and crackled, flushing Fabrizio's face.

"What will you give to your king?" he said.
"My loyalty and strength."
"What do you desire more than anything?"
"Love."
"How will you find it?"
"Through the Lord. Through grace."

"Then follow your king and the holy father. You will find this love you search for. You will find divine joy."

The emptiness of the Alps reduced the most cocksure to quivering loneliness. As vicious winds bit our faces and the cold crawled our blood, I took solace in our destination and St Peter's words. Adventures in a foreign land drive you to give more. To want more. To need more. In any journey there is a moment of transgression, a personal Rubicon, a line you cross from recognising someone to *seeing someone*. It is a look, a gesture, an emanation. A crack in the humdrum visage of existence through which holier light pierces. *Oh God, oh God...*

Armand was a few years older than me. Tall, muscular and taciturn, with cropped dark hair, strong blue eyes and a cool manner. He was icy in his command of others, withstanding the freeze with less clothes than most. At our route's highest peak, I watched him dismount his tired steed and stroke its mane. From a safe distance, I took the true measure of his figure. The winter sun splashed a pool of light around his physique and illuminated his beautiful, frosted face. Something stabbed at my heart. A devil or an angel. I imagined his sweat seeping from his skin and mixing with mine.

I'd seen Armand before, but not in this way. He was alluring and vulnerable, like the deer I used to hunt in Aquitaine's woods. The Alpine panoramas, mixed with a maddening desire to rest my flesh on another's, sent my mind into spasms of delirium. Head and heart besieged, I barely slept as we descended into the luscious green lands where that glorious empire took seed.

My fantasy lover became a tortuous mental puzzle I craved to solve on the sun-kissed journey south. Slowly he succumbed to my gaze. Through Lombardy we rode in silence two horses apart. Armand would move in then withdraw, never uttering a word. In Ravenna, as we assembled our weapons, he didn't flinch when I rested my palm on his knuckles. He was cold to the touch. Coy and unpredictable. He wanted me, that much I could tell. The only question was which one of us would strike first. The only thing separating people from destiny is the will to surrender to the impulse of the moment.

Twelve miles outside Rome, Leo III awaited. In danger of losing his papacy, the degenerate oaf had sent the king of the Franks the city standard and the keys of the confession of St. Peter. Frankish bishops gossiped the pope was a reprobate who drank, screwed and bribed his way to the Lateran Palace. In person he was a snivelling, pot-bellied runt with a deformed face. A man who shuffled rather than strode. Surrounding him was the real spectacle. The luxurious flourishes of his train, the inscrutability of the handsome guards and their lavish papal embroidery. Fabrizio served as the intermediary, passing ornaments, books and relics between the two powers. Charlemagne and Leo smiled blankly, nodding their heads, familiar friends in a familiar ritual.

Their courtship began the previous year. At Rome's Flaminian Gate, the pope's enemies sliced out part of his tongue and blinded him with daggers. Rescued by two of Charlemagne's envoys, Leo fled to Paderborn, where he weaved our credulous king a fantasy. *My liege, divine intervention caused parts of my tongue and eyes to grow back.* Yes, I believe in miracles. I also believe in man's infinity capacity to deceive.

The next day we entered the city of the Caesars. The true seat of empire displaced by the upstart to the east. As we entered the outskirts, a flock of ravens flew over our heads. I had travelled far, from those humble church steps in Aquitaine to the greatest basilica on earth. Something momentous would happen while we were here, as sure as two edges of a blade form the tip of a sword.

I expected Charlemagne to be feted like the Lord entering Jerusalem; we were welcomed only by indifferent rabble. A begging prostitute approached. Her skin was covered in lesions, and she stooped like she'd been punched in the stomach. I did not know her language, but I could see in her eyes she was possessed by some devil. Thirty pieces of silver, every evening.

Over the pale present, I painted the rich colours of the past. Julius Caesar riding his chariot in a victory parade. Augustus presiding over a festival of games. Nero cruelly consigning Christians to death. In the distance I saw the colosseum and imagined the terrible beauty of brutish men savaging each other, the cries of the crowd stirring them to slaughter.

As we crossed the Tiber towards the Lateran Palace, Armand conspired to be next to me in the march, so close I could feel his chilly breath.

"Am I welcome here?" he ventured.

"You are a Frank. We are all welcome here."

"To you I hope to be more than a Frank."

"More than?"

"Yes."

Clink.

"Everyone wants more."

"Do you wish to have more?"

"Yes."

Clink.

"As much as me?"

"What more do you wish to be?"

"Whatever you decide."

Clink. Clink. Clink. Riding behind was Fabrizio, his face turned knowingly to the ground.

At the Lateran Palace, power moved in whispers and glances through shadows. As the Scara, we accompanied

Charlemagne through a spectrum of sensory delight: mosaics, carvings and ornaments. Our tour ended in the state banqueting hall, outside which a porphyry fountain spouted jets of water. Inside, to the right of the papal throne, was a mosaic of St. Peter, Leo III and Charlemagne. The imitation of the apostle was feeble, yet it propelled me back to the woods where I once hunted with a child's abandonment. My quarry Armand was so deep in my mind I felt possessed by another changeling.

While Charlemagne stayed in the Lateran, our quarters were an empty hall half a mile from the palace. The Scara was kept busy with drills, exercises and marches. One moment Armand would smile. The next, he would look through me like I wasn't there. My gaze would shrink his stature, then have no discernible effect. Doubt and desire were all I knew in those cold December days.

Two days before Christmas, under our king's blessing, Leo took the oath of purgation. The charges were withdrawn; his opponents exiled. With typical flourish, Fabrizio orchestrated a group of knights to arrive from the Holy Lands and present Charlemagne with sepulchral keys from Jerusalem. Later that day while I guarded the king's chamber, a tailor arrived with a Roman tunic and pointed boots. History's strands were tightening. All I could do was stare into space imagining a disrobed Armand. Entwined, flesh on flesh, his lips owning me. In love and off guard.

On Christmas Day morning, we assembled in St Peter's Basilica. Hundreds stood in the grey cold of the church for the nativity mass. As Charlemagne prayed to the bones of St Peter, Leo crept behind him carrying a flash of light. I readied my sword, suspecting a blade. Leo whispered something to our king, then placed a circlet of gold upon his head and pronounced him Emperor of the Romans. Chorists broke out in Latin like the Holy Spirit had swept up their behinds.

"To Charles, Augustus, the God-crowned great and peace-loving emperor of the Romans, life and victory!"

Manufactured ecstasy rippled through the church. Leo grinned, widened his arms and prostrated himself before the emperor. Celebratory hymns soared to the basilica's ceiling. Charlemagne affected surprise but was a weak actor. He was the new Augustus, anointed by God's representative above the bones of St Peter in the city of the Caesars. What was conceived and choreographed in shadow was completed in light.

"Behold a Christmas miracle," Fabrizio crooned. "The sweetest unions. A gift to us all from the king of heaven."

Charlemagne's eyes changed. Not in colour but in depth. He was somewhere high now, closer to the Almighty. Detached in a dreamworld. His soul was seduced by a malformed pope pulling whatever strings he could assemble. Those pointed boots would leave indelible footprints on the conscience of the world. My mind swept our liege's empire with indifference, returning full circle to the only state which mattered absolutely. Armand.

What followed the coronation was a dark fairytale fit for a changeling. Even now, as I lie in this cell and recount it to myself, I am feverish. Deep within, I never wanted to be a Christian. Only deluded soldiers believe God is at their side during battle's frenzy. The only side any warrior is on is his own. And his only weapons are the sword in his hand, the courage in his heart and his desire to risk it all.

The rest of Christmas Day consisted of more masses and a feast of game. In our quarters, Armand and I stood among other soldiers and exchanged platitudes about this new political pact. My gaze bore into him. He too was feeling destiny's arm curl around his shoulders. I wanted to have done with it all. To press my lips to his cool mouth before our fellow soldiers. I have always believed in miracles. That Christmas evening, my wish was granted, and a different kind of crown placed upon my tender head.

Fabrizio summoned us both. Charlemagne would dine privately with Leo III that evening, leaving his chamber unprotected for several hours. He needed two Scara to guard the room, situated in one of the far-flung corridors of the Lateran. Sweet anticipation of solitude with Armand subdued my faculties to pacified mush. Only one memory survives from my walk to the post. The statue of the Capitoline Wolf. A tense, watchful bronze monster from which Romulus and Remus sucked, lost in their appetite for life.

As a gift, Fabrizio had placed a jug of wine and two empty goblets on a table outside the chamber. Nervously I drank the sweetness. Soon I heard Armand's boots tap and his armour rattle. His silhouetted frame appeared at the far end of the corridor. Candlelight cast him in a sublime golden hue. A Roman god sculpted in dragon fire and smouldering in the smoke. I could not stem the tide which flowed within. I still cannot. I never will.

I sensed Armand was a changeling like me, forever on the verge of revealing his true self. In the vulnerable places between his armour plates, I would chip away. When I poured him a drink and passed it to him, he accepted without resistance. For these brief hours we would be alone with the emperor's chamber. We would never be so powerful again. An opportunity. *A gift*. For if we could not be united now, we never would be.

"Come with me Armand. Come with me."

I gazed at him until he wilted. My partner's diffident eyes trembled, wrecked by rolling waves of longing. He was adrift at sea, another lost leviathan finding its companion in an endless ocean of loneliness. Feeling what I felt. Imagining what I imagined. The magic and the fire to be free. Coyly, I ventured backwards. My steps sure. My palms open. My beckoning eyes never leaving his. Pushing open the oak door, I savoured the billowing scent of royalty.

"Madness," Armand whispered. "Madness."

"I see you. I see beauty in you. I see all things."

We crossed the threshold and closed the door. The room was small, illuminated with candles and furnished with lavish tapestries, grandiose silverware and furs spreadeagled on the floor. Exotic perfume hovered, reminding me of Charlemagne's concubines.

On a table lay a map of the Italian lands. In the centre was the emperor's bed, draped in pristine, purple satin. To the left a rich red curtain closed off part of the room, where I imagined Charlemagne prayed. A starry, still Christmas night poured through slits in the wall. I wished three ravens would land on the ledge. Gifts from the other side, graced with a throbbing sword and dragon flames.

Lying on the bed in its scabbard was Joyeuse. The gold hilt gleamed. A delightful shaft of delicacy and deadliness, sinking into my guts. Light-headed, I recalled the surge of excitement in the basilica that morning. The winter sun soaking Armand's beauty in the magisterial whiteness of the Alps. All I wanted was to inhale him, then let the devil scrape the meat from my ribs.

I picked up the sword, surged forward and kissed Armand on the lips. He was still so cold to the touch. I gazed into his eyes until he crumpled, from stunned to softened to supine. He disrobed before me greedily. Armour clattered on the stone floor. Naked flesh. Beautiful, incorruptible. Not the kind daubed on church walls or described in holy scriptures. Real skin, blood, hair, sweat. Real yearning. Our eyes filled with flames and the chamber glowed in ethereal light.

I pulled Joyeuse from its scabbard and lifted the steel high. Slowly, I moved it towards Armand's throat, resting where I saw his pulse beating. I traced the tip down his chest, through the curling hair, to his stiffened loins. Armand lowered his hand, hooked his finger under the sword and raised the tip back to his chest. With a dark stare he leaned forward, pushing his flesh into the blade. He winced. Blood appeared above his heart. I removed the weapon. Armand ran his forefinger over the wound. Fluid dripping from the tip, he pushed his finger into my mouth. The sweetest of tastes. The salt of his fingers. The warmth of his lifeblood. The burning of his eyes. Armand dropped to his knees as I widened my arms to from the shape of the cross.

Our fires merged as we made love on Charlemagne's bed. Emperors of the world. All else fluttered into the abyss like phantoms fleeing holy light. My former life. My upbringing. The preachings of the church. The codes of the military. Union. *Sweet, blessed union.* To open your half-soul and let the missing piece travel inside you. I deepened myself into Armand until God conjoined us in my heart. *Our heart.* For we were not separate beings. We were one. We still are.

Clink. A sound. Through the heady fog. *Clink.* Another presence. From behind the curtain. *Clink.* I tightened. Armand was still lost in ecstasy's storm. A miraculous form reduced to writhing, sweating flesh, dragging me away from the intrusive sound. If Charlemagne, the ghost of Caesar or the lord of heaven had entered, I would have still quickened my absorption into Armand. Damnation rendered trivial by the white heat of lust. *Clink.* I continued. *Clink.* Away now. *Clink.* Into the flames. *Clink. Clink. Clink.*

We lay in each other's arms for a brief time, stroking each other's skin. A coolness hung in the room; love dissipated like steam from a cauldron. Armand was retreating into himself. He rose in a hurry and dressed, timid eyes searching the floor. I followed, gently placing my hand on his jaw and turning his eyes towards me.

"Do not worry," I said. "I will never do anything to hurt you. I love you."

From my neck I lifted the gold chain, gifted to me by Michel. Reaching down, I drew back the fingers of Armand's clenched right fist and slid the keepsake into his palm.

"There is no shame," I implored. "No shame at all in love. This was our miracle. Nobody else's."

We kissed, returned to our posts and stood in dazed attention. I could barely breathe. My body feigned alertness, while my soul wandered pastures of unimaginable beauty. I pictured us at St Peter's Basilica. A union blessed by Charlemagne and Leo III. Two guards relieved us, and we parted company by the Capitoline Wolf. I tried to steal a glance from Armand. He did not look around. To this day I cannot remember whether we returned Joyeuse to its scabbard.

Christmas Day ended in our quarters. We lay together but far apart in the same hall, separated by the beds of the other Scara. I visualised every beat of my heart sending tiny pulses of love to Armand. Pockets of trembling pink air, circulating the room and descending gently to bless my lover's chest. His touch still lived with me. I dreamt of a crucifix slowly descending through Charlemagne's crown, like how I'd slid Joyeuse's tip across Armand body. We were together, caressed by otherworldly breezes, in a room of a thousand flickering candles. The world of the changelings. That fleeting final contact of our lips. Then the dream terminated with the *clink, clink, clink* of money, locks and chains. The deadening sound of exchange.

The next morning, Armand was gone. When the bell tolled seven, Fabrizio ordered us to march through the city, no longer as royal troops but imperial warriors. The rest of the day was torture as I awaited my lover's return. After a long winter's day of marching and mustering, we were permitted an hour of free time before dusk to walk the city.

Armand stood alone by the banks of the Tiber, observing its uneventful flow, forearms rested on a wall. I walked up beside him. Holy light returned. The soft sheets of the emperor's bed. The murky taste of his lips. I looked around to see if anyone was watching us, then slid my hand towards his. He flinched. *Clink.* All light drowned in darkness. *Clink.* His bare neck filled me with sadness. *Clink.*

"Where is my chain?" I implored.

My lover returned only cold indifference, shrouded in silence.

"Do not deny this," I said. "Do not deny what you know to be true. What you know to be holy. What you know to be a miracle."

Armand flung my arm away. He placed his hand on the hilt of his sword, staring into me with demonic eyes. They were drained of beauty.

"We are discovered," he said. "Fabrizio witnessed our love. He will tell our king tomorrow. Unless we repent."

The revelation felt like it was happening to somebody else far away.

"They will tell you the union of the Scara and the empire matter more," I said. "They will tell you that the union between Charlmagne and the Lord is all that counts. But tell me they have ever made you feel like I did."

"We have defiled the bed of the emperor."

I placed my hand on his shoulder and looked him firmly in the eye.

"No, we blessed it. Our union matters more. I will die defending it."

"You are wicked and mad. Your devilry destroys a greater vision. There can be no joy if the joy is so short-lived. This is not joy. This is greed."

"But it has already happened. The only way we can live and be at one is by flying away. They will not find us."

My mind improvised a miracle. A disguise. A bribe. A ship. An escape.

"I will take care of everything," I pleaded. "Meet me here at midnight. We'll be out of the city and in foreign lands by daybreak. Where we are nothing to anyone but everything to each other."

"Leave me, devil."

"Devil? The only devil is the one telling you this is wrong. No sin would feel like that. No sin at all. Our union was pure."

Armand grunted. No words seemed to express the tempest in his head.

"Leave. Me. Be."

"I will not."

"You are mad. This is impossible. This cannot be."

"It already is. Even the most powerful keep secrets from the Lord."

"You are the devil himself. Seducer!"

Armand stormed away, like a wave crashing onto a rock and bursting into a thousand droplets. I stood alone in the city of the Caesars. A place where false selves dazzled in the daylight and truth brooded beautifully in the dark.

After dinner, a papal guard escorted me to Fabrizio's lair in the Lateran Palace. He sat behind a huge wooden table. To his right side stood a bloated, pink-faced cardinal. On his cheek he bore an inch-long knife wound.

To his left was Armand, eyes downcast. A trapped animal, like the ones I used to hunt in the woods. I re-imagined the room where our love exploded. Joyeuse, suspended above our heads and glinting in sepulchral light. A distant illusion, unfolding within a glass ball whose edges curved into vibrating softness. A fabricated land made for changelings, suddenly shattered by an icy hammer.

"You have committed sacrilege," said Fabrizio sternly. "A vile deed of perversion upon your fellow soldier. On Christmas evening, you poisoned this man against his will, and while unconscious, committed foul acts in the emperor's chamber. In the very bed of your master. Later that evening you made a similar seduction of the cardinal, while he was at prayer in his private quarters. When he resisted, you attacked him and fled. Leaving your mark at the scene."

Fabrizio threw my gold chain onto the table. *Clink.*

"Both will swear before almighty God the truth of the account. When the clock strikes eleven, your crimes will be reported to the holy father and the emperor. I anticipate execution by hanging. Or maybe we could tie you into a sack of wolves and hurl you into the Tiber, like they did under the Caesars."

Visions of my future flowed over me in waves of deadening black. They swept me back to the emperor's chamber. The coronation. The Alps. My military career. St Peter. Michel. A sword in a church door. A trio of ravens. An oak tree aflame with white fire. I saw no more beyond that.

"Yet we are prepared to offer you a gift," continued Fabrizio. "An act of grace. Your crimes will not be reported to the holy father and the emperor. Your absence from the Scara can be excused. On the condition you repent."

I recalled the moment when Leo placed the crown on Charlemagne's head. The way Fabrizio had watched us on the trek to Rome. The wine he'd generously laid on for us on Christmas evening. The mysterious curtain in Charlemagne's chamber. The *clink, clink, clink* of his voyeuristic trap.

"I will repent nothing."

Thhwhaaaack. I was knocked to the ground from behind. Blindfolded and hands tied, I was dragged across stone and cobbles and bundled onto the floor of a moving carriage. We bounced along to the sound of horses' hooves. I was carried upstairs somewhere. One of my assailants removed the blindfold to reveal a bed in a stone room. There was a single slat through which light streamed past a wooden crucifix on the wall and onto a barren floor.

The next morning, a rattle of keys. Two papal guards and the cardinal entered, affecting a pious look. He stood over me in pity, twisting his rosary beads. I wanted to slice the cut on his cheek wider and drain him of blood.

"I have pleaded with Charlemagne and the pope for clemency on grounds of passion," he said with a smirk. "I told them you were experiencing visitations and must come into the custody of the church. *This one is not like others*, I said. He is blessed, I said. A miracle."

He knelt beside me, like a thirsty dog about to slurp from a bowl of water. Surrounding him was an aroma of rancid wine and decaying meat.

"They have agreed to turn you over to me," the cardinal said stroking my hair. "You're a gift, dropped in my lap courtesy of our heavenly father. Your touch will protect me in the darkest of nights. Save me from this enduring chill. Serve the church, my child. Serve your God. There will be no greater joy."

While Charlemagne and the Scara returned north across the Alps, I stayed prisoner, a gift from an emperor to a pope. A plaything of the cardinal. Docile and accepting of his special love. On rare occasions, I was let out for walks into an airless garden surrounded by high walls and armed thugs. I befriended a fellow slave Luca, who heard Armand was at the cardinal's countryside retreat. Despite his betrayal, I was willing to forgive my lover. Every time you love a man, you carry his spirit inside you forever more.

In my cell that evening, I stood naked in the pose of the crucifixion. The wild visions returned. In the dead of night, I dreamed of escaping, stealing a horse and riding to the cardinal's retreat where I would pretend to be a messenger from God. There I would learn Armand, ridden with guilt, had taken his own life. The housekeeper would show me the dagger: a wooden crucifix, sharpened at the end. Armand had shoved it into his guts, with the same relish he'd pushed himself onto Joyeuse. I imagined what my love felt when he plunged in the cross. The ecstasy of death. He would make the finest of gifts, to heaven or to hell, or whatever awaits us on the other side. In my mind I burned the death house to cinders, then danced around its flames as the heat singed sensuously across my face.

I woke from my reverie to see St Peter standing over me.

"What do you see, child?"

"I see death."

"Where do you walk, child?"

"Nowhere."

"Who do you walk with?"

"Nobody."

"Where have you come from?"

"I don't know."

"Do you believe in the miracle of the Lord?"

"No."

"What do you believe in?"

"I believe in..."

"Speak it, child."

"I believe in..."

"Speak it, child."

"I believe in..."

... one thing only.

I lie in my cell, melancholic but becalmed. From the wall I snatch the crucifix and sharpen it against the stone. The Scara. Charlemagne. The church. Leo III. The body. The soul. None of these things would last forever. Not even God, for I had seen no evidence of Him. Except for the moment when Armand and I were one. The rest of it was just a show, as Michel said. The truth of this world is forever obscured in symbols, signs and suggestions.

A rattling sound. The cardinal enters my chamber, followed by a sneering Fabrizio. The couple move towards me with a *clink, clink, clink,* fanning to the sides to snare me in a trap. The Cardinal disrobes, his fat white blubber drooping over his waistline. I move my hand downwards in the weakening light, a gesture invisible to their lustful eyes. In my mind I turn them from men of God to ogres of Satan, trapped in scaley, sickening flesh skinned from monsters who stew in the freezing pits of hell.

"Charlemagne said you are our property," said the cardinal. "A gift. Part of his agreement with the holy father. I now gift you to another."

They leer above me with faces like starving ghosts. Fabrizio carries a wooden club, reminiscent of how Leo once carried Charlemagne's crown.

"My joy," Fabrizio said. "My joy."

Three ravens perch on a wall. Somewhere an oak tree catches fire. A sword is rammed into a church door. Reaching under my bed, I grab the crucifix and gaze at my attackers. My body is swallowed in dragon flame and I return in my dreams to the icy kingdom of the Alps.

I lunge at the cardinal, driving the sharpened base of the crucifix into his throat. Fabrizio, frozen in shock, meets the same fate. Both men crash to the floor like chunks of mountain rock. I could not hear their souls depart. No part of their essences was worth owning. Kneeling between their twitching frames like a penitent, I clutch the cross with both hands and raise it high above my head.

"I believe in the miracle of love."

Downwards I thrust. To my left. To my right. To my left. To my right. Armand's exquisite face flickers before my eyes. Candlelight casts him in a sublime golden hue. A Roman god sculpted in fire and smouldering in the smoke. I plunge deeper and deeper and deeper in a grim search for fulfilment. The blood flows towards the door where two guards appear, swords unsheathed.

I throw my crucifix down. Opening my chest, I spread my arms to form a cross. For the final time I shoot an unholy gaze straight into strangers' eyes. The guards raise their steel and plunge. What follows is a joyous occasion, in honour of a union between two changelings who gifted themselves to each other when ancient magic still held power over the earth.

Amrita

Springtime in Karnataka awakened the appetites of the gentlest souls. Nature's sweet light planted tender kisses on the earth's upturned cheek, drawing lusty colour from a pallid world too long cooled. On the Krishna's banks new life stiffened to the sky in shoots of green and yellow, as the holy river tinkled in the rays of the blessed sun.

Regeneration's fragrance caressed all, inclining budding lovers to lay their noses together and inhale the finest pleasures of the turning world. Those at the beginning of life's rotation thought it would last forever. The old, broken by fortune's wheel, knew otherwise. While nature's palette sent the young blind, aged souls saw through the haze to the pain of loves past. Listening to the Krishna hush and hiss, elderly wanderers contemplated their imminent return to the source of all things, dreaming of rebirth in a kinder world.

Beside the river, deep in the wrestling trees, lay the warlord Bhaavik's palace: an intimidating lair which rose through the mangroves in columns and domes of brooding grey marble. Bhaavik was the region's most venerated ruler, renowned for lavishing goodwill on loyalists and the ruthless oppression of foes.

Nestled above his stony face was a disorderly mane of black hair; below it an extravagant beard reaching his barrelled chest. Bhaavik was greedy and impulsive. On the battlefield, in the banqueting hall and on his bed, the chieftain consumed all before him, swallowing acquaintances into his body politic and spitting out scraps for swooping cormorants.

His wife Amrita was the only creature who could tame him. A gentle zephyr of ghostly blue eyes, polished skin and chestnut hair, she invigorated every room she swept with her sweet tongue and generous manner. Jealous ladies searched behind her opulent saris of brown, olive and gold for a blemish to her body or character. They found only frustration: a pious lady, skilled dancer and accomplished musician with a zealous conviction in the healing power of fine food. Romantic to the deepest wells of her heart, Amrita vowed to immolate herself on Bhaavik's funeral pyre when the time came, so their ashes would burn in a union no monsoon could extinguish.

Then one spring Amrita withdrew into her chambers, refusing food and water. Meek and sallow, she seemed unable to articulate the source of her pain. Medicine men were summoned to no avail. Her emaciated decline culminated in tragedy. One evening, after an unexpected walk in the palace grounds, she entered the kitchen, stole a bottle of snake poison used to kill vermin and locked herself in her bedroom. When Bhaavik broke down the door and ran to his lifeless queen, his howl was heard in the Himalayas. While Amrita's corpse lay in a white marble mausoleum in the prettiest part of the gardens, her spirit was said to possess the palace's food and furnishings. For the name 'Amrita' meant eternal life, and many prophesied their beloved lady would one day return to bathe the community in grace.

Bhaavik refused to leave his palace for months afterwards, declining even to hunt antelope on the plain. At court, he offered little except the slow nod of his head. Occasionally when it rained, he ventured alone into the palace grounds, catching the slanting water in his mouth. Onlookers speculated he was searching for Amrita's reincarnated soul among the trees, plants and birds. In the deepest pits of mourning for the end of his childless marriage, the warlord's talk turned morbid. To the mysteries of the holy river. To a premonition of drowning. To his deserved rebirth as the vilest creature in the cosmos.

The following spring, while the palace still lay in shadow, Bhaavik made a special announcement. To commemorate the first anniversary of his wife's death, he would broker peace with the ageing Ranbir, a rival chieftain. Both leaders hated each other, paranoid the other might launch a surprise night attack and slice his sleeping throat. Now a grief-stricken Bhaavik had lost his appetite for conflict and was inviting his old enemy to renew ancient bonds. The more cynical courtiers saw the move as a symptom of Bhaavik's degeneration. Most welcomed the news. The palace was missing its princess, the chief his wife, the land its happiness. Through this banquet Amrita would live again, reincarnated in a sumptuous feast unlike any seen beside the Krishna.

The palace cook would wizard this divine experience. A gentle creature, Azad was the mildest of seasonings compared to the fiery spice of his lord. His slim body and unblemished face rendered him fresher than his twenty-seven years. The cook was sober and fastidious in everything, from the twice-daily cleaning of his kitchen to the brushing of his glistening bun of brown hair.

Here was a man, the sages said, who taught himself to go without. Azad's only intemperance was an excessive thirst for water after a long day at the tandoor. When a friend asked him to leave his bubbling sauces to carouse, or a rival court offered him riches to serve, or a blossoming young lady invited him to stroll by the Krishna, Azad gracefully declined. Such insularity stirred no animosity. Those spurned retreated uplifted, praising Vishnu such a polite man was tempering an undisciplined world. Most beloved was Azad's smile, a sprinkle of dawn sunshine to lighten a monsoon day.

"What is your secret?" asked others.

"I have no secret," he replied. "My only desire is to be happy."

"What is it that makes you most happy?"

"Seeing others blessed the same."

Proudly unmarried, Azad was rumoured to have tasted the delights of woman only once. Some suspected even that was a falsehood to spare his blushes, concocted by friends in the market who sold him slices of goats, hare and boar. The only person Azad ever loved was his late mother, a poet admired for her elegance and feared for her temper. His father passed long ago from addiction to drink, while his only sibling was married to a lord in the mountains of the north.

As a boy, Azad could have sung devotional hymns in the temple or attended school with the Brahmins. But the fragrant lure of the tandoor proved irresistible. Food was the first thing in Azad's mind when he woke, the last thing before he slept. He sliced, chopped, stirred and seasoned with flourish, translating his mental visions into the sweetest dishes the realm had savoured. Restraint was his signature. He served no more than needed, nor revealed his special ingredients. Not even Bhaavik knew what awaited him at the banqueting table.

To fellow servants who observed him closely, there seemed two Azads. The first was a mild-mannered gentleman who relished spreading cheer on solitary walks. The second was a monomaniac perfectionist absorbed in his craft. Those who glimpsed through the kitchen door during feast preparation would catch Azad in the clutch of an unnerving trance. The dead eyes of a charging war horse overshadowed his famous smile, while his tongue ventured hesitantly back and forth through his lips, like a tortoise emerging from its shell. The impression was of someone in a hermetic daydream, greedy yet fearful, hypnotised into another realm of mind by an invisible snake charmer.

The tale of the two Azads began as a child. On a baking summer's night, one month after his alcoholic father was found dead on a dirt track by the river, Azad woke from thirsty dreams. Desperate for water, he tottered into the family kitchen. On the table was a succulent bounty of fruit his mother had laid the evening before. One item caught his fancy: a piece of plump flesh no bigger than his hand and speckled in brown, olive and gold. The fruit seemed to call out to him from the table, inviting him to caress its succulent shape.

Feed this desire. Feed this desire. Feed –

"Greedy boy," his mother screamed as she pounced from the shadows. She'd been sitting there all night, lost in grief. In her rage she slapped Azad again and again across the cheeks and pushed him to the floor.

"Deny yourself until the time is right. Restraint child. Restraint!"

As punishment, his mother pricked hot pins onto Azad's tongue every morning and evening for three days and forced him to prepare family meals for a week. He was restricted to water and forbidden to savour his dishes until each was perfect. Hunger submerged within him like a crocodile. Whenever his concentration at the tandoor failed, he sensed his mother watching like a vulture.

"Restraint is the second most important art of the chef," she said when his punishment was complete.

"What's the first, mother?"

"Surprise," she said, wafting a spoon of coriander chutney under his nose. "Now close your eyes, open your mouth and…. that's it, smiley, greedy, impatient little boy."

When Azad was eighteen, mother's wisdom and cruelty ended. During morning prayer in the Krishna, a jealous, hot-tempered man whose advances she'd spurned the night before held her head underwater until she drowned. It was said the plants drooped at her passing and even the river froze in defiance at the sun. Since then, every meal Azad cooked became a reincarnation of his mother, flavoured with the sweetness and sourness of her legend.

During his trances at the tandoor, mother appeared as a magic bird feathered with jewels, whispering support and scoldings from the courtyard before flying through the kitchen door into his heart. Her spirit bubbled up from his pots, mixing fragrant inspiration with vicious rebuke. When culinary perfection was achieved, Azad sipped water and heard her bruising laughter.

"A cook is many different people," she once said. "Servant of the lord. Master of yourself. Leader of all around."

"I have no servants. No armies. No riches. What then do I lead, mother?"

"People's desire, Azad. Learn to cultivate their desire and deny it from yourself. People who leave your table must not feel weighed down but ready to live more. That is what you give people. The gift of life. Remember you are a cook second. A leader first. A bestower and custodian of life."

As he grew to manhood, Azad's accomplishments caught the nose of Bhaavik, who appointed him as the palace's chef. Azad relished watching the court succumb to his spell. When feasting was finished and Amrita led the communal dance to the melodies of the veena, Azad watched coolly from behind a pillar, proud to have forged the channel through which the merriment flowed. During sleep, he fantasised about leading an army across the plain to save a captivating princess like Amrita from imprisonment. Together they would dine in the heavens, abandoning a real world as insipid as diluted milk.

Impressed by Azad's dedication, Bhaavik converted the cellar under the palace's kitchens into living quarters. To peer into this subterranean space was to see into Azad's soul. Bed, basin, table, cupboards and ornaments were impeccably clean and ordered. Azad was in exile and at home, withdrawn from the court's hustle yet the foundation of its spiritual life. A solo genius whose commitment to solitude burnished his mystique, he was an inscrutable man who could divide himself at will, nourishing the community with delights that depended on his mind residing in a darker world.

The morning after Bhaavik announced his peace banquet with Ranbir, the chieftain summoned Azad to his throne room. In seven sunsets, the warlord expected a feast worthy of Vishnu, Shiva and Lakshmi.

"Within your gifts we shall find Amrita," said Bhaavik. "Eternal life beyond samsara. No one should contemplate the pain of death."

"No, my lord," said Azad.

Without warning, Bhaavik's manner changed. The chieftain bored his eyes through the cook, his soul preoccupied by some distant, brooding unknown.

"What lies beyond, Azad?"

"I am a simple kitchen servant, my lord. I have neither the knowledge nor intelligence to say."

"I hope to see my wife again."

"As do I, my lord. We all want to see our lady again."

"Until then we have the finest pleasures of the turning world. Your feast. Her spirit shall live in every dish, bowl, conversation and dance. They tell me she may have regressed due to the nature of her demise. But that was not her. Some demon ravaged her. This land is possessed with... evil."

Bhaavik slipped deeper into melancholy.

"With this banquet, all will be purified. Peace will reign across the land. Will you lead us to that happy place, good Azad?"

"I fear you ask me to perform the duties of a deity. Your wife's qualities exceeded all the world's natural abundances. Not even food can do justice to the exultant power of Amrita's transcendent love. Yet I shall try my utmost."

"Of that I'm convinced, good Azad."

Bhaavik fixed his attention on his servant.

"Do you ever grieve, Azad?"

"For whom, my lord?"

"For your mother?"

"Never when I cook, sir. For food is the gift of life."

"Is that your secret?"

"No, sir, I have none of those."

Annoyed by Azad's tranquillity, Bhaavik unleashed venom.

"Your dishes are predictable and repetitious," he scolded. "Be warned, the most powerful people in the realm will be here. They will expect something very different too. Served with your winning smile. Do not fail me Azad, or the consequences will be dire."

Azad smiled, bowed and slinked away. After finding solitude in the palace gardens, he dropped to his knees with his head in his hands. Bhaavik was right; he was bereft of ideas. Dosakaya pachadi, uttapams, ragi mudde and chitrapaka. Rainbow platters of grains, pulses and vegetables. Raw mango, plantain, bitter gourd, jackfruit and sesame with black mustard-seed dressing. Dumplings of urad dal and pepper soaked in yoghurt. Every conceivable use of puran poli. Paruppu vadai and five-lentil fritters. Fried rohu, crab meat and countless other seafood. Fruits blended with buttermilk. Molasses sprinkled with pepper.

All stale, dry and unambitious. To disguise his creative paucity, Azad had resorted to sly reconfigurations of old dishes. Now master had seen through it. Soon nothing would cloak Azad's starved imagination.

When the sun set and the villagers retreated indoors, Azad paced the banks of the Krishna in panic, eyes flicking back and forth from the dusty path to the luscious mangroves to the river's implacable current. Underneath the soothing sound of water flowed another voice, bubbling up from the riverbed.

Feed this desire, Azad. Feed this desire. Feed this desire.

As if he was at the tandoor, Azad slipped into a deep trance, tongue twitching and eyes fixed. He floated back to the palace, wanderers averting their gaze as this sleepwalker crossed their path.

Soon he was back in the kitchen. Swallowed in shadow, he lit an oil lamp and crept towards the pantry. Opening the hatch in the floor, he descended the steps into the dimness of his living quarters. The pungent smell of rotting flesh pervaded the space. All three candles had burned away. Azad lit them again, glazing the room in sickly-gold light. Scattered on the floor were butchered carcasses of otters, rats and banded krait. From the bed, underneath the white linen, came the tormenting hiss.

"Feed this desire, Azad," it said. "*Feed me.* I hunger for more."

Lamp trembling in his hand, Azad pulled back the sheet. Coiled on the bed was a huge spiral of olive skin covered in brown bands. In the cellar's glow, two golden pupils flickered amid irises of ghostly blue. The king cobra raised its head, unfurled its tongue and exposed its fangs with menacing calm.

The creature had grown since it first slid into the kitchen on that hot evening months ago. Azad's first instinct had been to strike the intruder, but he remembered how the Brahmin offered milk and prayers to snakes. Since then, Azad welcomed the cobra like a pet, learning every inch and curve of its body and allowing it to circle him during dawn meditation.

The cook set the lamp down and sat on the bed. The snake slithered across his thighs, caressed the small of his back and crawled up his spine.

"Feed us, Azad," the cobra said. "We both hunger for more."

"I know. I cannot quench my desire."

"Then you must take it. Like you took me."

"I am afraid."

"The moment is ripe. The power within reach. Ease your pain. We can be united. No more secrets."

"I know."

"Be not afraid of your desire, Azad. Feed it. Feed me. *Feed us*."

"I know."

"Soon I will grow too big for this cellar. I beg you to let me out. Show the world our love."

"Our sin must be hidden, my love. I kept you alive so you cannot be reincarnated as an even lower form of life."

"Azad, I do not want to live if we cannot be together."

"I must go back to the holy river. To see mother. To hear her counsel."

"No more secrets, Azad," the cobra hissed. "No more secrets."

Still in the grip of his trance, Azad ascended the steps leaving the hatch open. Weaving through the village's sacks of rice, pulses, cotton and sugarcane, he made his way across the fields to the spot in the Krishna where his mother drowned. Resting on the riverbank, he prayed to Vishnu, contemplating the countless lives behind him and the countless lives yet to unfold. The previous year's ecstasy flooded his mind, mingled with terror that such a love may never resurface.

"Just as those bitten by snakes are vulnerable to suffering and death," mother once said. "Those bitten by desires suffer the cycle of births and deaths."

With a whistling sound, a brown, olive and gold swift landed on the Krishna without a ripple. Its feathers glowed like jewels. Mother appeared in the moonlight, floating on the water dressed in her burial sari. Old then young. Drawn then bursting with life. Stooping down, she lifted something from the river. A brown, olive and gold piece of plump flesh no bigger than Azad's hand. A swirling luminescent pattern flowed within the fruit.

Squeezing his eyes to stop the rolling tears, Azad stumbled into the river, the holy water reaching his navel. Only once in his life had he felt such yearning.

"Remember, you are a cook second and a leader first," she said as she handed him the fruit. "The moment is ripe. The power within reach. Ease your pain. Feed your desire."

"But you said desire is a disease. A poison to our souls. I must bring life."

"Do you feel alive, Azad? Have you *ever* felt alive?"

In the darkness his lover's voice returned, repeating the question she asked him by the tandoor when Bhaavik was out hunting. *What's your secret, Azad? The secret to your smile?* That sweet moment when their hands first touched; the first in a few brief afternoons of ecstasy that lifted Azad to a higher divinity.

In the holy river, clutching his mother's gift, Azad ascended there again.

"Feed this desire, Azad. *Feed this desire.*"

When Azad opened his eyes, mother's spirit was gone. Fruit in hand, he hurried to the palace.

Ahead of him in a clearing was Anaisha, a pretty village girl with a heart-shaped face and a perfume of disarming sweetness. Men courted her from sunrise to sunset, yet Anaisha refused them all.

"Azad," she said. "What don't you join me for a dip? The water is so cool. The evening so hot. Let me spend time with that beautiful smile."

"No, I cannot. I will not. I have business to attend to."

"With me, you will desire nothing more, Azad."

"Business to attend to. My work. My food. My *passion*."

When Azad arrived at the edges of the palace grounds, a figure stepped into his path and pressed a firm palm across his chest. He was a tall man with a scarred face, reeking of the stables.

"I am an emissary of Ranbir," he said. "I ask you to join his kingdom as a cook for three times what you receive from Bhaavik."

"No, I cannot. I will not. I have my master to attend to."

"Sir, I don't ask. I command."

"And I command the gracious and generous Ranbir to leave me be. My master is chosen. My fate sealed. I cook for one person only."

"You will have all you desire and more."

"I desire nothing else in my life, except to cook. To revive spirits. To honour the most ravishing lady who'd ever lived."

In the palace kitchen, Azad found Bhaavik slouched at the table, twisting the point of a carving knife into the wood. His master seemed tired and irritable, stinking of sugarcane wine.

"Tell me what is in your feast," said the lord. "I demand it."

"No, I cannot. I will not. I have my profession to attend to."

"Your profession is more powerful than your lord?"

"No, for if I were to denigrate my profession, I would be insulting my lord."

"Very well, Azad."

"A chef must build anticipation. Anticipation builds desire."

"You're like an ascetic who has retreated from normal civilisation. An exile from pleasure. But one whose life depends on giving it. Yet you smile through it all. Why do you smile?"

"Because I know what it is to love, my lord."

"And who have you loved?"

"My lord and all his people."

The chieftain staggered out, brushing the wall with his right shoulder. The clump of boots faded down the hallway.

Azad raised his mother's fruit in front of an oil lamp, its flame visible through the translucent texture of the flesh. Holding it above the neck of an empty bottle, he snapped his hand shut. Ejaculations of pale-yellow juice splattered in all directions, some sliding down the bottle's throat to collect at its base. With a few more crushes of the hand, the flesh was blanched. Azad raised his hand to the light and looked at the residual juice glistening on his knuckles. He went to lick then resisted. Carrying the bottle to the pantry, he set it down, lifted the hatch and manoeuvred onto the steps, tiptoeing into the dark.

"There there, my pretty," Azad said. "There there, my love. My beautiful, beautiful Amrita."

A rattling hiss drew Azad's attention to two ghostly blue circles hovering in a corner of the cellar. The reincarnation of his lost love was waiting in the same space where, a year ago, she'd slipped off her brown, olive and gold sari and feasted on his heart. The queen of the palace sucked at him greedily that afternoon, as if frightened her wheel of life could stop any moment.

During the twelve torrid sunsets that followed, Azad plunged into his master's wife like she was holy water. Yet beneath Amrita's cool refinement lurked emptiness and an insatiable hunger for danger. Like Azad's, her soul was a battlefield. As their corrupted bodies fucked, the lovers' warring impulses became conjoined. They moved as one conflicted animal spirit in a trance-like heat, forever yearning to shed their skins and lose themselves in a sensuous realm devoid of restraint. Inwardly Azad raged; outwardly his shoulders bore the weight of unbearable shame.

One day when Amrita approached him in the garden, he flung out his arms and barked at the queen never to look at or touch him again.

"No more secrets, Azad," she begged. "No more secrets. We must flee. We must exile ourselves from this place. Or soon we will be discovered and killed."

"I will not flee. This is my home."

"Bhaavik beats me. I cannot live with this torture of my body and mind."

"And I cannot live with this deceit."

"Then you must take it all, Azad. You must take it all. The realm itself."

"Impossible."

"I need more, Azad. I need more. Give me life Azad. *Give me life.*"

"You're a disgusting whore. A vulgar creature with no restraint."

"And you are demon disguised as a holy man," she spat, her ghostly blue eyes glowing. "I do not know you from one moment to the next. How I wish you could feel my pain just once."

"And how I wish vile parasites would chew you from the inside. On my tongue you leave only a rancid taste."

"Then if you do not take it all, I will take the only thing I have left."

That evening, while Azad stewed in the cellar below, Amrita entered the kitchen to steal the bottle of snake poison. As his lover was interred under pounding rain, Azad contemplated drowning himself in the Krishna, so he could join his mother's soul on the riverbed and blunt the fangs of guilt sinking into his defenceless mind.

One year later, in the darkness of the cellar, Azad nervously uncorked the bottle of juice borne him by the river. The cobra rose in anticipation, forked tongue extending between widening jaws. Azad poured the liquid into its open mouth and watched it swill and soak into pink, poisonous flesh.

"There there, my love. My beautiful, beautiful Amrita."

The cobra spoke like the dead queen. A lilting, seductive voice. Sometimes it would be close and sometimes it wouldn't. Festering faraway in the shadows, then lying in bed with him, coiling itself around his chest and neck to drip temptations into his ear.

"You are a leader first. A cook second. The moment is ripe. The power within reach. Ease your pain. We can be united and have no more secrets."

Every evening until Bhaavik's feast, Azad drifted in and out of the cobra's trance. The spells turned more frequent and unpredictable, less an act of will and more a wild fever dream. In his mind Azad kept returning to the river to collect more fruit, then fed its juices to Amrita. The snake swelled so long it was difficult to see where its fattening body began and ended. Azad often awoke in the middle of the night to find himself ensnared in its embrace. The sleeping head rested next to his, the forked tongue protruding and retracting rapidly as if trying to push away some constricting nightmare.

Bhaavik's feast day arrived. The palace hummed with excitement. For the first time since Amrita's passing, joy cascaded upon the land like a waterfall. Her lady's spirit had returned to bless the spring day, as drizzling winter shades turned into streams of bewitching light. The chieftain awoke early and bounced around in readiness for the celebrations. Wrestling matches, cock fights, ram fights and horse racing. A travelling troupe of acrobats, dancers, dramatists and musicians. A glorious feast of twenty-one noble souls, four of whom would be Ranbir and three of his trusted guards. Naturally his rival had sent a message saying he would be late. Even in his advanced years, Ranbir wanted to be the centre of attention.

Azad rose from his bed reborn. He washed, brushed his hair and flung open the hatch to let dawn's light pour into the darkness. Over the next ten hours he prepared the banquet alone. His only company was birdsong, his only indulgence slow sips of river water fetched by an errand boy. The surprise centrepiece of the feast would be Mother's Milk, a special golden sauce made from a holy fruit plucked from the Krishna's depths. Surrounding it on the banqueting table would be concentric circles of other succulent delights, representing the cycle of birth, death and glorious reincarnation.

When feasting time arrived, Bhaavik's servants flowed through the doors to take the supplementary dishes one by one to the banqueting hall. In a final flourish Azad followed, strolling through the palace like a peacock, holding the Mother's Milk aloft in a serving dish topped by a shiny bronze lid. *Mother, mother, if you could see me now. A feast fit for Vishnu. A leader first, a cook second.* He nodded to the guard to sling open the doors of the banqueting hall, beyond which sounded a booming voice.

Bhaavik was at the table's head. To his left were eight of his people, to the right eight more. Four places at the opposite end of the table remained vacant for Ranbir's party. There was much chatter and excitement as people eyed the food already placed. In the empty space at the centre, Azad placed his final dish.

"My lord Bhaavik," he declared. "I too loved Amrita. I will not forget how she inspired me to reach for the heavens.

To know what it is to love what I do. The craft of cooking. The art of passion. The essence of eternal life. I made this dish out of love for her. And for you all."

Azad whisked the lid away. The sauce bubbled and spat, shifting colour in the lamplights, from brown to olive to gold. Specks of ghostly blue appeared then dissolved. Underneath lay further disturbance, multiple ingredients floating and swirling to form mesmerising currents. The dish appeared in conflict with itself, the torment holding every guest's gaze.

"My name for this dish is Mother's Milk, in honour of my original inspiration," said Azad as he spooned a ladle into every empty bowl, seasoning each serving with his special smile.

"Yet today I rename it Eternal Life. Amrita's nectar. My only request is that you all taste it at precisely the same time. The moment the clock strikes eight. The moment when Amrita would enter the banqueting hall every evening. Until then you must savour only the smell. Restraint is the art of a chef. It was the thing I most admired about Amrita. And in honour of Amrita's love of her people, everyone in the palace must sample Eternal Life too."

Azad bowed, exited the hall and walked serenely to the kitchen. His beautiful smile beamed brighter than ever before. As the palace clock clanged eight, his mind and body flowed in bliss like a holy river reaching a tranquil sea.

Outside the kitchen door, a used cooking pot was upturned in the corridor. Reddish-brown sauce was splashed on the floor and dripped down the wall opposite the door, like the pot had been thrown violently from the kitchen. Inside more dishes and pans lay scattered amid the fractured clay of oil lamps. Cupboards were flung open. Spices, preserves and seasonings had been smashed from their containers. In the pantry, the cellar door was ripped off its hinges.

The cook grabbed the only lamp still untouched, slid down the steps and rotated the light. The bed was empty, its sheets cast aside. In the semi-darkness, there lay a clump of what looked like clothes. As fine and delicate as a sari, dropped to the floor by a reckless lady hungry for tenderness. Azad lowered his light and inspected the tissue. Snakeskin, stretching to the cellar's darkest corner.

"Give me life, Azad," hissed the voice of Amrita from the riverbed. "We must show the world our love. Come to terms with what you desire. To see inside yourself. To see what you really want."

Azad dropped the lamp, clambered the steps and raced through the palace. Dizzy and panting, he flung open the banqueting hall doors.

All guests were slumped motionless in their chairs. Some face down. Some with necks craned sideways. Servants and guards lay still on the floor. All faces were ghostly white and all eyes vacant. Each throat bore two tiny punctures of red. Bhaavik sat dead in his chair. Unfeeling hands gripped the armrests. Unseeing eyes lay blank under his furrowed forehead. Coiled around his torso and neck like the cruellest of vines was Amrita. Her mouth hovered above Bhaavik's head. Moving slyly from side to side, she goaded Azad with the ghostly blue irises of her gaze and the seductive sliding of her tongue.

"I was entranced by your looks, charm and skills," purred the snake. "Your mastery. Then you desired me no more. Yet I continued to live. Like your guilt continued to eat you from inside. Now you have all you desired. In your trance you poisoned them all. So come and claim your place. Deep down that's what you always wanted. To rule the country like you ruled the kitchen. A cook second. A leader first."

Azad walked funereally to the chair. Easing her muscles, Amrita released Bhaavik. The cook heaved his dead master from the chair and threw him to the floor like a gutted carcass.

"One final kiss, Azad," she hissed. "One final kiss to swallow us both."

Steadily Amrita curled herself around Azad as he took his place at the head of the table. Gripping his ankles. Pressing his thighs. Locking his arms. Squeezing his neck. As the cobra finished her entrapment, she lowered her head down towards Azad's crotch, her forked tongue tracing elegant patterns on the pristine white fabric of his banqueting gown.

"One final kiss, Azad. One final kiss to swallow us both."

Amrita rose again, suspending her head a hand's length from Azad's face. A sickly-golden moisture slid from her jaws. In the blueness of her eyes, Azad saw the Krishna's currents ebb and flow.

"One final kiss, Azad. One final kiss to swallow us both."

From the far end of the table, Azad's mother watched in cold fury.

"The moment is ripe boy," she scowled. "The power within reach. Ease your pain. Take your Mother's Milk. Forget all restraint. A cook second. A ruler first. Take your milk. Good, smiley, greedy, impatient little boy."

Azad looked at Bhaavik's bowl. He dreamed the sauce was holy water from the Krishna and lowered his head to sup. With a ferocious lash, the cobra clamped her jaws on Azad's scalp. The cook's face turned white, as the apparition sucked and sucked. Two streaks of blood streamed down his face and collected at the corners of his mouth. In a frenzy of feasting, Amrita's guts expanded and retracted until she consumed her lover whole.

Ranbir arrived at the palace gates in a flurry of hooves and trumpets. The elderly lord lowered himself with a wince from his horse and looked upon the home of his old enemy. Unsettled by the stillness, he instructed his guards to patrol the palace swords unsheathed.

"Heavenly Vishnu preserve us," one guard screamed.

Ranbir limped to the source of the cry. His stomach turned rancid as he beheld the banqueting hall. Sitting on the throne was Azad, stone dead and sporting that beloved smile. Surrounding him were the corpses of the entire court. Faces pale. Lips swollen. Eyes gone. On the floor beside the throne, Bhaavik was sprawled like a slain soldier.

After sweeping the palace, one of Ranbir's guards returned with a bottle from the kitchen. A puddle of sickly-golden liquid stewed at its base. Ranbir wafted the neck under his nose. Snake venom. Presumably administered by the kindly cook sitting dead in his lord's chair.

Believing such a gentle man as Azad would never sin, Ranbir conjectured Bhaavik had forced his cook to lace the banquet with poison. Azad had never wanted anything else in his life, except to cook. To deliver a spellbinding experience to revive spirits and honour the most ravishing of ladies. Bhaavik was another beast. Someone who never escaped the pain of his past, nor his pessimism towards the future.

The warlord camped for the night in a field near the palace. Before he sunk into sleep, Ranbir recalled the cruel smile on Azad's dead lips. He sensed there was more to that young man's story. On his journey home the next day, Ranbir ordered his party to stop by the Krishna. Sorrowfully he kneeled on its banks and looked into the flowing water.

Through the buzzing and purring of the countryside came the river's quiet hiss. The Krishna's murkiness cleared. On the riverbed lay two young lovers in a naked embrace, faces obscured and lips locked together. Beside them lay another couple, then another, then another. An entwined tapestry of drowned flesh spread from source to mouth. The bodies were white, petrified by the harshest of winters. Their jaws still twitched. A mangle of corpses, sucking life from each other like newborn babies at their mothers' breasts.

"The finest pleasures of the turning world," Ranbir muttered.

"My lord?" said a servant. "Are you ill?"

"No, just full," said Ranbir. "Full of this life. This land is possessed with evil. I am sick and tired. I have swallowed more than I can take."

"Do you need water, my lord?"

"No, my good friend. I do not need to drink. I only need to know what lies beyond. I'm sure I will taste that mystery soon enough."

Upon return to his palace, Ranbir sank into a trance. He told the story of Bhaavik's feast to his servants. They told it to the villagers, who told it to the realm. Soon the legend spread across the land that, on the first anniversary of their queen's demise, Bhaavik's court performed collective suicide. So laden with grief from Amrita's death, their only desire was to banquet with their reborn queen in another world. And for those who heard the tale, their darkest wish was to drown softly in a river of eternal peace, their appetite for life finally sated by the cool, sensuous deep.

Rumi

I'll tell you its name, as long as you don't expect to hear mine. A khamsin it's called: a giant sandstorm blanketing markets, mosques and mausoleums in blinding swathes of ochre. A thing with no face or shape. Exceeded in power, according to some, only by the breath of Allah. But I don't believe in the divine. Dirty air is the only thing blowing through my hollow body.

As afternoon fades, a khamsin sweeps Cairo. The breeze stiffens. A hush slithers the streets. Bartering ceases in the souks. The city empties of ritual and every abandoned pot, place and pathway is suffocated by the desert's veil.

I emerge from the bazaar to confront the beast. Storm winds blast my slim frame. I shield my eyes with the back of my hand. My headscarf covers the rest of my face. In my profession, it doesn't pay to be recognised. Stooping, I cup a handful of sand in my palm. Removing the scarf, I blow tiny desert shards back where they came, observing them scatter, dip and disappear.

So with sand, so with people. People, politicians, princes. Husbands, wives, lovers. They come. They go. Only two powers thrive in a khamsin. The first is chaos. The second is me. I know how to be in the right place at the right time. In Cairo, you learn to grasp whatever there is. See opportunities where others feel fear. If you don't, life beats you into a corner, where you cower at the mercy of a deranged shadow who screams at you not to move.

Every day I circle the Qasaba. Through the stench of sweat, spices and incense, I sniff for easy wealth hanging from low branches like ripe fruit. The sandstorm within never settles. I am the world's thirstiest person. Not for water, but for coin. The precious circles around which everything revolves. My wispy motions slip unnoticed through crowds. My sound is soft; my disarming eyes forever watch the world. *Let me lead you on a merry dance*, they say.

A beggar buys a date. He drops the money into a pot. A boy slips his arm inside, snaffles the coin and runs into a bazaar past a woman thieving fur to seduce a soldier. She steals into an alley and steps over another beggar. The wretch hasn't received anything today, until a city official throws scraps to him on his way to prayers. Treasure chests all of them, ready to be unlocked. I draw so close I can smell my prospects' breaths. They barely notice me, until they waken to what's happened. Pickpockets must be as cold as the Nile in winter.

Many revere the mystery of the pyramids. I idolise the legend of the Sphinx. Freedom lies in perplexity; the art of sending my victims' minds spinning. Especially those too naïve for Cairo. My only emotion is disdain. My only impulse greed. My only path flowered with profit. The one thing I won't steal is someone's breath. Not even my former master's. There is not much sport in murder. The victims can never look back and realise what's been taken.

Tonight, the khamsin is my only companion. As people huddle inside and pray to the invisible, it's the perfect time to thieve. I need to be quick. Forever shifting like the desert sand. There is no joy in stopping. I learned that from my master who wanted me to stay fixed. Sometimes I didn't see his attacks coming. He certainly didn't see mine. Since I vanished with his pride, I've been addicted to seizing what doesn't belong to me.

I escaped with nothing. I became nothing. I appear to the world as nothing. Two layers of clothing, even in the maddening heat. My outer garments are raggedy and old, so I blend in. Underneath are clothes from my previous life. Shrouded beneath those is the body I was taught to loathe. One day I may steal more than pride from my master and complete the circle.

Since leaving him, I sleep on the streets, in a different corner each night. I do not want a home. They have walls forever pushing in. Only one spot in Cairo is truly mine. A chest in a hole in the ground in a ditch on the city outskirts. In there I bury my possessions deep. Coin and trinkets I neither spend nor wear. Treasures I will protect with my dying breath.

The khamsin howls. All else is quiet, from Bab al-Futuh in the north to Bab Zuweila in the south. Deeper into the storm I venture. My pace slow, my head dipping. The wind stings. The sand billows. The city is blind, so it's a good time to see. The storm surges quickly. In their haste, people leave things unguarded. Open market stalls. Clothes, carts, sacks and flasks. Scraps of food covered in flies. The petty debris of short, grasping lives.

Everyone is indoors except for me. These insiders believe in community and higher powers. I do not. I have no identity, faith or family. I'm a material person only. If you cannot see, taste, touch or smell something, it is not there. And I'm sharp enough to know all material things disappear. Such is the dance of life, the rhythm of stealing. The call to possess which afflicts us all. The imams would say I defile my nature. In my thirty-fifth year, I'm wiser than they think. I follow my nature every day.

"Gold," came the wail. "I tell you I've seen gold."

A familiar voice, from an alleyway by the Al-Aqmar.

"I tell you I've seen the golden house."

Through the ochre haze I see a figure. Head tilted skywards, back to the wall. The poor fool is laughing and singing. Shakir, a fellow thief. Once he suggested we partner, so I cut all ties.

"Summon yourself, idiot," I shout. "Have you lost your mind?"

"I've no mind, no place, no body. I left them in the golden house."

"Which house?"

"The one outside the city. Such riches I've never seen before."

My breath quickens. Sand whips into my widening eyes.

"Where?"

"Everywhere and nowhere," he laughs. "It moves. I tell you *it moves*. Never in the same place more than once. First the north, then the south, east and west. Its people too. Always moving. *Always moving*."

"Which people?"

"Gold, I tell you. I've seen gold."

"Other people like us?"

"There is no one like them. They came with the storm. They are empty of all things. We are dust. All of us dust. Dust. Dust. Dust."

They. In a city where everyone is out for themselves. Whoever they are, they've stolen Shakir's mind. I step away from him. Something has entered Cairo which needs my attention. A house that moves. A golden house. One ready to be spoiled by a thief who moves even faster.

"When did you last see them?"

"A few miles or so beyond Bab Zuweila. Be quick. What they offer is beyond measure. So quick. All is light. Light upon light upon light."

The khamsin yields to my will. I drive into the storm with my right shoulder, charging through the Bab Zuweila gate towards the desert. Gold will shimmer like nothing else out here. Once I imagined life beyond Cairo. In Arabia, Persia or India. Maybe I should roam their cities next. A spirit of no fixed abode, with no lock on my door. Nobody will see me depart. Like nobody ever sees me coming.

Exiles Incorporated

As I leave the city, the humming returns. The same tune sung by Shakir. A melody circulated by the storm, across my front, behind and to my sides. A dark form rocks back and forth, like a wounded bird trying to spread its wings. I move closer. The man is curled on the ground, tipping gently side to side, knees tucked to his chest. His arms cradle his shins. I encircle, then venture in.

"Are you insane?" I shout. "You'll perish out here."

"I will not. I am only breath. Only breath. Listen to this music."

The man is dressed in rags. His face wears a grizzly stubble and craggy lines. I kneel before him and wave my hand before his wounded eyes. He does not flinch. I look about this blind man's person to see where he keeps his money. His humming continues.

"What tune is this?" I press him. "Where have you heard it before?"

"In the house. The golden house. Where I breathed my last. Now the only breath I pass is Allah's."

"Where is this golden house?"

"There is no gold. Only light. Endless light. Light upon light upon light."

"Where?"

"The wind will take you there. Follow the wind."

"The wind is blowing all over the place. Speak sense."

"There is only one wind. Only one true breath. *Listen to this music.*"

Enraged, I push him to the ground. My hands pat his legs, hips, chest and ankles. Nothing but shabby cotton, frail skin and decrepit bones.

"The golden house has robbed you, eh?" I scorn. "Your mighty Allah's wind will rob you of your life now."

"How can someone steal what doesn't exist? The wind has taken everything I have. The wind has taken away all things. I... see... now."

"Shut up with your riddles," I shout, spit from my mouth evaporating in the violent air. "What is this golden house?"

"To the east. To the light in the east. Wind and light as one."

"Fool. Is there nothing of worth on you?"

"Only the breath of Allah. His joy. His peace."

"Did these golden people rob you?"

"No. They made me. Out of nothing more than air and movement."

"Imbecile!"

I leave him to perish. My mind will not tolerate trickery. These insurgents from the golden house are likely illusionists, dispossessing people of their wits. Mysterious adversaries controlling simpletons with gibberish. I contemplate returning to kick the beggar in the ribs. But I don't waste time on idiots. Neither do I indulge violence. Its outward bruises may heal; the inward ones endure.

The wind hurries me eastwards. Soon I am engulfed in a void. The storm screams. My eyes sting with sand. Through the raging abyss, I hear my master's summons. His slow, deliberate steps and his breath crawling up my neck. My head and shoulders curl in supplication, bracing for his blows.

"Submit," he whispers from the past. "Submit to my will. *Submit*."

I stumble, rise and stumble again. Forever fleeing. Through the desert. Through the night. Through the shrieking dark. Thoughts swirl and devour each other. Nightmares return. The moment the master smothered me. A dark, towering figure pressing a blanket across my face. His heavy hips trapping my waist. The furious writhing of my feet. My arms thrashing his face.

In the pitch black I see a flash of motion. It dances and dives, flickers and folds. A man appears laughing and twirling, playing a flute. That same maddening beggars' tune.

"Who are you?" I demand.

Silence. The man swoops in circles around me, no more than three horses' length away. Dressed like a vagrant. Drunk on something. A delirious apparition drawn from another world.

"Who are you, devil? What is your name?"

"No name. No person. No thing. Only emptiness."

"Explain yourself, madman."

"I've been touched by the light."

"Where is the golden house?"

"The house of light is just ahead," he cries, spiralling into the darkness. "They will take your breath away."

How long I wander, I do not know. The khamsin lashes me onto my back. I shrink into a ball and wait for the ferocity to subside. I picture my chest. My pretty chest housing all my treasures. I cry for vengeance on the world, yet my words die on ceaseless waves of sand.

Through the blizzard, my master extends an invisible hand to choke me.

"Submit to my will. *Submit*."

I've robbed so much of Cairo, yet my clothes, body and mind still belong to him. All I have left is the defiant dance in my lungs. The more my master squeezes, the more my breath deepens. The more he tries to silence me, the more I sense a strange rhythm inside. My heart, pounding against the lock that's sealed all tenderness from the world.

I wake at dawn, lying on soft white sand. All around in the distance, the khamsin's turbulent air surges and soars, curling sand on the horizon like fists of wrath. I cannot even see the pyramids. Yet the space I inhabit is serene. A pocket of stillness the storm can't penetrate.

Far away, yet within the vacuum, a smooth mound of sand glistens in the shimmering heatwaves. A short, white-walled building that twists from the earth like a bloated minaret. Circling its perimeter are seven men and seven women dressed in white. Heads bowed, they drag their palms along its exterior, like they're stroking the belly of a revered beast. There is no chanting or talk. Only quiet revolutions in the brilliance of morning's light.

Steadily I stalk the vision. The surface of this spiralling shape slides and turns, reforming to unfelt wind. I spy an entrance but will wait for nightfall. Until then I lie still and let the sun beat my back. Sleep comes and goes. Waves of thirst and hunger roll then retreat. The day passes. The rituals end. Darkness settles.

I move on my hands and knees, then walk upright with long strides. I do not know why I am here. Who these people are. Or what I expect. I may not even thieve a thimble. Yet some passion drives me. The same passion which drove me into the khamsin, and which swept me from my master's home at midnight.

I circle the building, running my left hand over its warm surface. The structure pulses gently, as if breathing. The walls emanate a soft glow, like they'd absorbed the previous day's sunlight and now radiate it back into the desert night as a spectral campfire for wanderers.

Inside, the hallway is dark. No furnishings or ornaments, only bare ground and walls. Ahead lies another opening, symmetrical to the entrance, leading to a central chamber trembling in golden light. I creep down the corridor. To my left and right are openings to smaller passageways, circling inside the house. Over my shoulder comes the master's breath. The wheezing voice. The smell of his vices. The thunder of his fists.

"Submit to my will. *Submit.*"

I turn round and see nothing.

In the central chamber, a concentration of starlight descends through a hole in the ceiling like a waterfall. An enchanted lullaby of pale gold, floating to the ground and rippling into a radiant pool whose edges gently surge and subside. I breathe in the light. A serene breeze sweeps my body.

Movement stirs within. I orbit the pool of light and stare into its reflection. Soft reeds and sunlight. The lapping of water. The sky above. A woman's face. Unblemished, unbruised and unbowed. The beggars' tune returns. My breath quickens and slows. Its music circles me as I circle myself, spreading my arms and spinning slowly. In my chest comes the whisper of another's breath. Not the master's breath. Someone else's, inspiring me to dance the way sunlight coaxes flowers to life.

I have stepped into the windpipe of the world.

Submit.

Him? No. Another. My mind and body spin. Gone is all grasping. So too touch, taste, smell and sight. Only the music of this new breath remains.

Submit.

I collapse into the pool of light.

Submit.

Not the sleep of dark.

Submit.

The sleep of light.

Submit.

A sleep within sleep.

Submit.

Pure, white and blissful.

Submit.

A melody in my heart.

Submit.

Through the dream I track a figure whose back is turned. Slight in build and raggedy in dress with disarming eyes. *Let me lead you on a merry dance.* I follow my prey, trying to glimpse the face. The coins in the pockets clink, so I reach out to snatch them. The figure vanishes and reappears a few steps ahead.

Submit.

A breath on my shoulder.

Submit.

My pockets emptied.

Submit.

The thief spins away, face hidden.

Submit.

I grasp at the air.

Submit.

I reverse my motion.

Submit.

The target remains elusive, picking my pocket every time. I feel naked, recalling the bruised mornings after my master's attacks. When I would examine my body with disgust, pitying it as a prison caging shallow, worthless breath.

Sunlight stirs me from sleep. I lie spreadeagled in the golden house's central chamber. Traces of sand drift to the ground. The pool of light is gone. In its place is a marble floor decorated with black and gold swirls and spirals, entwining elegantly towards the centre where I rise to my feet.

The beggars' tune swells: a distant friend whispering four simple words.

"Listen to this music."

Through side doors in harmony, three men and four women step softly. They are dressed in white skirts and wear hats made of camel hair. Their faces are smooth, strange and faraway. Seemingly in a trance, the figures traverse onto the marble floor and form a circle around me. One of them steps forward. A tall, handsome lady with hypnotic eyes. She is the only person to wear a black cloak, which she lays gracefully on the ground behind her.

Spreading her arms and twirling slowly, she begins to dance. Her companions follow. Soon seven strangers orbit me in a cyclonic whirl. Their faces are soft and calm; pale reflections of some unseen power which strums their bodies like finely tuned instruments. The right hands are directed to the sky, the left to the ground where their eyes are fastened. One dancer twirls faster than others. The tall lady floats to him and touches his skirt. He slows. The same is done to three more dancers, until all move in equilibrium.

Once my master dragged me into a courtyard to dance, his drunken friends laughing as I was sucked into a whirlpool of shame. Among these new dancers, I am lifted upwards. I lower my left arm to the floor and raise my right to the sky. My rotation begins in the ball of my left foot. My right takes a circular step and drives the motion. A breath steals my old voice and replaces it with a new one.

You have been created with love to love. Submit to this love. Submit.

The beggars' tune surges. My speed accelerates. A tug of my clothes corrects me. Fragrant wind cools my face. Light pours into the room, flooding my soul. I long to throw off my layers until I soar to whatever is the wellspring of this power. Ascending with me are my fellow thieves. My victims. The strangers I see in Cairo whose stories I yearn to know. They move in harmony, pure threads of sunlight woven into each other like satin. A blast of warmth erupts within. Its shockwaves fly apart my former self like sand to reassemble me as something else. What I become, I no longer understand. Language fumbles feebly at the treasure I've received.

You have been created with love to love. Submit to this love. Submit.

I am touched by something. Kissed. *Breathed into*. Not by a man or a woman. By a wind that wraps my body. A sensation as hot as the desert sand and as cool as a shower of rain. Its fluidity hugs tight, forming around my figure. More precise and intimate than the clothes I used to wear in my former life. The power holds me in its grip, with the softness of lips and the insolubility of stone.

Steadily the force soaks into my skin, penetrating deeper. All my surfaces, everything I once clung to, are stolen away like a layer of cheap garments from a corpse. *Away, away, away.* I become only my essence, a distilled speck of myself. *Away, away, away.* Surrounding me are so many others. Hundreds and hundreds of tiny irreducible cores swirling forwards on some wild, incomprehensible power. *Away, away, away.* I move with them. We are one. All of us precious. None to be forgotten. Never to perish in the tumult of this blissful embrace.

Submit to this love. Submit. Submit. Submit.

The dancers disappear. The golden house dissolves. Their motion burns inside me like coals on a fire. I am alone again in the desert. For hours I wander, wishing the sweet music would return. I'm no longer a thief nor even a person. Just a speck of sand, blown in synchronicity with a million others.

Humming my beggars' tune I arrive in Cairo, travelling in circles around merchants, market traders and malcontents. All wanderers, oblivious to the nascent illumination within. My memory takes me to the only place in Cairo that was ever mine. I arrive at the end of a narrow street. I enter through the narrow gate. I kneel on the narrow ground.

I reach into the narrow ditch. I imagine the golden house's pool of light rippling around my toes and hear the rhythm of the dancers' feet. The touch of the leader on the younger person's frock. The steadiness of her breath.

Submit to this love. Submit. Submit. Submit.

My treasure chest is a simple wooden box brimming with coins. The currency of survival. Normally my heart beats and my skin itches as I cradle my prize. Now with the calm grace of a kindly elder guiding a naïve youth, I open the box. There are no circles of gold. No dark, demanding eyes. No trace of my master. No hunger to be sated. Just an explosion of ochre, rushing into open air from bottomless space.

"Listen to this music," I cry. "Listen to this music."

I follow the storm into the street, chasing the grains of sand as they transform into tiny crystals of light. They sprinkle the citizens of Cairo. The rich, the poor, the broken, the mad. Those who've experienced the dance and those who haven't. I weave between them all.

"We are only breath," I say. "The wind of Allah's love circulating all around. Dancers, whirling in the motion of His universe."

My dance takes me to the Bab Zuweila gate and to a new life beyond the city. Waiting for me there is my master, squatting on the ground. His arrogant face sneers at the sky. A vision of frozen black fire, swirling in a vacuum of hate. Once he smothered me. Now I move past him until… something tugs at my clothes. The lady with hypnotic eyes from the golden house.

Submit to this love. Submit. Submit. Submit.

I return and circle my old master. I lower my left arm to the ground as I raise my right to the sky. My rotation begins in the ball of my left foot. My right takes a circular step and drives the motion. I sweep around his decomposing spirit again and again and again until it disintegrates to dust. *Away, away,*

away. With the force of a thousand khamsins, I puff the memory of my husband into the past.

I am a woman again. The air in my body is no longer my own: it belongs to the universe. I release it freely into space. Neither do I possess these wifely clothes. I twirl through the city's outskirts and into the silent desert. With a pickpocket's glee, I remove my headscarf. My eyes, cheeks, mouth and hair glow in the sun. I slip the other rags away, inviting the light to heal the flesh and pores on my slender arms and legs. *Light upon light upon light.* Through the dunes I dance, singing the beggars' tune, my delicate curves swaying amid the rolling banks of sand.

"Listen to this music," I cry. "*Listen to this music.*"

The wealth of the desert calls me. An ocean of serene iridescence into which I will swim. My pale tears surrender to its crystal sea. I trust its waves to guide me east. To the land of the prophet, peace be upon him. To the city of the holy rock, around which I will walk seven times as Allah breathes the power of submission into me. There I will flourish in the fountain of His love. Taking no more than needed. Wanting no more than I have.

My fine heart breaks, buckling under the pressure of joy. Through the fragments rises the rhythm of Allah, soaring high to form a sound sweeter than the one which led my dance. Under His sun, I cast no shadow. In His world, I am but a mirror reflecting His divine love. And through His words, I become but particles of air passing through His flute. The music is light, gentle and final, whispering the sacred words I longed to hear from the moment I first drew breath.

"I love you," it says. "I love you. I love you. I love you."

Janeiro

Drifting towards each other from opposite directions, the two strangers arrived at the blackened plant in the wasteland together.

The charred tree stump jutted six inches from the ashes, like a dark fist punching through the earth. It was the solitary landmark in the grey, waterless plain, save for the depression in the ground where the river once ran.

"The source of the signal."

"Could do with watering."

"Your kind have a sense of humour, then."

The stump's top, shorn flat during deforestation, was a smooth black surface without growth rings. The moon's reflection lay suspended in its centre.

"You really think this is where it happened?"

"It was a different time back then."

Together they imagined an emerald landscape of trees, villages and colonial ships prowling the coastline. Now there was no coast. Greed and fear had long since burned away nature's nervous system, leaving only a petrified expanse smothering the earth.

"At least there's nobody left to torch outsiders."

"This resisted the fire."

"Just about."

"Why them? They were nothing special."

"Special enough to induce an extreme reaction. The last of its kind."

"Or the first."

The strangers let their breaths intertwine over the burnt wood.

"It's still alive."

"How do you know?"

"We've started speaking the same language."

***

Everyone understood the command, no matter where they came from. The Governor-General demanded mercenaries pack the cannons with gunpowder. Grim circular faces of heavy iron cylinders pointed across the bay, so militia on the fortress turrets could unleash fire on rival colonialist ships. After all cannonballs were exhausted, the men would count the driftwood on shore. Routine would return. Unoccupied hours watching the rivers emerge like open veins from corpulent emerald country.

A fragile peace held on this strip of South American coast. Swords and smallpox had quelled the indigenous Tupis. Taking their place were merchants, artisans, farmers and slaves. *Degregados* too: miscreants fleeing their motherlands to suck the breast of the new world. Compliant Tupi lived in new mission villages on the plateau. Several toiled at sugar plantations up the coast. Others slaved on ships bound for Europe, loading the vessels with nature's bounty from tortoise shells to topaz. Many had fled deeper into the brooding forest.

The settlement was named Rio de Janeiro. River of January. A natural wonder first seen by European eyes on the first day of the first month. A new channel through which earthly riches and God's love could flow in abundance. Spearheading the advance were the Jesuits. They'd braved the Atlantic to teach Christianity, Portuguese and Latin to the Tupi, so the savages could savour the sweetness of God's language on their tongues.

Some settlers were less convinced. Lonely exiles from the old world sensed holy words might run aground here. In the stillness after supper, drifters meandered towards each other around jittering fires. Speculation ensued as to what lay in the forest's guts, from two-headed monsters to voluptuous witches drinking the blood of their young. Some conjectured the forest may even be one enormous creature. To wound one leaf would be to wound them all, provoking an earthly wrath that would freeze speech and curdle the soul.

Under a full moon, tensions thickened. Mirthful evening chatter tapered to silence and ended with twitching gazes into the dark. Panicking flickers of white light appeared in the trees then dissolved. Seething spasms of sound rumbled from the unsettled water. Branches creaked and stretched, like the forest's nerve endings craved new sensations in the tender air.

The last to fall asleep dreamed the moon and the earth were in dialogue. The two celestial objects shared an alien language, the visions went, channelled through primeval waterways that pleaded for an intimacy neither describable in words nor conceivable in the mind.

***

"You may be the best linguist, brother," Luis told Enrique as they set sail from Lisbon. "But you're far from the most authoritative. And it's a long journey for someone so *mature.*"

The leader's last word hung in the room like a butcher's hook. Luis was a taciturn man with a cruel streak. He was ten years younger and six inches shorter than Enrique, but unafraid to cast doubt on his fellow Jesuit.

"Language is an advantage," continued Luis, sitting squat as a bullfrog behind a barrel. "But what these ungodly people require is *firmness.*"

Enrique knew Luis didn't trust late converts. Every night, Enrique slept apart from his companions, shrivelled up in a cramped vessel battered by the malevolent Atlantic. In the adjacent cabin, Luis, Goncalo and Christiano spat and slurred court gossip, tongues tinged with sadism.

"I've been watching you," said Luis to Enrique on deck one evening. "There is something about you I do not understand. Something inside you I do not like. You aren't comfortable in your own skin."

Enrique suffered violent bouts of vomiting during the voyage. He slept only four hours each night. Two days before they docked in Rio de Janeiro he was all packed. Priestly accoutrements, a Bible, a Latin dictionary and Portuguese grammar books. Like King Sebastian, Enrique carried a copy of St Thomas Aquinas's writings on his belt. More precious was his private journal of blank pages. A void of faith still waiting for God to show him what to write.

Forty years old, with black hair thinning at the crown and a chiselled face accentuating dark, far-seeing eyes, Enrique was often mistaken for a man of destiny. Yet he'd volunteered for the expedition on a whim, then succumbed swiftly to sickness. Every morning, he would clutch his rosary beads and inspect his skin condition. The itchy redness, a parting gift from the lady in Lisbon, had spread to his navel. Liberal application of drinking water cooled the tenderness momentarily. For hydration, Enrique preferred rum.

"Do you know the difference between temptation and true calling?" probed Goncalo one evening after prayer.

"Neither can be put into words," Enrique replied.

"You have a fiery temper," said Goncalo. "A nervous disposition. And you drink too much. Mark my words, these will be hazards in the new world."

The ship docked as dawn broke. Luis led the Jesuits through a patchwork of wooden huts and nascent farmland. Heads turned to survey the new arrivals, including a young Tupi servant lady who smiled shyly at Enrique. He cast his eyes down and let the flutter within cease.

After a day's rest, the party set off. They would follow one of the rivers at the north of the bay through the forest towards the hill. On that mount a new chapel would be built, so the beasts could bask in a beacon of the Lord. As the group ventured into the trees, Enrique recalled his final night in Lisbon, when soothing streaks of moonlight broke through the shutters onto entwined flesh.

"What does your God feel like?" the prostitute said in the upstairs room of the tavern, running her fingers professionally across his corrupted flesh, curls of her hair resting on his bare shoulders.

"This good?"

"No."

"What then?"

"He feels like..."

The silent city waited.

"What does love feel like?" he replied. "Sound like? Taste like?"

"This was not love. You know it."

Enrique's first and only time. A thirst he'd tried to quench. He wondered who she was entangled with tonight. Like she wondered who he was. And how in the nervous dark of the night, he'd never been able to tell her.

***

Alone in the darkness, Jaciara listened to her husband snore in the other woman's bed. As the river's music trickled through the forest to her ears, she decided to flee once and for all.

"Can you hear this?" she whispered. "Which one of me will hear this?"

There was always more than one Jaciara. The one who couldn't see past the next duty. Another frightened of her own shadow. Then one who laughed secretly at authority. Who wanted to step through the deepest trees to explore a foreign realm. Who craved to know the source of all living things.

Water, that might be the answer. On long hot days, Jaciara would pause her chores and listen to the river's purity sweep her mind to faraway places. Searching for the great sea which had brought forth the outsiders. Those who arrived in boats wearing shiny clothes to drive her people into the belly of the land. Hungry ghosts, dealing in hurt. Part of her wanted to be hurt. And by being hurt understand. And by understanding, learn strength.

Turning from the village for the final time, Jaciara entered the forest and crept to the river. Slowly she slid down the bank and rested the soles of her feet on its cooling currents. Nature growled. The trees, branches, twigs and leaves, normally so still, trembled. Hidden creatures lay everywhere, teeming below the swirling surface.

She lapped the river's water across her body. Over her breasts. Down her arms. Into her face. Between the legs. Soothing her flesh from the soreness spreading across her belly and thighs. No men had seen those places for a while. Her husband had lost interest. Lesser men mocked her weight. The cruellest claimed an evil spirit caused her some undefined disfigurement. And when she spoke, her words lay stagnant on the ground like puddles of unwanted rain.

Jaciara had never been beautiful, unlike the river. That was eternal. Its wonder came from how it stayed true to its direction. In dreams she followed its course, leaving the forest's tentacles to soak her ageing flesh in healing sap.

"We don't like what you've become," said one of the elder women. "We do not understand what you've become. You are... troubled."

Since the death of her only child, Jaciara's sole purpose was to mix ingredients for meals. Sometimes she would hear the river and experiment with the earth's produce. Soon the leaders no longer trusted her to cook. She was a person who mixed up her mind and her words. Too anxious, too distracted, too... sensitive.

Tonight, she would follow that impulse. The river spoke to her in a way no person could. Would her little girl be there too? For no life just disappears. It becomes something else. The god of nature taught her that. Life forever flows somewhere. Where hers was going she could not say.

In the morning, sunrise stirred the displaced Tupi from sleep. They rose in unison, part of the land's rhythm, like the growing trees and the passing of the seasons. Except for Jaciara, who was long gone. Down the river. To the pale ghosts from beyond. To begin again in a new world.

***

Put out this fire. I beg you put out this fire.

After breakfast, Enrique drained the last drops of rum from his flask. The burning under his skin was too much, the alcohol's rippling warmth too pleasurable. Blades of sunlight slashed through the trees onto the Jesuits' faces. Enrique limped on, aggravating the ankle sprained during an intoxicated night odyssey through Lisbon. Red patches were forming on his arms and legs. Soon every part of his tender body would be vulnerable to infection.

Christiano, a timid, waif-like man, wheezed five paces behind. Bringing up the rear was a dour mercenary with a simple mind whose name Enrique kept forgetting. In front was the drooping figure of the sanctimonious Goncalo, a shake detectable in the fingers of his right hand. Ahead strode Luis, accompanied by another mercenary. Together they followed a tamed Tupi guide with a shuffling gait, numb face and busy eyes.

"Does he know where he is going?" said Luis.

"Ask him yourself," said the mercenary. "Sometimes they tell the truth."

"I do not trust them."

"There's no such thing here. These savages have no system. They live according to nature, finding and taking all they need from the forest. Appearing from nowhere. We shouldn't dawdle."

"Do not presume to command me."

Prickly and impatient, Luis despised the drudgery of invasion. He only wanted to teach Tupi the poetry of the gospels. Out here, language evaporated in the heat. Conversations sagged as soon as they began. The logic and clarity of Latin were slim solace when minds fell apart.

Enrique imagined God's renewing breath surging through each leaf, branch and sprinkle of light on water. There were enough stories to fill a thousand journals. Yet with every turn of the page, the prostitute's face bled through the paper, her sobering voice resurrected amid the trees.

"This was not love. You know it."

Old world, new world. Enrique couldn't say what either meant. Wiping his mouth and grimacing from his limp, the pretend Jesuit listened to the river run. He wanted to slip under its surface and extinguish his burns forever, until his seared nerves couldn't sense anything at all.

***

Jaciara withdrew behind a tree when she saw the other Tupi. Three young men, armed with arrows and oblivious to her presence, fanned the other side of the river. Branches curled around their shoulders. Vines crawled underneath their feet. Killers, poised to strike ghost men who stumbled through the trees. The more they murdered, the more they hoped to quell their fear.

Her husband was like that. Afraid of what the sea had sent. In the wake of their daughter passing, he rolled onto Jaciara like a slab of rotting meat. A cold man, similar to the women she once called friends, who seemed less like people and more like dark caverns filled with icy eyes.

When hollow love finished, Jaciara huddled her bruised body and mind, like she'd once held her daughter's diseased corpse. Maybe the ocean ghosts who'd claimed their land had claimed her only child too. The little girl might still exist with the invaders, singing of an enchanted land where mother and daughter would reunite in each other's embrace.

Jaciara changed course, leaving what remained of the track. She stepped softly into the undisturbed labyrinth of luscious green, mesmerised by how its contours and depths rematerialised in the needles of light. Quiet rippling reverberated all around; the ruffle of some swift creature burrowing unseen, or a freakish breeze lifting the forest's tissue to expose repressed tenderness underneath.

She gasped. A spherical thicket of vines and branches, seemingly without root, hung suspended in the air at chest height. From within came flutters, flaps and flickers of white light, insistent sparks of stifled energy. Slowly Jaciara approached. She opened her mouth to speak. No sound came. Parting the branches with her fingertips, she peered inside.

Two birds lay next to each other on a web of twigs. Four wings of matted grey feather, pulsating with white light, beat frantically against each other. Inside their translucent bodies were bones, organs, veins and tiny tendrils of nerves. Together they twitched, searching for strength. Jaciara reached into the dark to cup them in her hands. Their frail bodies were warm; the skeletons shuddered. Jaciara gently tipped them upright. Their heads were fused at the temples. Four bewildered eyes blinked rapidly. Not two animals but one. White light beat in tune with the thumping of conjoined hearts.

Phhwwwooooshhhatatatata. The creature shot through the gap in the foliage. Jaciara squealed and dropped to her knees, hands over her head. Stillness settled. The animal's only trace was the sound of wings beating distant trees. The hidden forest was coming to life, speaking a language she could not fathom.

***

"Fly!" screamed Christiano.

The first arrow struck the lead mercenary though the neck. His hands flew to his throat, his gasping body swayed from shock. Two more arrows pierced Luis's back, driving him into a tree. He slid down, face grazing the bark, arms extended like a crucified man. A third arrow entered Goncalo through his mouth, the missile's tip splintering the back of his twisting head.

"Fly!"

Enrique fell to the ground. An arrow shot through the space where his chest used to be. Two, three, four more. The last one struck a tree only a few feet from his head. From behind came a scream of pain and a thrashing of leaves. The other mercenary's legs lay prostrate, fingers twitching in the undergrowth. The guide was gone.

Hail Mary, full of grace. Hail Mary, full of grace. Hail Mary, full of –

Another arrow flashed past. Enrique scurried into the forest on his belly, rose into a stoop and ran. Conspicuous in black, Enrique tore away his garments until all he wore was underwear and a crucifix swinging across his bare chest.

Delirious, he imagined host of animals staring at him through the leaves. Monkeys. Vultures. Foxes. Lizards.

Toucans. All God's creatures. All shrinking into the forest's dark from insane invaders. He wished he could see the world through their eyes. A thousand simultaneous perspectives. But he could only feel a thousand suspicious stares, pricking his raging flesh.

***

Night fell as Jaciara entered the clearing. The space was perfectly round, like a miniature sun had descended to singe all plants into formation. She gravitated to its centre. Her light steps barely sounded on the parched earth. Leaning back her head, she closed her eyes, basked in the black sky and let her face absorb the moonlight. Cool air encircled her body. The great ocean rumbled. It couldn't be that far away. In the morning, she hoped to climb the trees and see the edge of the world.

Lying on the ground, Jaciara drank from her water pouch. She nibbled on fruit she'd picked, relishing its sweetness on her tongue. The leader once told her she was no longer able to bear fruit. Her figure was changing. Her mind was changing. They mocked her gentleness towards animals. Ridiculed her desire to know the ocean. Other mothers knew what was expected. To cook. To nest. To be quiet. To understand when they'd fallen from favour. To be comfortable in their own skins.

Jaciara removed her clothing so the chill could soothe her sores. In the daytime they burned. Under the moonlight they glistened, thirsting for moisture. As she drifted to sleep, her bare breasts rose and fell amid the tranquilising purr of a thousand insects. Upon her came dustings of powdery white light. Inside, a vision of amorphous bliss swirled past her mind's eye. If not her daughter, then a lover. If not a lover, another kind of ghost.

***

Come Enrique. Be with me.

On the run, as always. From the Tupi's arrows. The cold-eyed disappointment of his landowning father. The few girls who tried to win his heart. The grit and grime of real labour. Commerce. Family. Friends. A planned future. The church's code. The sin he'd committed. A lady of the night. Her sweet voice. Running forever. Always from himself.

Normally Enrique would flee into books. Markings on paper. Words. Language. Noises from the mouth. Broken. Disjointed. Meaningless. Into the dark he muttered some more. Prayers, utterances, grunts and sighs. They clanged to the ground, like junk thrown from a window by a trapped priest in a burning church. Except the house of God was his own infected body.

He mourned the dead Jesuits with whom he'd crossed the ocean. Their panicked lunges. The terrified eyes. The twitching arms. Their slow slides into nothingness. Gone now. To heaven or to hell. The forest had spat out its contaminants. Enrique would bury himself in its leaves. Then like a cowardly beast, slink to the river. To Rio de Janeiro. To a boat. To sea. To Lisbon. To…

Damnation. An unfathomable pit of decaying flesh. Love paid for with pouches of coin. His conversation with the prostitute was accruing interest. Her satanic touch had caressed Enrique through the pestilence. How he burned for her still, while drunk on the need to forget. He was ready to die in this place or become something else, blessed or cursed under a sheen of lunar white splendour.

Come Enrique. Be with me.

***

Jaciara's eyes flicked open when she heard the gentle crunches on the ground. A creature in the clearing. Alone. Bare-chested. Tall. Strong. Lost. No weapons. An ocean ghost. A man magicked by the forest.

A dizziness returned, not felt since her daughter. Not fear or danger. Absorption. His flesh was marked with redness too. *Put out this fire*, it screamed. *I beg you put out this fire.* Moonlight graced his muscular curves. In its pacifying rays his sore flesh glowed, like the scales of some mysterious sea creature.

The entwined trees formed a protective nest around them. Together they would be hatched birds learning to fly. Or clinging reptiles, shedding their skins. Their tissues would bristle, back and forth, back and forth, until both outer layers flaked away to unveil ravenous nerves underneath.

***

Enrique traced swirls of holy water with the fingertips of his mind across the lonely lady's exposed skin. Her eyes burned deepest brown. *Come. Be with me.* He circled her slowly as the trees meshed tight, entranced by her absent-minded smile and inhaling her earthy scent.

A thousand invisible eyes closed their lids. The only sound was the drumming of Enrique's heart. From Coimbra to Lisbon to Rio de Janeiro to the forest. *To her.* A cyclone of anguish once packed so tight unspooled. He knew not where its pieces would be flung.

Put out this fire. I beg you put out this fire.

Soft foldings. Into each other. Bountiful nights tucked between spells of austere sunlight. *What does it feel like? Sound like? Taste like?* No words were spoken. Language, or the lady's name, no longer mattered in this strange new world free of time and consequence.

***

Jaciara sunk her nails into his skin and guided him in. He was as fluid and as beautiful as the river. No body. Just spirit. Here. Now. Forever. Through this gentle man's embrace she would return home. Be rid of her old shell and inhabit this new one. Smooth and strong and tall like the sheltering trees. His breath husky and deep. She longed for his fluid to tingle across her stomach, and for her husband to witness their flesh wax and wane in rebellious harmony.

***

Enrique saw God in her. In this small clearing. In the warmth of the forest. In this speck of new earth. He would devour her until his spirit swelled beyond himself, so he never suffered his loathsome skin again. They anointed each other with sweat, juice and tears. Every drop dowsed the burns inside. How quickly she'd opened her body, worn with the wrinkles and sags of a wearying life. How quickly she'd opened her arms. Her legs. Her heart. Prison. Lisbon. Church. Pouches of money. Death itself. Oceans away. Dreams drifting through smoke rings on a mountainside thousands of miles distant, beyond an empty sea he'd traversed many moons and lifetimes ago.

***

The forest enclosed around the speechless couple. They were locked in a sphere of vegetation hovering a hand's width from the ground. Sketching out each other's stories in their minds, they slid fingers over each other and plucked the opposing souls like the strings of a harp. Together they floated in a fragile vacuum, clasped bodies sheltered from dry, loveless space.

Their red patches of flesh expanded and coalesced. Armies of skin cells weaved as one, turning from violent red to silvery light. Their scales peeled away until their brown and white flesh became indistinguishable.

Slowly they fused. A nebulous moon-coloured form centred by four eyes blinking in unison. Curving, rotating and floating, like welded foetuses in an amniotic water springing from the deepest of reservations.

If a stranger from any world, old or new, wandered into that clearing, they would witness the birth of a new species not yet seen or imagined on earth. The creature spoke a new language, understood only by itself, and nature fell silent in reverence to its alien words.

***

"Do you feel this?"
"Yes."
"Where?"
"Here. Now."
"Always."
"Forever."
"Who are you?"
"This."
"Where are we?"
"Nowhere."
"Where should we go?"
"Nowhere."
"What do you see?"
"Us."
"What do you hear?"

"Us."
"We can begin again, can't we?"
"We can."
"We will."
"They will come for us."
"I know."
"I won't leave you."
"Never."

***

The sun set over the grey plain. The two strangers sat by the charred stump and sipped from their vials. They rewrote this barren world, imposing on it fantasies of tempestuous waves hurling ancient winds onto their worn faces.

"Fusion must have happened quickly."
"Yes. Frightening."
"Or liberating."
"Do you think they talked?"
"They understood each other. Even if others didn't."

The explorers' hands moved closer through the comforting silence.

"The end came too quickly."
"That kind of love always does."

***

Two scouts, one Tupi and one Portuguese, drifted towards each other from opposite directions towards the creature.

In the evening light, the sphere of vegetation was still adjusting to itself, rippling with supple movement. Flares of fizzling white burst through, rolling sheets of coolness across the onlookers' skin.

Raising their weapons in shaking hands, the scouts approached. Sweat slid down their creased temples. Within the nest they glimpsed the union. Grey whirls floated on white liquid. Four peaceful eyes appeared in the milky miasma, fluttering and at peace.

The scouts fled to their camps, gesturing to the moon and shouting the same words in opposing tongues.

"Evil is here. Evil is here. Evil is here."

***

The two tribes agreed a temporary peace. A new beginning, balanced by silent agreement they shouldn't mix. A few fading voices argued they didn't need to form alliances. Yet both parties understood there was an element of the other's magic in this. Neither found the words to explain what had happened between the two runaways, or why the forest's demons imprisoned them in this way.

Whatever was spawned did not belong in their worlds. Together they would burn away this grotesque abscess. There was enough safe distance in the clearing between the disease and the rest of the trees to avoid spreading the calamity.

At dawn the next day, the Tupi and Portuguese circled the creature with blazing torches. Leaders on both sides nodded their heads. Newly arrived Jesuits prayed for deliverance. Tupi blocked their ears, frightened the earth would scream. Jaciara's husband held his hands over his eyes as the fire decimated what was left of his wife. He would not miss her. Christiano turned and faced the ocean. He felt guilty about abandoning Enrique during the attack. But running away was for the best. The Lord's language would forever elude these savages.

As the inferno engulfed the union, nobody spoke a word. Its mystery perished from the earth as quickly as a solitary flame on a windswept coast.

***

The lovers drowned in each other's sweetness, the sacred fluid inside them extinguishing the cruel heat.

"Don't…"

"…say it. Please don't…"

"…be afraid."

"Can we escape?"

"We already have."

"Where?"

"Into each other."

Eyes fused as flesh melted. Barely flinching, they burned as one, nerves forging like iron in voracious white fire.

"Is it over?"

"Soon."

"Where will we go?"

"I don't know."

"You're slipping…"

"…into me."

"You're running..."

"…into me."

"Do you feel it?"

"Yes."

"Where?"

Together they pushed their thirsting roots deeper into the earth's flesh.

"Here. Now."

"Always."

"Forever."

Ripples of light doused the blaze. White smoke rose from the clearing.

"Who are you?"

"This."

"Where are we?"

"Nowhere."

"We can begin again, can't we?"

"We can."

"We will."

"Where?"

Phantasmic clouds lingered in the sky long into the morning. All that remained in the ground was a charred stump, jutting from the soil like a tombstone. Confused words swirled around this spot for a while, until their original source became shrouded in time. Witnesses chose to forget the story of Jaciara and Enrique. The nervous language of its telling could never express the quaking beauty of its truth.

***

The strangers held hands at the blackened altar. Since the inferno thousands of years ago, the remains of the two lovers had emitted an imperishable signal, inaudible to the ear and imperceptible to the eye. It had journeyed through the nerve centre of the universe to touch two other lonely souls. Together they'd travelled towards each other, fleeing all they'd known for uncultivated harbours.

"Do you think theirs was real love?"

"It was more than that. A new beginning. A new species."

"Why them? Why here?"

"I don't know. Some higher power must have been involved."

"One that let everything be destroyed?"

"Not everything. We're here. So is this."

"Where do we go now?"

"Let's stay. There's no one else."

"But we look different. We come from different worlds."

"There is *some* resemblance."

The couple's skins glowed red, the nerves underneath trembling like the edges of a forest under warming winds.

"We're both looking for the same thing."

"Why us? Why now?"

"Why not? Somebody must start this place over again."

"Do you think we can?"

"Yes, we will."

"Where?"

"Here. Our first day. Of our first year. In a new world."

The strangers loaded their vessels with new language, sending their cargo in two opposite directions. Their message was simple. *A new land has discovered us. We have discovered a new land. Love exists and it's within planet Earth. Planet Earth exists because love is within.*

Turning to each other, the strangers smiled and kissed. Beneath their fusing forms, water seeped from the dead centre of the moon still reflected in the solitary tree stump. Slowly but forcefully, it trickled across the ashen ground, seeking solace in the burnt-out space where the River of January once flowed.

Genjo

"Master is gone," screeched the monkey as it danced around the well's mouth between the encroaching weeds.

Genjo spied the unwelcome guest from his tatami mat on the veranda. He kept his eyes open during morning meditation. Embittered rivals could easily slip through the crumbling garden walls and slit his throat, their vengeful laughter rattling through the cherry blossom trees.

"Master is gone. Master is gone."

The monkey flitted and bobbed; a whirling apparition of grey amid tangled green. As head gardener, Genjo was obliged to tend all parts of Daimyo Keiko's estate. Letting it descend into an overgrown mess was unbecoming of a samurai, even a retired one. These days, keeping his affairs in order was like trying to carry the ocean in the palm of his hand.

"Master is gone. Master is gone."

Keiko had indeed gone. Sankin kōtai required all daimyo to reside in Edo for six months every year. Genjo managed the land in his master's absence: a mighty exponent of bushido reduced to dealing bushels of rice and timber.

To relieve the boredom, Genjo often gazed across the landscape from Keiko's hilltop estate and envisioned his younger self, galloping through a sea of red and yellow banners scything down his enemies. Sometimes he sketched his past glories onto canvas, transforming the halcyon scenes swamping his mind into feeble charcoal shadows he could gift to servants.

"Invasion. Abduction. Violence," screeched the monkey. "Your master has gone, I tell you. Your master has gone."

A talking monkey. Of all things. But these were unusual times. Rumours bubbled up from the valley's peasants that a strange madness had gripped the land, the source of the poison unknown. Japan expelled foreigners years ago yet remained tormented by ghostly sightings of fantastical beasts. Bearded men with bodies of dragons wallowing in rolling red fog. Flying fish attacking birds. Squid-like creatures squelching through woods, eyes glowing in the dark.

The monkey hopped and squawked. Genjo contemplated snatching the irritant's tail, twisting its neck and tearing it in two like a sheet of paper. Rising from his knees with a grimace, he wiped the saliva from his chin and watched the garden sway like a ship's deck in a storm. He placed his palm on the marble statue of Lord Buddha and let the dizziness pass.

"Mind your head," hissed another voice. "Mind your head."

Startled, Genjo scanned the length and breadth of the garden. A faraway ripple of queer laughter, then stillness. Apart from himself and the primate, the estate was empty of sound, save for the dripping of residual rain from the roof shingles.

Not bothering to tie his maroon silk robe across his sagging belly, Genjo strode to the well. It resembled one from a queer folk tale he once read as a child. A hole in the ground from which strange monsters might slither, their slimy tails curling off the page to encircle his mind.

"Monkey man, you imbecile," he scoffed as he parted the waist-high weeds. "I know your kind. A sly devil. A symbol of foolishness. A weedy string of an animal. Yet you attempt to worry a samurai. And most heinous of all, you disturb him while in meditation with Lord Buddha."

The monkey stopped dancing. Standing on its hind legs, tail drooping between its feet, the visitor waddled to

Genjo's side of the well. The creature pushed its face to the samurai's nose and yawned, a damp stench wafting through grimy yellow teeth.

"Oh you must worry, my gentle Genjo," it said. "The realm you cherish is possessed. Your daimyo has been captured while journeying back from Edo. An evil spirit has claimed Keiko."

"Keiko? Captured? Where did you hear this?"

"From your master directly. The spirit is wily, but it cannot silence your master's tongue. Keiko's plea for help can be heard around the land. Your daimyo is fastened to a tree in the middle of a large swamp. Every day the water rises higher. Soon your master will drown in the boggy earth."

"What is the nature of this spirit?"

"Chaos, good Genjo. Pure chaos. A darkness is spreading across the land. Like black ink spilling on paper."

"Darkness?"

"Men's minds are no longer their own. The soul of Japan is under attack."

"How come I have not heard of this?"

"The spirit intercepts all messages. We're cut off from ourselves."

"Except you, I see. Why should I trust you, monkey man, with your squealing voice and silly dances?"

The animal arched its eyebrows and prowled to the far side of the well.

"Look," it said, pointing downwards. "See for yourself how your master is in peril. How our land is infected."

The well was deep, about the height of three men. A cold wind circulated within. A putrid smell rose from the black trembling pool at its bottom.

"Look, Genjo. *Look*."

The ripples rearranged. Contours appeared from the blur. A familiar face, painted on water. Trapped below the surface, visage twisting, was Daimyo Keiko. The master was upright, fastened to a maple tree, cloaked in red mist and gnashing teeth at unseen assailants.

"Sorcery!" cried Genjo. "How do you concoct such vile apparitions?"

"Sorcery indeed. Our land is possessed by some phantom. A loathsome parasite. Only Genjo has the presence of mind to save his lord. For you fought valiantly for decades against every manner of evil."

Reeling from the well, Genjo dropped to his knees among the overgrowth. His hands ran over his bald head, through knotted strands of grey hair and cradled his slackened jaw.

"I did, good monkey," he muttered, tears swelling. "I remember that world. I know that world remembers me."

Over the tips of the weeds, Genjo could see the hills he once mastered. Floating into view came memories of horses, heraldry and heroes. The kind who never die. The ones never forgotten. Genjo recalled the sweet smell of blood and the war drums pounding to his racing pulse. Through the vision leaked the cackling of old foes, still lurking in the cherry blossom.

"The jealous elite cut me down in my prime," Genjo continued after the dizziness ceased. "Trumped up charges of treachery. Now I'm here. Demoted to gardener. Trimming hedges and pruning flowers. A paper man in a two-dimensional world. My punishment for being too much the samurai."

"Our world was not ready for your kind," whispered the monkey. "You owe a duty to your lord. And your lord needs you. A samurai not loyal to his master is no samurai at all."

The weeds rustled. A ghostly warrior appeared before Genjo. Gallant, muscular and as fluid as a mountain stream.

The Red Devil. Skin tingling, Genjo paused to colour in his vision. Imagination overflowed his mind like a river bursting its banks.

"Where is Keiko?"

"The far side of the island. In the great swamp. Oh Genjo, you must hurry."

"I've not fought for years, monkey."

"Return, Genjo. Be the Red Devil you still are."

The sun emerged from behind a solitary cloud. Golden light throned the garden. The morning dew evaporated. A warm breeze bent the tall grass towards Genjo's feet, scattering the dead chicken feathers not yet swept away.

"Be ready, monkey man. Be ready."

Genjo's body raced his mind back to the mansion. He stomped across the veranda, knocking over his cup of sencha. The tail of his billowing robe slid over Buddha's head. As his footsteps slapped down the corridor to the armoury, side doors slid open in deference. Beyond were the powdered faces of four geishas, semi-dressed in silken gowns, their slender curves reclining on beds.

"Master us Genjo," they cooed in chorus. "Come and master us. We are so lonely. We crave to be mastered. We thirst for your love. Do not go. Do not fight. Stay. Be our master."

There was no time. Genjo could only handle one girl each session these days and he'd lost track of his favourite. With a heave of both arms, he slung open the armoury's iron door to reveal spears, swords and other serrated edges. The Red Devil suit, with its lacquered breastplate and golden-horned helmet, radiated from the room's centre. Resting next to it on a wall bracket was his favourite samurai sword, a gleaming curve of silver steel longer and wider than the others.

Squeezing into the armour took a while. The abundance of wine and cake at Keiko's mansion would have broken Lord Buddha. Genjo's manservant usually assisted, but he was carrying buckets of water up the hillside as a punishment for mocking his master's snoring. The samurai considered calling the geishas to help him into his battle wear, then feared they may laugh.

Ungrateful vixens. Only ever nice when they want something.

Genjo tugged, twisted and tumbled into a row of axes hanging on the wall.

"My lord," called a geisha. "Do you need help in there?"

"Be gone, vile hag. Or I shall do much more than master you."

Soon Genjo was back on his feet. Fully armoured and croaking battle cries, he waved his sword until his shoulders ached. Slinging open the door he surged down the corridor. Sweat beads slid down his temples. The geishas lined the walkway, scattering lotus petals at his booted feet.

"The likes of which the world has not seen," they sighed.

Outside Genjo's black stallion awaited, scraping its hooves in anticipation. The monkey bounced up and down on the saddle with glee, tugging excitedly at the reins and squawking feverishly.

"Victory will be certain, Genjo. The master will be freed. All will be well. Japan bows low in gratitude. Our hero has returned!"

"I never thought I'd don these sacred items again," said Genjo. "Truly they fit me like a second skin. My sword is long. My will is hard. Onwards, monkey man, you dancing fool. To the swamp. To the master. To glory. Let the face of a new legend be drawn over the fading visage of the old."

Clambering into the saddle at the fourth attempt, Genjo kicked his unruly horse in the guts with both heels. The stallion shot forward as if fleeing fire. The monkey clung on to Genjo's right shoulder plate. From the terrace the geishas waved farewell; blurred faces behind silk cloths that fluttered in the breeze. Genjo would see them again; each lady conquered by a more brutish sword, stiffened and sharpened with the throb of overdue combat.

"Mind your head, dear Genjo," the geishas sung. "Mind your head."

"Carry water and chop wood, idiot boy," cried Genjo as his manservant swung open the gate. "Tomorrow, we feast our victory in Master Keiko's honour. It is time for one last heroic dance."

They swept past the cherry blossom and round the track's satisfying curve into the valley. Genjo had drunk too much sencha, so stopped half a mile later. Waddling into the woods, he realised his armour was on back to front. Only the monkey's dexterous claws prevented Genjo from urinating over himself.

"Suspend your laughter, simple creature," he moaned, the proud arc of his piss curling like a samurai sword into a kerria bush. "A mocked warlord is a very dangerous thing."

"We must delay no longer," pestered the monkey. "Your master needs you. Your realm needs you."

Across the country they raced in a typhoon of red, black and gold. Clods of dirt flew up in torrents of air swirling in their wake. Genjo passed the sites of his most famous duels. Once again, he vanquished the ageing warlord with fading reflexes. Decapitated for a second time the young charger distracted by a bee. Relived the day he sliced the legs of a trio of warriors from under them with a single rotating swing, throwing their dismembered corpses into the river.

Genjo first recalled these tussles as line drawings, then imbued them with watercolours like grand paintings in his mind's gallery. Slowly his artist's eye for noticing the infinitesimal returned. A colony of ants ascending a tree. A fluttering leaf indicating the wind was blowing north northwest. The wispy trail of a distant cloud forming the shape of a sword.

Manmade Japan was different. Witnessing its ugly new castles, homes, roads and bridges was like traversing through sludge. His country was unworthy of his sketchbook. If he met a fellow ageing samurai, they would look at each other yearningly from the daze of shared dreams. All fight was pacified. All honour gone. Only shallow laughter remained. Vile, vicious laughter.

"How far to the swamp, monkey man?" said Genjo.

"Soon," replied the monkey. "Follow your instincts. Trust in your skill."

"How will I know I've arrived?"

"When the country fits in the palm of your hand."

Genjo arrived at a narrow river. Ahead was a rickety wooden footbridge, crossing the water to a village of ramshackle huts. Beyond was a dilapidated castle, owned by a daimyo who'd neglected all maintenance during sankin kōtai.

A bizarre spectacle was unfolding in the courtyard outside the castle gates. Four scrawny boys moved in a circle carrying a ceremonial palanquin, from which lolled a drunken daimyo slurring war songs and grinning like an imbecilic monkey. His subjects were busy trading clothes, trinkets and treats, laughing in a cold, uniform tone. Their faces bore no distinguishing features at all.

Genjo's stallion reared up on its hind legs, brayed loudly and galloped over the bridge, dislodging a few slats into the dark river. The villagers flocked to Genjo with imploring eyes, clutching at his legs and making suggestive strokes of the horse's coat. In fury, Genjo unsheathed his sword and raised it skywards, glancing across the crowd to gauge their admiration at its size.

"Ingrates! Detestable, base ingrates. I have riches for you."

Galloping round the courtyard in circles, Genjo whipped the deranged crowd into frenzy. The faceless peasants gave pursuit. With a sudden lurch, he diverted back over the bridge. The horse's hammering hooves dislodged more slats. The pack followed in blind delirium, falling into the river one by one to sink. Arriving on the opposite bank, Genjo doublebacked and leapt the width of the river to land in the courtyard.

"Be gone serpents," Genjo cried. "Slither not across the face of this fair land. Entwine yourself around no more esteemed warriors."

"Bravo Genjo," said the daimyo from his palanquin, raising a small glass of amber into the air. "Our protector. Our master. Our true Lord. Our –"

The drunken lord sipped, hiccupped and vomited milky white fluid onto his lap. He slid out the tilted palanquin and landed head-first on the cobbles. Over he rolled, through the castle gates which closed with a piteous clang.

"I shall return, simpletons," roared Genjo from his steed. "We shall return Japan to its former glor –"

"Mind your head, Genjo!" came a scream.

The samurai ducked. A spear sailed through space. Attached to it was a boy, dressed in black, no older than twelve and with a ferocious grin. The would-be assassin continued his trajectory into the river, spraying a plume of dirty water over the assembly. He never resurfaced.

"So quick, so handsome, so strong," carolled the crowd to Genjo.

"You see monkey man," he smirked. "The finest of warriors can vanquish his foe and seduce the masses without engaging in combat. You don't always need to thrust away like a moron."

"Onwards to victory, brave Genjo," crowed the monkey, as they careered along the dirt road.

The next village was covered with the corpses of samurai. Parasitic poultry incessantly pecked their faces. High above, on the terrace of the tallest building, sat an overweight fudai daimyo peering down a rifle barrel and chuckling at the mayhem. One geisha massaged his feet; another soothed his brow with a fan. The fudai fired at random, the crack of his rifle and explosion of white feathers followed by hoots of laughter.

"Butchery!" screamed Genjo, charging into the throng of chickens and dispersing them with thrashes of his sword.

Enraged, the fudai strapped the rifle to his back and performed a perfect somersault from the terrace. He landed on his feet before Genjo, his robes splaying behind him as he rose to eyeball his foe. The fudai lifted the rifle and fired at Genjo's face. *Crack. Crack. Crack.* The samurai parried each bullet with his sword, advancing closer to the fudai with each defence. *Crack. Crack. Crack. Click. Click. Click.* Out of ammunition, the fudai smiled bitterly.

"So calm, Genjo," purred the geishas. "So controlled. So cunning."

The fudai's head was soon rotating on a feasting spit in the village's main square at a banquet held in Genjo's honour. The two geishas, who transpired to be the fudai's daughters, postponed their grief to enjoy romantic dalliances with Genjo. One came under the table between courses. The other during a ceremonial sword dance. Upon climax, both lovers patted Genjo on the head like a confused dog as the saliva dribbled from his mouth.

"Mind your head, Genjo," they said. "Mind your head."

The samurai departed with a swirl of his sword, an unsullied geisha chasing him naked down the boggy track. Mildly embarrassed, Genjo threw her a pouch of coins and blew her a kiss. He fantasised dancing with all three ladies while unveiling a towering artwork of his likeness in the village square. An etching into a painting into a statue, still standing while the rest of Japan sank into the sea.

"Keiko used to say I was not equipped, monkey man," scoffed Genjo. "That I don't have the skill anymore."

"Your master will feel your power soon enough."

The trio rode up the hillside to a village bisected by a huge waterfall. Houses either side quaked in its thunderous flow. Behind the avalanche of water, a group of muscular, semi-naked men prowled the cliff edge, wearing monkey masks and brandishing whips. In unison they lashed servants, who kneeled with upturned buckets catching water, tipping it behind and repeating the process, their groans barely audible through the roaring surge.

Genjo weaved through them, following a track lined by barrels painted with the words 'the chaste'. From each container popped geishas' heads, faces caked in mud, brown water flowing inexhaustibly from the barrels.

"Such vigour, such power, such strength," they sighed. "Master me, Genjo. Master us all."

Peace came at the summit. Sky and land stretched serenely into white space. Genjo stripped naked and bathed in a stream up to his waist. His sculpted torso, lean abdomen and fulsome hair sent the highest-flying birds into a swoon. Apart from the horse and monkey, his only companion was a lonely attention-seeking samurai on another peak, turning a sword into his belly and contemplating whether to fall.

"It's hard to cope when every woman craves your seed," he said. "Not all gardens can be tended, you see."

"You are only human," said the monkey.

"Yet I worry I lack… potency."

The monkey fell quiet.

"These younger samurai are quicker, stronger."

"They lack finesse, good Genjo."

"They do indeed. Artistry. Grace. Courage. The willingness to grab a thing by the hand and do it themselves when times are hard. Keiko will see."

"Yes, when the country can fit in the palm of your hand."

Genjo lifted his hands from the water and flexed his fingers, enjoying the coolness trickle down his wrists.

"Enough monkey," he snapped. "You vex me with your tiresome riddles. Get me to the swamp and I'll hold the world in my hand. The sky. The sun. The stars. Every secret of the earth. Keiko and I will hold dominion over everything. Restored to my rightful place by my master. The water is rising around us all. Now help me dress."

Together they assembled Genjo's armour, straining to stretch the steel over his titanic muscles. When finished, the samurai leapt on his horse in a single bound without grabbing stirrup or saddle, then galloped down the mountainside onto an open plain shadowed by darkening sky.

"Mind your head, Genjo. Mind your head."

A ghastly squawking rained down. A swarm of crows in the shape of a spear plummeted towards Genjo. With swift elegance, the samurai dismounted, unsheathed his sword, closed his eyes and kneeled.

"Let my weapon penetrate the heavens," said Genjo.

As the first crows closed in, Genjo rose with his sword pointing to the sky. Swivelling on his heels, he rotated his wrists furiously, scything every single bird at lightning speed. Flurries of black feather showered down in a thundercloud of screams and screeches, until the plain was darker than coal.

"Your sword is long and fierce and true, good Genjo."

Beyond was a vast lake. It had no discernible shoreline, like it was painted on the landscape with a single, lazy brush stroke. Matted with black feathers, Genjo, horse and monkey charged into the water to cleanse themselves. They sank slowly, holding their breaths as they pranced through fishes, seaweed and shafts of sunlight illuminating the drowned corpses of foreign invaders.

At the lakebed's deepest point was a bubbling black hole. Bursting out came a squadron of green sea serpents with needles for teeth. Genjo wrestled each to the ground with one arm while fending off the remainders with the other. One by one he choked them until they disintegrated.

A thousand and one zombified soldiers waited behind a bank of seaweed, armed with rifles and mouths foaming with yellow pus. Maggots writhed in the holes where eyes used to be. Many fled in fear at the sight of Genjo. Some fired at the trio with bullets. Each missed the target by such distance it seemed providence had intervened. Genjo swam towards them, his sword acrobatics eviscerating them into a collective grey smudge.

Through the charcoal blur, he spied a track winding enticingly to the brow of an underwater hill and a hand-drawn clump of trees floating underneath the waves like a mirage.

"This is a strange land, monkey man. Is Keiko close by?"

"Yes, good Genjo. The swamp is nearer than you think."

"Will Keiko love what I have become?"

The monkey remained silent.

Pools of dark inky water wallowed within the aquatic woods. The trees rippled into each other; a slow entanglement smattered with tiny pockets of light. On the lakebed, bracken and bark coiled together like slow-moving snakes. The vision was as thin and two-dimensional as the blinds in Keiko's pleasure rooms. It moved too, forcing the samurai to duck as branches swung like axes at his head.

From the depths sprung four noblemen, swimming back and forth and side to side, swords raised tentatively. They formed a circle around a lavish carriage, tangled in seaweed and marooned lopsided against a rock. A sixteen-petalled yellow chrysanthemum was painted on the vehicle's rear.

"Help me," cried a sobbing voice, muffled by the water. "We are doomed. The water is rising. A monster haunts my land. My dreams. My mind."

Genjo swam towards the carriage. The four guards attacked, their contorted faces issuing silent screams. With a single swoop of his rope, Genjo whipped them from the lakebed. They crashed and he was upon them, lassoing and trussing them into a floating heap of defeat.

Inside the carriage on his knees, eyes full of desperation, was the emperor. He was a frail main with a wispy white beard, drawn face and mucus hanging from his nostrils. Next to him was a naked geisha with a jewel-encrusted blanket over her chest. Unperturbed by the shenanigans outside, she stared at Genjo with crazed lust, tiny bubbles popping from her mouth, nose and ears.

"Oh Genjo," said Japan's sovereign, scrabbling towards him and clinging onto his right calf, resembling a toddler refusing to let go of his mother. "At last, you've come. Our land is doomed. We are fleeing. Fleeing for our lives."

"Fleeing? From what?" asked Genjo.

"Oh please no," screamed the emperor. "Mind your head!"

A stream of ice singed the right side of Genjo's armour. The blast froze the carriage and turned the trussed-up guards to black ice. Above the water was the hazy shape of an enormous dragon, swooping in circles. Genjo propelled himself to the surface to meet its attack. Parrying the ice shards with his sword, he somersaulted over the serpent's head and landed on a passing cloud. Samurai and dragon wrestled each other from one side of Japan to another, rolling and writhing like two warring storms. The awestruck populace watched as the two figures spun ethereal ribbons of orange and red, sending spectral trails into the cosmos.

Eventually Genjo prevailed, thrusting a dagger into the beast's side as they grappled at the edges of space. As the dragon screamed, Genjo reached into its mouth, tore out its tongue, wrapped it round the creature's throat and squeezed. Standing triumphantly on its back, Genjo guided the dragon under the lake using its tongue as reins, while strangling the steed to death. The beast expired just as Genjo rested its corpse gracefully beside the emperor, the snout of its nose a hand's width from the old man's feet.

"Genjo, this land is yours now," the emperor said. "Take this. It is the key to my throne room at my palace in Edo. Whatever is in there is yours. Return to the past again and make it right. Take Japan back to its glorious past. Banish those malevolent forces contaminating our minds. I declare to the world you are my one and only son. A real man. A real hero. A hero who will never die."

Genjo studied the key in his palm. It was very small. Slender, light and sculpted from golden water, curling at the end into tightening circles. It reminded Genjo of the doodles he used to draw.

"Only when the country can fit in the palm of your hand will the master appear," said the monkey, dancing on the stallion's saddle with one hand behind its head. Genjo's companion was translucent, a ghostly surface traced against the evanescent trees.

"Your riddle has come true, monkey. I hold Japan in my hand. Now, where is my beloved master?"

"There," said the monkey, pointing lazily behind Genjo. "In the swamp."

The emperor, geisha, dragon, carriage, woods and lake dissolved. Thick white mist engulfed Genjo; a new enemy formless and unreadable. Somewhere behind the wall of white, his stallion neighed timidly. Tentatively Genjo followed the sound into swampland with a *phwuck, phwuck, phwuck*.

"Master?" cried Genjo. "Master? I come to find you. I have missed you."

No sound returned. The fog unveiled a familiar shape with motionless hooves and a slouched head. Genjo mounted his tired steed and lurched it forward, sword raised in one hand and the monkey perched on his opposite shoulder. With every attempted trot, the horse's hooves oozed further into the bog.

"Who is your lord?" chirped the monkey.

"Monkey, you know that. My lord is Keiko."

"How will you recognise your master?"

"I will know. I hold all of Japan in my hand."

Genjo looked at his palm. The key had dissolved into a puddle of grey water. In his other hand was his sword, shrinking in the mist.

"Master?" he said, his voice breaking. "Where are you? I beg you speak."

"The water is rising," jeered the monkey.

The stallion reared up, threw Genjo and bolted. He tumbled down a steep ravine. With each roll, a piece of armour dislodged. Finally, the momentum waned. Genjo found himself semi-naked, peering back through the mist at a huge mountain. The monkey was laughing at him. Vile, vicious laughter.

"Master, I am coming," said Genjo.

The samurai trudged upwards through the swamp. The air was filled with the battlefield smell of blood, shit and rotting flesh. Genjo only made ten steps before the ground rose to his calves. He retreated down the hillside into the deep, white void, pushing his hand into the thickening blankness.

"Help me, monkey man. Help me. The water is rising."

Five feet away, a figure rose from the sludge through the white vapour. Keiko. More versions of the master rose all around. Some grimaced, some grinned, others screamed without sound. A hundred Keikos, flittering into white.

"Mind your head, Genjo," they hissed. "Mind your head."

"Keiko," Genjo said. "Please dance with me. The water is rising."

Whaaaapp. Something below the surface seized Genjo's right ankle. The Keikos' features dissolved into white oval surfaces with black slits for eyes. They retreated as one, twitching and turning into the distance until the mist erased all. The force below tightened its grip. Something knocked Genjo's weapon clean from his hand into the abyss.

"Please dance with me."

There was a loud splash, then a huge whack to Genjo's forehead. A constellation of stars formed a circle in the sky. Everything beyond its perimeter was pitched into darkness.

"Mind your head," screamed the monkey. "Mind your head."

Whaaaapp. The underground enemy clamped Genjo's left ankle. The samurai lurched forward only to sink further. He reached into the swamp with both hands to grapple whatever was fastened to his feet. *Whaaap. Whaaap.* Tentacles locked his wrists. Soon, Genjo was submerged to his chest.

"Master, master!" he cried. "Where am I? Where am I? Let me see you. Tell me where I am. I only wanted to dance. Please, the water is rising."

A ripple in the water, six inches from Genjo's face. A green vine, of the type he used to hack down in the garden, coiled calmly around his neck.

"We told you to mind your head," hissed the plant.

The vine unfolded at the tip and prised open Genjo's shivering lips, forcing its black inner stem deep into the samurai's throat.

As he slid into the earth, Genjo looked to the sky. In the ever-decreasing circle above, Keiko appeared. Blurry at first, the contours slowly appeared as if painted on water. A familiar face. Cloaked in a red mist, streaming with tears of grief. It was a more authentic visage than anything Genjo could draw.

"Master is gone," the face said. "Master is gone."

***

"Master is gone," shouted the two boys as they ran down the track to meet the lady of the house. "Master is gone."

Their panicked eyes and waving hands set Mistress Keiko's mind racing. *What's he done now? He only had to look after the place for a single day.*

"Come," said the shorter boy, dragging her by the hand through the outer gates. "Come now. Master is gone."

Keiko did her best to keep up with the boys, despite the long trek from the neighbouring daimyo's home. The trip was a sad one. His lordship was pleasant enough, sipping his discoloured sencha and listening to Keiko's worries with patience. Both agreed time must take its course.

"Have you little scamps been spying again?" Keiko scolded the boys. Sweet children who dreamed of being samurais. How easily it can turn sour. Keiko was in her forty-seventh year, tired of absorbing the violent fantasies of overgrown children. *Children playing with swords. Stupid. Worse than Genjo on a difficult day. Even he is gentle at times.*

"You should be at the schoolhouse," she continued. "Not creeping through the cherry blossoms laughing at your elders."

"We saw him fall," said one, eyes flooding. "We cannot reach him."

A sickness rose in Keiko's throat. *Please don't say it. Please don't let it be.* Another accident, like the one which started this mess. When a foolhardy Genjo charged into war to prove himself to his father. Frightened at the first sight of the enemy, he'd ran into the woods, tripped over weeds and hit his forehead on a tree. They carried him back to camp like a baby. *Mind your head*, they taunted him with cackling laughter. *Mind your head.*

"What do you mean, boy? Tell me what happened!"

"This way, Mistress Keiko."

She followed the boys through the hallway, past the drawings Genjo created to cope with his funny turns. *The water is rising*, he would cry in his sleep. *The water is rising.* Underwater mountain ranges. Flocks of crows shaped like spears. Ghostly swamps. Dragons. Emperors. Serpents. A mocking monkey. Dead men walking. A paper chain of mental decay. In the rooms behind the screens, there were more pictures. None of the ladies were drawn very well. The men were comically oversized. *Samurai. Obsessed with sword length. Always have been.*

Keiko stepped into the garden. Genjo was not where he should be, in that peaceful spot on the veranda. There was still a half-drunk cup of tea next to a vacated tatami stained with dried urine. Even Lord Buddha looked preoccupied.

"We watched from there," shouted one of the boys, pointing to the cherry blossom. A vantage point from where they could see in vignettes the ruined estate and the decline of its master. Like when Genjo fell out of his garden chair and rolled down the bank into the shrubbery. When he confused chickens for his own soldiers but slaughtered them anyway. The time when he declared war on all birds, then pleasured himself under a table growling like a dog.

"Quickly, Mistress Keiko. Quickly. We must help him."

I should have been kinder. I should have done better. He needed more help.

The taller of the boys marched back, grabbed Keiko by the hand and pulled her through the knotted overgrowth. The other boy was on tiptoes, looking down the well. A putrid stench of damp wafted towards her.

He will be fine. We will be fine. All will be fine. Everything will be fine.

"He looked silly, like he was in a dream. Swishing a pretend sword. One time he fell. It was like he was drunk. Then he got back up and…"

But you know it won't be fine, don't you? You know this time he's gone. Because the boys are afraid, the air still and the sun so cold.

Keiko peered over the edge. Genjo lay crumpled at the bottom, wearing his morning robe. Dark water rose to his nostrils. Strands of air matted his bald, twisted head. The afternoon light rippled over unblinking eyes. His right hand was clamped into a fist, suspended defiantly in the air, like he was clinging onto something precious that may unlock the secret to his state of mind.

Gone. Finally. All that's left are silly drawings and pretend worlds.

Kindly folk said he was possessed by a malign spirit. Harder hearts claimed cowardice. Children sniggered from behind trees at the local lunatic. Nobody attended him. Only her. Keiko. A distant cousin, whose family and friends had been massacred during another petty squabble between rival clans. Even she pushed Genjo away in the end, unable to control her laughter when he disrobed and grabbed her hips, desperate to hold another's flesh in his hands.

"Shall we dance, Mistress Keiko?"

The cremation took place on a rainy afternoon. Keiko was one of only two attendees. The other was an elderly man from Edo, arriving by imperial escort to lay a yellow chrysanthemum on the veranda.

"If the emperor had recognised his son, come by just once, his life would have been different," Keiko told him through sheets of rain. "It was too much for him. For me. For anyone."

When the ceremony concluded, Keiko led the imperial envoy across the garden into the house. They spent the afternoon dumbstruck by Genjo's drawings. Outside the heavens lashed down.

"Why did you stay with him?" he said. "For so long?"

"Because he needed help. Care. Calm. Nurturing."

"You sacrificed so much."

"I believed in a paper man. In dreams. In peace. Maybe I'm mad too."

"Who will you become now?"

The red-tinted rain continued that evening, dousing the hillside in its tears. Keiko lay awake in bed, listening to sadness drip through the house. Everything in her world was distorted, like she could only perceive life through the filter of a polluted stream.

"I don't know."

The next morning, she scattered Genjo's ashes amid the cherry blossom, at the same time of day he would patter onto the veranda to drink sencha and meditate. She flung the contents of the urn as far as she could. The ashes fluttered and floated to the ground. Genjo would no doubt have sworn the trees were shedding their leaves in pity.

Far away Keiko heard the tearing of paper. Her companion was gone, swallowed into the undiscovered sea awaiting everyone. Above ground, nature bloomed and withered. Seasons came and went. Daimyo rose and fell. The violence continued, while boys fought with sticks. People drifted on, autumnal leaves at the mercy of careless currents. And on that lonely hill, in a secluded spot of this withdrawn island, the cackling of laughter could still be heard at night, creeping like a mad monkey of the mind through the tangled swarm of trees.

Attu

"Tell me a story that will protect me forever."

The girl's whisper drowned in silent dark. She snuggled deeper into her blanket. *The further I go, the more daddy will want to come back.*

"I will always protect you, darling."

A voice from the blackness. Her mother. No shape, smell or touch. But she was there. Always would be, even in memory. Like the ground beneath her feet and the air lifting her lungs.

"Ours is a love as old as the hills."

The warm words cloaked the child like soft armour. They were each other's protectors. Safe in secret spaces only the two of them could go. The deepest cave. The highest peak. The quietest, most contemplative corners of their hearts.

"What if you don't stay? Like daddy."

Mother was thinking about that too. That sleep with no end.

"There will come a time when you won't be here," probed the girl. "Then I will need your story. For comfort and courage."

"Comfort and courage. They're different things."

"The best stories do both, don't they? The best people give you both. Like daddy. Before he went away."

"They do indeed. Very well then. A story. For comfort and courage. A tale you can wrap yourself in till the end of your days."

Mother's magic spun slow and terse. She weaved the story from thin air and the confluence of all nature offered. Lapping waves. Hurtling storms. Stubborn rock. Winds blasting barren terrain. A tale as immovable as a mountain; a sleeping stone giant cradling a tiny, fragile mystery within.

"Where are you now, child?"

"I'm with you, mummy."

"No. That's not how stories work. Where are you now?"

"In a far-off place."

"Yes, that's right. An island."

"What's it called?"

"Attu."

"Where's that mummy?"

"In the Aleutians. A chain of islands between Russia and Alaska. They curve the top of the Pacific like jewels in a necklace. Attu lies at the most western end. For some it would be nearest east. A lonely place, shrouded in mist."

White lights blinked in the child's mind. Twinkling and twisting through patches of thick grey, like ancestral beacons guiding her to safety.

"Attu is called the birthplace of the winds. The Pacific's warm air meets the frigid currents of the Bering Sea to create huge gales and…"

"And what mummy?"

"No. You need to imagine it yourself."

Beyond the grey, the little girl saw the island materialise through sheets of hail. The land's contours rolled like the rise of the hip and the swelling of a breast. Through the tumult came the soft curves of a girl's face. She had a pretty nose, hungry mouth and dark, fearful eyes.

"Once upon a time, there was a woman in Attu called Amka," said mother. "When she was a child, her father went away and didn't come back. But she learned how to protect herself."

Squawking birds. Splinters of rain. Violent tides ripping on the rocks of blackened bays. Lanterns glowing within tiny shelters made from grass. Families seeking comfort in treeless land. Plants swaying with the whipping winds. Men on shore and at sea, clothed in animal skin. Hunting for crabs, cod and walrus. Mountains crowned in snow, even during the warm seasons, when flowers rushed from the ground under oases of sunlight. Colours died as quickly as they sprung, beauty surrendering to seething gales.

"How did she protect herself, mummy?"

"The secret came to her as a little girl during a bedtime story," said mother. "Just like this one. A story told by her father. He was tall, strong and gentle. Loving and kind. One night he wrapped her tight in a wonderful gift. To keep her warm from the winds and forever in touch with the land. A magical piece of fur…

***

…not from the otters or bears, little Amka. From a special creature. The last surviving one of its kind."

Father's eyes burrowed deep. Compressed oceans of purest blue in a cragged face. Time hunted him. There was a stoop to his shoulder, a stiffness to his step. A wisdom to his voice. Amka loved him so much she thought her heart would burst.

"I saw it. Tracked it. Across inlets, bays and hills. Until I found its home high in the mountains. In a cave within the rock. But deep down I know the creature found me first. It lifted me upwards to its lair on a magic wind."

Father raised his upturned hands above his head. The wispy white hairs on his knuckles. The grooves on his weathered palms. The sudden clench of a fist as he grappled with resurfacing pain. The same hands that brought home animal skins, soaked them in piss and stretched them on stakes. Which sliced the muscle and fat from dead intestines with his bone knife.

"The creature was the hungriest thing I've ever seen. I skinned it, Amka. Now I give the fur to you. For comfort and courage."

In the twilight, the fur didn't look special. Another dead otter, perhaps, one of many which lolled and lapped in the ocean's foam. Father lay the fur across Amka from chin to ankles. His breath turned grey in the cold hut. She closed her eyes and imagined the creature. It had a frightened stare and a gasping mouth.

"Do you mean as hungry as a big bear?"

"No. This was not a bear. This creature came from an older time. When we lived in harmony. When the land was pure and protected us. When we didn't need boats or spears."

Father often talked about the past. Amka was never sure what he meant.

"This creature was a phantom of the earth," he continued. "The one earth to which we're all connected. The one God. Nature. It binds everything and nurtures all. Everything in nature has a spirit and wants to be cared for. Even the creature. That too was searching for love."

"Why did you kill it, then?"

"I didn't. I only took a layer of its fur. The magic wind would have cloaked it again. The creature still lives, you see. In the mountains. In the deepest parts of this land. It also lives in this fur. In you. Nature's way is to pass power to another. Like passing a story on through generations. Love works the same."

Her father kissed her on the forehead and patted the fur down.

"The land is where we come from and where we will go," he said, losing his gaze in the strands of brown. "Hold true to its power, little Amka. Always."

In restless nights to come, she imagined every hair was an island of its own. On each would be tiny people like them, believing they were on lonely rocks abandoned at sea. Bound together in a harmony they couldn't comprehend.

"Bigger powers may come to own the land," father said. "The earth will always be hungrier. There will be times when you feel all alone. Wherever this fur is, you will be at home. At one with the land. At one with nature. At one with me. Remember there is a special strength in you. A fire that wants to live."

The sea roared, the shelter shook, the lantern flickered. The two of them. His bed opposite hers. The hunting equipment in the corner. A knife. A lance. A spear. A net. A safe place.

"Will I be a good hunter?" said Amka.

"Yes. You have the aggression. The instinct. The desire. I see it in your eyes. The hunger to survive."

"I'm scared."

"A good hunter is like the wind, little Amka. That changes all the time. But you never see it. You only feel it. Sometimes when it's too late."

The next morning, Amka saw her father for the last time. He strode broad-shouldered into the icy dawn to set sail in a baidarka. Later that day, the elders came to Amka. The sea had taken her father. If he'd worn the magical fur, he might have floated back to her. For comfort and courage. As it was, Amka's world was awash with tears.

She wore the fur during his burial. Fellow hunters moved with strength and grace. They placed stone and earth over the mound to protect his body. Not a grand burial, like the caves used for chieftains. A simple goodbye for a simple man. Amka knew father was not that. He'd skinned the magical creature. The hungriest thing he'd ever seen.

As the ritual closed, Amka wondered which of the hunters would make the best father. Many seemed younger. Bigger in the arms and chest. There were a couple she liked.

When a woman placed a comforting hand on Amka's shoulder, she struck the lady in the face so hard she drew blood. Frightened, Amka ran to the shore and swore loudly at the sea.

The villagers passed her to a placid, diligent family. They taught her to weave fine baskets from sea-lyme grass. She made special coats called kameikas. Women wore the skin of seals or sea otters. Men wore the insides of bears, walruses or whales. The women sewed with needles made from the bones of seabirds, twisting thin strips of seal intestine to make thread. Amka would lose patience. She yearned to be among towering figures who killed and skinned.

Besides, she already had her kameika. A special one from the creature. She slept, cried and bled in it. The fur sent her back to a windy night, a bedtime story and hunting equipment glistening in the corner. Sometimes she would clothe herself in the fur and wander to the shore in search of father's memory. The sea was empty, bereft of passion. She hated it.

As weeks, months and years passed, the fur grew thicker and broader. No one else noticed; Amka only unfurled it at night. She grew too, maturing into a beautiful, preoccupied figure with an impenetrable face. Men circled her subtly. Women's eyes narrowed with distrust. The air grew cold wherever she walked.

"You have the desire," Amka told her first and only lover. "Just like me. I see it in your eyes. The hunger to survive."

Aput. Tall and dark-haired, with a boyish face. Anxious for something. On their first night of union, Amka wore the fur. She let it slide gracefully to her ankles, enjoying Aput marvel at her naked form in firelight. She was full of softness and hunger. At one with the land. Amka devoured her mate that evening, scared he would never return.

She wore the fur when she gave birth, on a rainy evening when the wind threatened to scatter the village. Tonraq, they called him. *Tiny man*. Amka swathed the baby in the fur and blessed him with the earth's spirit. Ear to his chest, she listened to the magic wind which bore the rhythm of his heart and lungs.

Her lover could not find such depths. Aput was impractical and uncertain, shadowed by some past he hadn't the courage to face. When confrontation was demanded, he sought peace. A man who could not use a lance. Who missed with his spear. The village men recognised Aput's weakness, like they sensed his wife's hunger. In the evening, Amka sometimes left Tonraq and wandered past the returning hunting party, placing herself in their field of vision, her back teasingly turned and silhouetted by the sunset.

One night, the hunters struck. They plied Tonraq with drink, left him to sleep on the beach and invaded his home. The two strongest men grabbed Amka while she was sleeping, shoved a rag in her mouth, stripped her and tied her legs to stakes, stretching them like an otter's skin. The men took turns while Tonraq slept. After they left, Amka crawled under her fur and wept, fighting the urge to skin herself alive and set fire to the flesh.

Everyone in the village denied what happened. Especially the women.

"Amka is crazy."

"Ever since the sea swallowed her father."

"She provokes men."

"Torments them."

"Devours them."

Amka fled, swaddling Tonraq in her fur and leading Aput inland. Safe from the sea's clutches and the venom of the village. She found peace in the foothills, at a clearing between two inclines where blue and yellow flowers grew. Amka showed Aput how to build a shelter. Together they dug an oblong pit, collected driftwood and erected walls with a grass roof. She made a spear from wood and stone and propped it in the corner.

Every evening, Amka tried to heal Aput's shame. But his lovemaking was never as deep as she wanted. The spirit of the earth was nowhere to be found in her husband. Aput refused to sleep under the fur, fearing its hold over his wife. While he crawled into the corner to cradle Tonraq, Amka lay awake, stroking her father's gift. She would surrender to its swirls and curls of brown, savouring its smoothness on her body. The magic fur that knew every pore of her flesh.

Amka swelled again; Aput doubted he was the father. When the little boy was born sleeping, Amka unleashed frenzied howls at the sea and tormented wails into the wind. Wrapping her son's corpse in the fur, she longed for its magic to bring him to life. If she curled into the coat far enough, they would find each other alive. They never did.

Aput became too timid to hunt. Too clumsy to comfort. Too broken to fuck. He was frightened of Amka, Tonraq and being isolated near the mountains. He would not stay the course. Tonraq neither. They would not protect her. Only the fur could do that.

"You're no longer a woman," Aput said. "You grunt and hiss like a beast. And you crawl inside that otter fur looking for sympathy."

"This is not otter fur. It comes from a magic creature."

"Idiot stories from your idiot father. The whole village despised him. Just like they despise you. The fur stinks. So do you. I should never have followed you here. You eat at my soul."

"You cannot face them after what they did. You cannot face me. You're not strong enough to protect me. Me or our son."

"Liar, I will show you my strength," shouted Aput. "Fucking whore."

He struck her with his right fist. Amka's head snapped back and she collapsed to the ground. Seizing her spear, she sprang towards her husband and pushed the weapon's tip to his throat.

"I do not want you," she spat, forcing him back against the wall. "I do not need you. Somewhere on this island there will be a place to feed my longings."

Amka snatched Tonraq and moved higher up the mountain. On a small plateau, she used rocks to build a new retreat. Tonraq sat quietly and watched. The wicked sea, and the men who worshipped it, were faraway. She wished the wind would obliterate them for good. Down below she could see Aput stewing in their family home. A shrinking speck of a man shuffling like some timid insect.

One day, a man from the village visited Aput. Amka grabbed a knife and descended, ready to tear this intruder limb from limb. He was an elderly man. The gathering wind bent his body forwards over a stick. He was not one of those who'd scarred her. But he wore the same cruel gaze, his shallow eyes subtly roving her body.

"Your husband is needed," he said. "We're being attacked by invaders from over the sea. They have weapons that blast fire."

Aput left the same day. Amka did not care if he came back. Whatever came from foreign lands would not penetrate her. She returned to her makeshift pile of rocks, leaving their marital home as prey for the elements.

A few evenings later, while Amka carved a sleeping Tonraq's likeness in stone, a fox prowled into their space. She hurled a wayward spear. The fox attacked, rammed its snout towards Amka's neck and scratched her cheek. As it thrashed and slashed at her raised hands, Amka squeezed its throat and slammed it to the ground. The fox rose, stunned. She retrieved the spear and buried it in the animal's back, twisting until the tip lodged in the earth. She savoured the fox's final gasp for air and fancied she could see its spirit depart. The next day she hung its skin on a rock to be purified by the winds.

Days later, a bear came. Amka had spent the day hunting for food, Tonraq nestled on her back in a pouch made from the fox's skin. When they returned, the bear was rustling inside their home. Setting Tonraq out of sight behind rocks, Amka crept up on the beast and drove a spear between its shoulder blades. Nimbly, she stayed behind the bear as it swayed from side to side, lashing at the air with its arms and screaming in agony. *A good hunter is like the wind. You never see it. You only feel it.* When the bear collapsed, Amka waited patiently for its last breath. Then she hacked off its head, disembowelled the body and prised away the fur.

There was no magic in these new coats. Not like her own special fur, which grew larger. When laid out flat, it stretched beyond her head and her feet by a hand's length either side. Amka cut holes in the middle through which she could place her head and arms. With the excised fur, she made shoes and gloves.

Years passed. Tonraq reached manhood. Mother and son rarely spoke, communicating through grunts and glances, lost on waves of turbulent dreams. Amka became like a destitute queen. Nothing or nobody was good enough, except the solitude of the island and the memory of her father.

One day a young man with matted black hair and a pale face visited. He was short of breath and rarely blinked.

"Aput is dead."

The invaders had stabbed her husband in a skirmish on the shore. Two things were noted of his demise: Aput bled out quickly and called Amka's name as the ocean rolled over his face. She only believed the first part.

"They're killing us all," he continued. "They poison and rape."

The messenger's eyes hovered awkwardly over Amka's face.

"They've captured an old woman and a boy who they use as translators. They force us into labour. They come to strip the land of its fur."

"Did he fight?" said Amka coldly.

"Yes. Aput did fight. Bravely."

"Everyone does. Did he fight for the land? For its spirit? Was he hungry?"

"He fought for our people."

"Why do you tell me this?" she growled. "I'm no longer one of you. I belong only to the land."

"I do not come for you, Amka."

Tonraq wanted to leave. To hunt. To kill. To bond with men. To know women. Sometimes he would wander away from home for days on end. Every time, less of him came back. They collected Tonraq the next day so they could train him to fight. But Amka knew these people didn't have any real fight in them. Her son didn't know the world, nor the islanders.

She retreated into her fur. It still smelled of the day Tonraq was born. When she looked at the fur long enough, on those rare sunny days when the warmth of perfect light soaked her shoulders, Amka could see even greater depths. The entirety of nature. The presence of the one God that harmonises everything.

Amka was beyond her fiftieth year when Tonraq returned. Her son had embraced the invaders' way of life, learning fragments of new language. On the other side of the sea were two places called St Petersburg and Moscow, bound by the memory of a man called Peter. Another tall, strong leader greater than anyone.

"We're part of a bigger world," Tonraq said. "Their ships, the way they hunt. We can be safe if we join them. There is no point fighting the wind and the sea alone. Come. Join me."

"I belong here," Amka said. "My spirit belongs to the island. With this fur. With my father."

Amka never saw her son again. She knew in her heart he could never be a real man. No doubt he would drink, turning his beautiful world numb. Deaf to the call of the wild. In her solitude, she found wood and carved. Small figures of a father and a child, staring into space from the rock's edges. Miniature hunting equipment glistening in the corner. In dark sleep, she imagined herself lying next to Aput, when their future swelled with hope. During the day she wandered into unfamiliar parts of the island and waited for the wind to speak.

Her dried body was changing. Flesh wrinkled over her withering body. Once ravishing hair turned grey. The fur continued to thicken, trailing the ground like a cloak. She was pricked by invisible splinters every time she moved. Hot flushes came and went, violent and unpredictable. She screwed the insides of insects out with her thumb; crept upon resting birds and bludgeoned them in fury. Wilder animals retreated. In the exposed land, all Amka felt was suffocation.

"Get away from me," she screamed, tearing at the fur. "Get away."

The fur would not loosen. Over time its strands had burrowed into her skin, spreading to the soles of her feet and the palm of her hands. The inscrutable dark beautiful face that once excited men was cloaked in a film of wispy brown hair.

Amka wandered the island, talking to the wind. Some days it roared back. Other days it whistled and hummed. She pelted across terrain, forever shifting course, hungering for nature's bounty. When the urge to kill faded, she became listless and lost.

"You live," she cried out. "In the mountains. In the deepest parts of this land. In this fur. Passing through me. I will not leave you. I will never leave you."

Home, her father, the creature. They must be here, in some shape or spirit. Yet the island sent back only the flattening emptiness of the wind. Time and gales declared a war of attrition. All around was sea, imprisoning the island in its eternal chokehold.

One morning, while she scuttled along a ridge in search of dead birds, a Russian confronted Amka. He was tall, bulky and handsome. There was a knife in his belt. Over his shoulder was a metal rod that unleashed fire which killed things from afar. There was greed and cowardice in his face, lust for fur in his eyes. Amka imagined consuming him like she once consumed Aput. Or lashing him to the rocks at the mercy of the wind.

"What do you hunt for?" she barked.

Amka watched the man flee in terror, tumbling, rolling and crawling behind a bank of rocks. No better than an animal. More of them would be coming. Armies of them, spat at her by the sea.

There will be times when you feel all alone. Remember there is a special strength in you. A fire that wants to live.

"Come home, Amka. Come home."

At her time of most peril, the magic wind breathed into her. The creature was summoning her at last, like it had with father a lifetime ago. A hushed, melodious sound, lifting the fur and seeping its warmth into the centre of her soul with the quiet assurance of a delicate lover.

Whether the opening discovered her, or she discovered the opening, Amka could not say. Deep within she knew where it was all along. The cave was two thirds up Attu's highest peak on its north face. Flowers nested round the opening, somehow enduring the climate's violence. She was able to enter without stooping. A warm breeze blew from inside. A lullaby from her father. His lantern and hunting equipment glistening in the corner.

"Come home, Amka. Come home."

The inner walls narrowed. She lowered her head and placed her hands on the interior of the cave. It was damp, lined with thick fluid. Moisture from above tip-tapped onto her head, soaking into her magic fur. Warm air circulated. She fumbled forwards in the scant light afforded by the distant sun behind.

"Daddy?"

Ahead, a formation jutted from the ground. The front part of the rock had two depressions at the top half: large, circular and in perfect symmetry. Beneath was a tall, narrow gash. Beyond that the shape widened, spanning to the edges of the cave and into blackness.

This was not a rock. This was a skeleton. The head of a creature long deceased. Time had fused its wings to the walls. Ever so gently the edifice moved back and forth, like the mountain itself was breathing.

"Daddy, where are you?"

Amka breathed softly. She placed her hand between the crack and stroked its surface. With a pitiful crack, the skeleton crumbled to dust. The cave ended there. Amka lay on her side, clutching her knees and raising them to her chest.

"Don't leave me alone. Don't leave me alone."

She stayed there for a long time, opening her mouth and catching the drip, drip, dripping of cave fluid on her lips. The fur spread too, rabidly climbing the walls. Soon she was lifted and suspended in stasis. The magic wind that spoke to her came not from the ocean, but from the belly of the earth.

"Give me your love," Amka replied. "Give me all of your love."

The island breathed as one. Amka grew sensitive to every creature's pleasure and pain. The Russians were coming, casual and arrogant. They'd not experienced motherhood; the miracle that brought her closer to the earth. She would savour their last breaths.

Steps outside the cave. An intruder with a lamp. In the swaying light she saw a rod of fire sticking out from his waist. Four steps away. Her mouth watered. A tug in her belly. Three steps. A knife in his belt. Two. His bare neck. One. Hesitancy. Another one not man enough to reach all the way inside.

Amka pounced, locked her jaw into his jugular and ripped away a chunk of flesh. Streams of warm red slid down her throat, pooled into her lap and soaked into the fur. His last breath tasted like the freshest of hillside flowers. Sunset broke through the cave entrance, illuminating her evening feast.

Two sunrises later, three silhouettes appeared at the cave entrance, waving fire and shouting strange words. Amka waited. Her face felt the warmth of the flames and the dregs of their breath. Slowly she let the fur curl around their ankles, wrists and necks, ensnaring them in her space. Into their mouths the fur crawled, seizing their spirits and depriving them of voice.

She calmly feasted on the first man, draining his blood and crushing his bones, relishing how the other two lost their minds through observation. By sunset, all three men were consumed, traces of their remains collecting on the cave's ground like sediment on the shore.

Time passed. Amka lay cocooned in the cave's depths, waiting. More greedy men ventured inside to be digested. Smarter ones stayed outside and fired their guns. Amka absorbed the bullets, as the ravenous fur swelled to the cave's entrance.

There it stopped, turning into knotted bracken singed by the sun. What was once alive and insatiable turned withered and grey. Soon it became indistinguishable from the rock. Yet deep inside the hunger remained. An emptiness. A promise. A story. Soft, yearning words of absence…

***

…carried to sea by the wind, to be told one day to another little girl in some distant place."

The night was black. Sleep would come soon. The girl clung to her blanket, her lifeline to the waking world. Everything seemed floating and ungraspable. Her mother especially. A tired, frail voice.

"What happened then mummy?"

"The Russians left. Europeans passed by, assuming Attu was barren. The Japanese and Americans fought a terrible war there. The Americans won but withdrew after a time. They still claim it as their own. Attu is uninhabited now. Everyone has abandoned it. Like your father abandoned us."

Mother paused. Her silence spoke of regret. Of old age. Of being smothered inside some huge mountain of deep, everlasting hurt.

"Except one person who still lives there and calls it home. The last surviving one of her kind. Every island is a story, hungering to be told. Every person too. Some desires always stay with you. Like stories. They take on a new shape. What lies within is always the same."

"The fur Amka wore," said the girl. "Is that the fur I'm wearing now?"

"Maybe it is. Your fur. From the land. From nature. From what has come before and what will continue to be. What story it tells will be up to you."

The girl's mind was already over the sea.

"I love you, mummy."

"I love you, too. Is that courage and comfort enough?"

"That's all I have. So it will be. It must be. She was very brave."

A troubled current in the blackness. Maybe the girl had not fully understood the tale. Was her mother trying to warn her?

"Get some rest, little one," said her mother. "You may feel different about the story in the morning. Or when you're much older."

"Can I just have one more story? *Please*."

"That's enough for one night. Some tales must wait. Some places are left well alone. Some corners best not visited. Not yet anyway. We all must learn to..."

The wind whipped. The cold air bit exposed flesh. The weary world was volatile still. Everything could change direction suddenly and the girl wouldn't see it coming. She dug her nails deep into the fur, grinding her teeth. When the rage passed, she spoke.

"Will daddy be coming back?"

"No, my love. Daddy won't be coming back. He's gone away. He decided to search for love elsewhere. Where he's sailed, I cannot say."

The hunt began at midnight. In her dreams, the girl woke in another world, drifting over the waves to the barren island of Attu. One day she'd leave mother. This home. The four walls surrounding her. To search for love. To awaken her own hunger. To find the hunting equipment glistening in the corner.

"Tell me a story that will protect me forever," she screamed to the island as she reached its shore.

The terrain lay undisturbed, as the sound of her cry shuddered through the mountains with an insatiable hollowness craving to be filled.

Loki

I held the young man's gaze as long as I could. His black face was serene and guileless, like he was in private audience with a choir of angels. I love to read complexions. This one's meaning I could not decipher. It was an itch I could not scratch. Amid this freak show, the African seemed at one with himself.

Lowering my eyes to the ground, I wondered what his breaking point would be, or whether he even had one. I desired him to speak as he would in the jungle, without this exhibition's artifice. To hear his authentic cadence. The tenor of his strangeness. That singular combination of notes unique to every person. A secret melody that would inspire my fingers to dance over black and white keys in a concerto of calm.

When in the mood, I can turn my hand to anything.

There were about sixty semi-naked savages from the Congo Free State on show in Brussels. The African pavilion, a grandiose art nouveau tableau of wooden vines and elephant tusks, was the centrepiece of King Leopold's exposition. I found the spectacle ridiculous and shallow, like tying a prehistoric fossil in a silk bow and placing it in a boutique window.

Lurid chatter accumulated over afternoon tea in decorous salons. The curious and cosmopolitan, fattened by leisure, scoffed at these black exiles. Their privileged faces conveyed vacuity, the blotches of their swollen skin a metropolitan excess bottling deep anxiety.

"Brainless creatures. Easily led."

"What scenery though. How threatening. How primitive. How inspired."

"Yes, yes, yes. How *artistic*."

There are few things I despise more than bourgeois taste.

I'm a different kind of artist. A con artist, plundering Europe's capitals. I own nothing I call my own. All objects on my person once belonged to someone else. Even now, closer in years to sixty than fifty, my appetite is as unsated as my demeanour is sly. People only appreciate me when I'm gone, possessing something they hold dear like money or jewellery. Fears. Secrets. The most precious parts of their soul. I'm not like them though. Never will be. If you followed me closely, you'd swear there was nobody here at all.

My stock is mixed. Part French, part German, with Italian ancestry on my mother's side and Hungarian on my father's. Rumours circulated in the lower aristocracy that my mother enjoyed a tryst with a lusty Spanish pirate nine months before I was born. My father, a drunk Bavarian gambling connoisseur, was none the wiser. I've never been north of Hamburg, yet my unruly shock of blond hair evokes the Scandinavian spirit. For now, call me Loki. A trickster. A shape shifter. An ageing man who plays it low key.

I've looked at my face countless times in the mirror, trying to piece myself together. To create a signature tune that tells my story. But the only signature I scratch is one with my right hand when I check into a new hotel with someone else's money. I always take a moment before deciding what to write. Blending into the upper classes isn't easy. So much so that time and fate led me to seek myself in another kind of jungle.

My journey to the Congo began with an unedifying poker game in a Pigalle brothel. Two rotund merchants from Montparnasse with faces like bank vaults caught me teasing a replica Jack of Spades from under my shirt cuff. Beetroot-faced and waving cigars in fury, they strained forwards in their armchairs to protest. I used the time afforded by their lethargy to retreat to the open window. Swaying towards me through an opium fog brandishing a revolver was a sultry Senegalese courtesan, whom the proprietor had ordered to chaperone proceedings. Her face twitched like a neurotic sparrow. Clearly, she bore a motherlode of unresolved pain and hungered to lodge a bullet in my groin.

Inching towards the window, I threw my arm in a diversionary gesture towards the corner of the room and let out an effeminate squeal. While their eyes roved the floorboards, I grabbed the outside sewage pipe I'd spied when entering the building and began my silky descent down four storeys of Parisian townhouse. As I reached midway, the pipe came away from the wall, for I'd enjoyed too much good food in St Germain at the expense of a naïve dowager grieving her dead husband. I landed awkwardly on the cobbles, spraining my ankle while the courtesan rained bullets and curses from above. I limped into the shadows, imagining a faceless Gallic crowd greeting me with unbridled applause.

Bravo, Loki, bravo!

Those Montparnasse hogs were well acquainted with the gendarmerie, which meant the city of light would soon turn its search beams on your lovable Loki. I boarded a train that evening from Gard du Nord and arrived in Brussels at dawn. A timid official asked for my papers. His hesitant voice and creased brow smacked of an abusive childhood. Preying on his eagerness to please, I persuaded him I was a down-on-his-luck stockbroker from St Tropez who'd lost his identity documents in a panicked night flight to visit my dying mother in Anderlecht.

The Belgian capital was a grimy place. In a grubby bar outside the railway station, a sloppy pianist, drunk on proletariat beer and nose buried in the cleavage of his past, was massacring a Bach concerto. A provincial bunch, these Belgians. Typical Europeans. Their insipid faces tell their own stories. Narcissism. Greed. Cynicism. Shallowness. This whole choking continent struck a prolonged bum note; its turgid drone provoking a desire to soar, soprano-like, to purer plains.

Harmony matters. In isolation, constituent parts may be light as feathers, but when cohered correctly they acquire the grace and velocity of a bird of prey. The majesty and danger of a leopard. Or the animal magnetism of these handsome blacks. Perfect specimens unspoiled by civilisation. *Wholeness,* that's what they communicated. Nature's sequence. The chord progression of the divine.

I'm a pianist by profession. At least I was thirty years ago until the Trauma of Trieste, where the feeble-minded elite jeered my alternative rendition of Beethoven's ninth. My mother, who taught me to play, was equally appalled by my performance's licentiousness. There was no tune she could not master. No men who could say no to her charms. No financial wheeze she could not orchestrate. Yet the only music she left me was cacophonous laughter, chuntered through rotting teeth.

Today she floats on my shoulder still, mocking my fall from grace, louche men sniffing her perfumed neck. That woman taught me how to take revenge on the world. To glory in deception and the sheer thrill of surprising susceptible people. The kind of dullards swept up in the mumbling muzak of their minds.

I let go of my love for mother long ago. Yet I've never relinquished my adoration of the piano. The self-possession you need to master the instrument is synonymous with the skills required to rise in society. To move between delicacy and darkness. Pianissimo to fortissimo. As it is with the black and white keys, so it is with conning people. A case of pressing the right buttons. Striking the right note. Rising them high while hitting them low. One day I may even trick my real self, if I knew who that was.

In Brussels I drifted, spinning yarns to gullible tourists conspicuous in their idiocy. I fled expensive restaurants without paying the bill, chuckling as the protestations of irate waiters faded into the distance. Eavesdropping in coffee houses led me to the African pavilion. There, the clarion call of a thousand trumpets summoned ambition from its slumber. The primal nakedness of promised savannahs scorched away the damp superficiality of city life. These blacks. *Oh these blacks*. Their docility. Their physicality. Their opacity. The contrast of their ebony skin with the ivory furnishings. Ivory, ivory, ivory. White, smooth, pure. Billiard balls, knife handles and grand pianos.

Yes. The ivory trade. In the Congo Free State. If I couldn't master the piano myself, nor the courts of Europe, I would conquer the savages of Africa. Beguile natives with my vocal intonations. Bamboozle them with the soft patter of civilisation. Scratch away at this unusual race until the mystery of that beautiful boy's expression was revealed. From the depths of the dark continent, I would climb the scale again. Make my fortune, then sell some savages as slaves in the harems of Cairo or as water carriers in Casablanca. Lounging in some mock Côte d'Azur compound, I would coerce my other captives into exotic dances, while I conned opium-addicted millionaires using a deck of cards and my natural charm.

I played my hand that afternoon. At the recruiting office for the Force Publique, the ragtag of bandits whom King Leopold had charged with extracting the Congo's treasure, I met a scruffy, bespectacled oaf with his belly bursting from his shirt. He sweated behind a heavy desk loaded with drab secretarial accoutrements sourced from God only knows what flea market. Bureaucracy's tyranny was trod in tedious tramlines all over this wretch's face. I treated him to a whirlwind of theatricality, transforming myself into a merchant seaman with many decades in the Far East, financially obligated to a destitute five-child family in Ghent.

"It takes a solid man with an even temperament to survive out there," he said. "A man of your vintage may… struggle. There is opportunity. But only for those who dig deep enough."

"I am younger than you think," I said. "My teeth dig very deep."

"How far would you like to go?" he said through a smirk, the question swinging back and forth like the pendulum of a clock.

"As far as possible."

The fat man scribbled on the authorisation documents and tossed them at me like he was disposing of dirty laundry.

The next day I travelled to Antwerp, wearing a white linen suit and white fedora. In my hand was a stolen and mostly empty valise initialled JC. In the port's alleyways, I muddied my suit's ankles and elbows. People take more pity on a wealthy man in decline than a poor man on his way up. After slapping some sense into the slow-minded harbour boy, I soon found my home for the voyage: a dilapidated steamer called La Sirène.

Home. Always another place. For I am groundless; a perennial traveller powered by fabrication's winds. So many characters I have played, flitting to and from the stage. The hoodlum in a brothel. The financier in transit. The merchant in the commercial district. The coloniser in the jungle. Oh yes what a sound to my ears. *The coloniser.* This time I will do more than pretend. In the jungle *I will compose*. A harmony born in the heart of darkness.

As the boat cleared Zeeland, I stood on deck and doffed my hat to the diminishing coast, span it round my head thrice and crowed some words in Italian. A genteel lady with a parasol blushed and moved slowly away, no doubt unsettled by her awakening lust.

The four-month voyage was tedious and turbulent. We stopped at A Coruña, Vigo and Lisbon. Then onto Africa. Dakar. Freetown. Liberia. The Gold Coast. The French lands. I scratched myself more than usual, needled by the vindictive heat and gnawed by exotic insects. A journey marred by sleepless nights and turgid conversation with money-grubbing adventurers from the lower classes. A motley crew of custom officers, soldiers and degenerates, with rattlesnake voices and eyes glittering with speculated gold.

There is nothing more powerful than a posh accent to seduce such social climbers. I owned them all, mesmerising my audience with gorgeous stories about my past and hypnotising them with flourishes of my hands. In the process I convinced them to fund my plans for a philanthropic music school to civilise the Congolese. I often say there is nothing finer than the music of the piano. But there is. The music of money. The jingling of coin. The soft sound of bank notes pressing together. For good measure, I beat my seafaring companions at poker on a ten-night winning streak. Their faces wore no filter, so I didn't need to use my covert Jack of Spades. But I did anyway. Victory is sweeter when you cheat.

At night I shared a room with three dim-witted mercenaries masquerading as entrepreneurs. To shut out their snoring and the steamer's exhausted droning, I closed my eyes and summoned Chopin, Bach and Liszt. Rising from my bed in semi-sleepwalk, I dressed in imaginary coat tails, powdered my face, coiffured my shimmering blond hair and ascended the stage of Trieste's opera house. On a cabin stool before a cheaply framed sketch of Victoria Falls, my fingernails scratched the sideboard. My companions deemed me insane. A doddering man on a last quest for glory. A wisp of a figure who would evaporate on African soil. How they underestimate the power of the insubstantial.

Granted, I'm not an impressive specimen. Short, fat and ruddy faced. Save for my blond locks, there's nothing attractive about my personage. Weaker men would have given up with such an inheritance. But it's the thrill of the chase which drives me to the dark. To the pursuit of boyish mastery over another. Sometimes I still imagine myself a Napoleonic swashbuckler. On sunny afternoons in the Bois de Boulogne, I liked to burn insects with a magnifying glass. My Norse tendencies mean I'm ready to swing an axe if needed. And I hear people coming before they even do themselves. Nobody hears me though, as I scratch towards them through the undergrowth. They won't in the jungle either. I will die putting one over somebody. Where my soul goes then is anyone's guess.

From the ship, I didn't scrutinise the African lands by sight. When I visit new place, I close my eyes and listen to its music. The chatter, rhythm and beats. In the dark continent, the hacking of the trees, the firing of guns and the murmur of native chants coalesced into a terrible din. Underneath it all scuttled a low-key scratching that reminded me of… discord. The place was hot too, devilishly hot. I would lose another stone before I acquired my first tusk of ivory.

During the slow, sweltering journey down the clawing isolation of the Congo river, I succumbed to fever. My companions' chuntering and the grinding operations from the steamer's belly haunted my waking moments. When darkness fell, the Senegalese prostitute from Pigalle plagued my dreams, transforming herself into a giant leech that sucked torrents of blood through my penis.

The day after my fever broke, our steamer chugged to a stop on a desolate strip of sand banking the river. Thinning, hungry and bristling with contempt for mankind, I stepped onto the soil with my valise. A man of means. A successful coloniser. A gentleman of the court. Those who survived out here, I decided, would be those who told themselves the best stories.

The Force Publique station was a disparate chain of one-storey huts reminiscent of farmyard barns. Next to the dark lustre of the jungle, the buildings seemed as vapid and untethered as a mirage. The complex comprised an administrative office, counting-house, stores, shipping facilities and a cemetery. Cloaked in uniforms of pristine white, the Force Publique officers were mainly mercenaries from across Europe. They brandished rifles and bull whips made from hippopotamus skin. Shuffling around them were famished minions from Zanzibar, West Africa and Arabia, chains around their necks and ankles, scarred flesh stretching across jutting bones.

A diminutive Force Publique officer greeted the navigator. After a flurry of paperwork and indecipherable whispering, he told me and a few other wanderers to reboard the steamer. We sailed further down the river, passing three more stations in two days, each one smaller than the last. More travellers disembarked at each one to be swallowed by the trees. Soon I was the only traveller on board.

Journey's end finally came. The innermost station was a squat, one-room ramshackle shed smelling of dried blood. Within the lair sat its sultan. The captain was a sweaty lump in an ill-fitting beige suit with a ridiculous spotted red tie over a pink shirt. Eyes swelling, teeth blackened and nostril hair rampant, he barely blinked as he scanned me up and down. He sensed I wasn't who I claimed to be. Nobody was here. *Go ahead. Test me.* I'd paint him a vision so brutal his hair would turn white. When in the mood, I can turn my hand to anything.

"Why have you come out so far, blondie? You seem a little… antique."

"So far?" I said, dryly. "I was hoping the boat would go further."

"Ah, the confidence of youth. *Mon dieu*. We have an adventurer on our hands. Either that or a fucking idiot."

In the office corner was the source of the pungency. A wicker basket, full of a dozen severed black hands, flies bedding into severed flesh and veins.

"Our trophy collection," said the captain. "I ask my boys to give me one black hand for every bullet fired. Helps save ammunition. Too many of them are trigger happy. Sometimes I pay a bonus on the hands I get, sometimes I don't. Flesh is a major currency here. But I assume you'd know all about that."

I hit him with a salvo of sailoring exploits. Hong Kong. India. The Caribbean. Each tale was so perfectly pitched, I could have convinced him I was the bastard son of King Leopold. One fraud mesmerised by the handiwork of another. He rewarded my silver tongue with a revolver, machete, white uniform, warm bed and power over a bunch of beautiful blacks. My task was to ensure they ripped rubber from the trees.

"Rubber?" I enquired. "Not ivory?"

"There's none round here," laughed the captain. "Only the red ivory. Rubber is what we need. And rubber is what you'll get. Lots of it. Enough to fill these baskets. Or you may find it's your hands going on a journey."

Rubber. Cheap, nasty, rubber. For those new-fangled bicycles everyone was riding. I'd followed a tissue of lies across two continents. The devil laughed at me from deep within those cursed trees. Or maybe the mockery came from Lucifer's headquarters in the satin sewers of Trieste.

"Get going, blondie. You'll see what's involved."

"Now?"

"No. Tomorrow. Tonight, we savour the scenery. Don't stay awake too long and let your mind play tricks. One fellow shot himself the very first evening."

"Is that supposed to scare me?"

"You look scared. Are you sure you're not too long in the tooth for this?"

"My teeth are indeed long. They go deep. Deeper than this vile continent."

"We shall see Long Tooth. We shall see."

I slept in a small shed to the rear of the station. The air was chewy and the smell marginally better than a latrine. My roommates were Hercule, a slovenly drunk from Marseilles, and Antoine, a man from Toulouse who shared vulgar anecdotes about fucking high-class hookers in Tangier. Hercule's *pièce de resistance* was to brag about filling a fishing net with large stones and unruly Congolese, then sinking them to the riverbed and relishing their screams.

"May I invite you to join me in a game of poker," I said, fingering the replica Jack of Spades tucked into my sleeve.

"What's on the table?" snapped Antoine.

"The honour of being the first tomorrow to blow a black's brains out."

"Done," chipped in Hercule. "Currency?"

"Bullets. They count more than coin here."

I won every game. While a vanquished Hercule and Antoine slept, I lay on my bed, endured their snoring, scratching the insect bites peppering my body and smiling to the imagined sounds of Chopin. They knew I was a conman. We all were. How long before we all lost this game of bluff?

At dawn I strolled the station to meet my men. The pack was led by two gormless Force Publique officers whose names I didn't ask on principle. But the blacks. *The blacks*. They were something else. Three of them. Statuesque yet emaciated, with drooping lips and shoulders. A palpable equanimity resided in their brutalised bodies. They were *grounded*, like their souls speared so deep through the soil they had fused with the earth's crust.

I trudged beside them in grinding fascination as we ventured into the darkness. Our feet squelched; our ears pricked for the rustle of leopards. Underneath it all came the persistent scratching.

"Watch your steps," an officer said. "There are snakes everywhere."

I remembered the ludicrous ostentatiousness of the Brussels exposition. The ornate carving. The twisting. Oh yes, they'd been right about the twisting. The Congo screwed your perceptions out of shape, stunting your sight and distorting your hearing. Everything I touched was laced with the residue of greed. The stench of vegetation, at first fresh and vital, grew nauseating. And the sounds. Clinking manacles. Dragging chains. Distant, inexplicable screams.

Yet there was something here for me. What it was, I could not say. My life to that point was only masks and mirrors. Out here was a chance for something deeper. An untapped power. Opportunity arises every day; so many fail to seize it. In Africa, I would swoop, scratch and stab until it was mine.

A native had shimmied up a rubber vine and was slicing away to release the sap. *Scratch, scratch, scratch.* He descended and waited for the creamy liquid to drip into a pot. When he collected enough, he smeared the juice over his body.

"What the devil is it doing?" I said.

"They're scared we'll kill them as soon as we have the pot," replied one of the officers. "They rub it over the skin, peel it off and roll it into balls."

"Why don't you stop them?"

"Because when they peel it off, they take a lot of their skin with it."

I was overcome with shame at my admiration for these disgusting beasts. To cleanse my conscience, I acted immediately.

The violence lasted as long as it takes to sweep up the winnings at the end of a poker game. My victim was a stooping black simpleton with an impudent expression who loitered after everyone else. *If this tree falls, the rest will fall too.* As we moved deeper into the jungle, I fell behind him, bringing up the rear of the party. Drawing closer, I lowered my left hand and swept its palm across the upturned blade of the machete strapped to his back.

"Scoundrel," I cried, holding my hand theatrically before my face, affecting a look of horror as blood streaked down my wrist. "Black, vicious dog."

The two Force Publique officers span round, hands placed on the butts of their holstered guns. The three natives turned too. My victim was a picture of sluggish confusion. I paused a moment so they could all comprehend the scene, then reached for my pistol with my unwounded right hand and fired a bullet into his guts. The savage crumpled to the floor, arms outstretched, trembling fingers clutching the ground. I cracked another shot into the back of his head.

"One hand for every bullet spent," I screamed, tearing the machete from the strap on his back. Raising the blade above my head, I brought it down twice. *Hwacckh. Hwaacckh.* I picked up the two severed hands and threw them at the Force Publique officers. Lifting my injured hand to my mouth, I sucked the blood and eyeballed my companions. That day, the blacks scraped rubber like Satan was on their tails.

Bravo, Loki, I heard the jungle cry. *Bravo!*

"Long Tooth certainly can bite," grunted the captain when we returned to the station, the two amputated hands decorating his desk.

"I can turn my hand to anything," I said coolly.

"Indeed you can," he said. "A card-winning, negro-killing old timer. As good at killing as you are at poker. *Mon dieu*, what are you like at fucking?"

The captain took a final drag on his cigarette, stubbed it in an ivory ashtray and lit another one. In the exhaled haze of his first drag, he opened his arms wide and invited Hercule and Antoine into his aura, like a penny dreadful prophet delivering a sermon to the slums.

"This is my kind of maniac, *mes frères*," he said. "Let him loose into the wild. He'll send the natives scampering all the way to the Nile."

"Then I must have as many bullets as you can spare," I said.

"Then poker it is, my murderous friend. Tonight. Hercule and Antoine say you're formidable. Then again you haven't played me. The more I win, the less ammunition you have. Get used to wielding that machete. For I play cards like I hunt for rubber. I take no prisoners."

For the first and only time, I played my overlord at poker. I won all ten rounds handsomely, if not honestly, and enjoyed his smug face turn sour as he relinquished his bullets the next morning. I suspected he'd drunk brandy all through the night, cursing how I'd upturned his tiny empire.

"Proceed to this inner station," he said, fingering a hand-drawn map scratched onto the back of a telegram sent by the Belgian crown to mark Leopold II's birthday. "We lost contact two weeks ago."

"I thought we were at the inner station," I replied.

"You are, old timer," chortled Antoine. "Now you're going to the inner, inner station."

"Everyone thinks they're the centre of the universe here," the captain said. "Until they realise there's no centre at all."

"No centre to anything," chimed Hercule.

"Very well," I said. "Whatever's needed."

"*Très bon*," wheezed the captain. "Scuttle off, you dog. Secure the station. Fetch me what you can. Be like a tiger. No tricks at all, you understand. And if you get in a corner, don't expect us to save you. We're all dead men walking anyway. We gave up on justice a long time ago."

I departed with two packs of ammunition and three natives under my command. Their faces told me they were too enfeebled to disobey. I delegated navigation to the shortest of the three and moved to the back of the party, training my revolver on their broad, smooth backs. I let my machete hang loose from my belt like a pirate's cutlass. There was perverse delight in being alone with these sinewy foreigners; their semi-nakedness stirred my libido.

Days passed. The further we trudged, the cloudier things became. Fatigue set in. The station proved elusive. That infuriating scratching sound resurfaced. The natives had partly filled their buckets with limp, thin rubber, but it wasn't as red as I wanted. I grew restless and angry.

I'll kill these primitive beasts one by one. We'll go down together. Straight into the deepest pits of the earth. For the black key is always subordinate to the white key. Always.

"Get on your knees," I barked at the least productive man, placing my pistol to his temple and splattering his face with my spit.

"Hands forward, onto that rock. Head down."

The trembling slave submitted, while the other two slinked into the trees.

"You're too slow," I sneered. "Far too slow for Loki."

I lifted my machete, fancying myself a conductor raising his baton before a hushed audience. The river, trees, jungle, country, continent and world fell under my possession. That elusive melody of myself, forever promising to form in the tepid air, took shape. My bravura stroke of butchery would be heard in Europe's grandest palaces.

I'm capable of anything at all, you know. *Anything at all.*

Unleashing a Wagnerian war cry, I aimed for his wrist and slammed down the blade with all the force I could muster. The only noise greeting me was the spark of metal whacking stone. The black hand was gone. A bolt of excruciating pain shot up my arm into my brain, sending my entire body into a quiver concentrated at my knees. My wrist was broken. I squealed in rage and drew my pistol with the other hand. The black rat was fleeing into the trees. He was no more than ten yards away. I took steady aim and fired three times. Unfathomably, traumatically, the negro continued upright at pace and vanished from my sight.

"We were getting on so well," I cried. "So very well indeed."

I set off in pursuit, my injured hand limp and my gun cocked in the other. The machete was slung over my shoulder. They would be finding pieces of this filthy mongrel centuries from now. Loss of face will not do for a man. Even one who has so many. Your Loki can change like the wind and be whatever my environment wants me to be. Even an African one. I recalled salon chatter in Paris about how we all descended from apes anyway. Humanity is as predatory as it's always been. We just make prettier sounds these days.

Exhaustion soon overwhelmed me, as did the mocking sounds of the jungle. The slicing of the hand. The scratching of rubber. The low note of the piano. Noise, disassociated from source or corresponding movement. To save my reputation, I needed only six black hands to take back with me. Any would do. I just needed to lie low. In the low key.

I retreated behind a pocket of vegetation to rest my wrist. Savages may soon wander past. If it was one, two or three, I would gun them down. If there were more, I would still kill the lot. I may be lucky, and the gormless idiot who escaped might wander into my trap. That night I failed to sleep. My skin felt alien and loathsome, harbouring a dark desire to have it scraped away by the blacks in the same way they scraped rubber from the trees.

In the thick of my gloom, a new sound carried. A strange, sonorous hymn, booming from the jungle's heart. Deep and mournful, the earth's bowels seemed to sing in lamentation and shudder my core. Towards the concert I trod. My wounded hand dangled to my side, the other grasped into the dark. The music swelled. A melody formed. A vocalised version of that interminable scratching sound burrowed into me like a tapeworm.

Soon the source was revealed. Around twenty Africans stood in a circle around a rectangular pit. A quadrant of flaming torches illuminated their peaceful eyes. One by one the women peeled away to dance before the menfolk, who stamped their feet and slammed their spears into the ground. Their bodies pitched and ranged in smooth vibrations, descending and ascending allegro. Unseen instruments rattled and throbbed with masterful precision.

Like a sonic hurricane, the camp's collective energy swirled and soared into the jungle's trees. The women withdrew to form a circle around the men, who repeated the dance, their eyes fixed to the trembling ground. This was the object of their worship, I realised. The earth on which they stood, their spirits attuned to their origins by the music's unbreakable umbilical chords.

Sweet lord, it was fierce, beautiful and sublime. And those faces. Indivisible, not through lack of individuality but *because of it*. I saw it all in their eyes. Hope. Fear. Friendship.

Philip Parrish

Love. Longing. Loneliness. Features different yet interchangeable. Together they were like a polyrhythmic orchestra reaching crescendo and losing control, acquiescing to a single original sound over which they held no power.

The party danced then dispersed, drifting past me trance-like to vanish in the trees. The beauty of the African's voices hung like braids of liquid ivory from the branches. Still mesmerised, I wandered to the pit. Inside lay the corpses of eight black and white men next to each other like piano keys. Natives and colonisers, joining hands. In this supernatural night, I swore the walls of the pit rose around me, as if the earth sought to nurture whatever remained of my soul.

I closed my eyes and dreamed myself a member of their congregation. The dead rose and danced with the living. The petty world evaporated into air. I wished to throw myself into the abyss with the dead men, for they seemed the most sanctified things in the world. As it was, the memory of the music spirited me elsewhere through the jungle. Eventually I collapsed far away from everywhere, drowning in dreamless sleep.

At daybreak I awoke to gentle hacking. A man was making his way through the jungle. A black, lonely figure some distance ahead. He was strong, beautiful and without an ounce of fat. Slowly I rose, caked in mud. I followed him into a clearing. For a moment, last night's rapture returned, along with my desire to lie beside my black and white brethren. I let the urge roll over me and dissipate.

"Stop. Right. There."

The man turned slowly like he was in a trance. His left eyelid was partly closed, his right eye slanted. He stared at me in tranquillity, like he'd already seen both our futures.

I raised my gun and fired. The pistol's crack sent birds fluttering to the sky. My target showed neither fear nor injury. The devil strode towards me with open arms. I unleashed all my bullets. The tiny capsules of death must have swerved around him, for he was soon upon me. He grabbed the wrist on my gun hand and twisted my arm. I crumpled to my knees and rolled onto my back. The African pinned me to the ground, pressing his insurmountable face towards mine.

Gently he shook his head. Adrenaline in his eyes gave way to tenderness. That face, like the one which stared out at me from the exhibition. I wanted to kiss him. *Yes*. A kiss on those lips. He was complete, beautiful and heroic. My boy in Brussels. A pure thing, as smooth as polished ebony. Sculpted like a statue, redolent with grace. No wonder the bullets diverted in deference.

"Let me go," I said. "Please. Just let me go."

The African looked deeper into my face, searching for my soul. I continued to shrivel like flotsam, adrift in the luxurious brownness of his eyes.

"This is not who I am," I muttered. "Please. I beg you. I am lost. Terribly lost. I do not know who I am. I have no… heart."

Without word or change in expression, the African lifted me with him. In a daze I was carried at the mercy of this specimen's power. The land yielded to my saviour's footsteps. The pain in my wrist subdued. My current body, semi-naked and white as a sheet, followed obedient and unshackled. Day surrendered to the night surrendered to the day until I lost all sense of time and place.

In the distance, a Belgian flag sagged between the trees. The captain's station drew near. My mother continent's contempt for the natives burrowed back into my mind. *Scratch. Scratch. Scratch.* Past faces flocked like hungry birds of prey. *Scratch. Scratch. Scratch.* The front row of the audience at Trieste. *Scratch. Scratch. Scratch.* My pitiful condition and ineptitude with a gun. *Scratch. Scratch. Scratch.* My lust for these exotic creatures. *Scratch. Scratch. Scratch.* He had beaten me. This fucking black had beaten me. I was being led. *Led.* By a savage. *Scratch. Scratch. Scratch. Scratch. Scratch.*

As we reached the main track to the station, my companion turned, smiled and took my hand. The nerve of this neanderthal. The dark witchcraft in his animal heart. Scattered along the track were discarded rocks, quarried from the earth and cast aside for Lord knows what purpose. As my guide let go of my hand and turned to look up the track, I saw my chance. I grabbed the biggest rock I could lift with my functioning hand. With a howl of vengeance, I slammed it into in the back of his head. He sank to the ground in a balletic swoon, a gentle whisper of acceptance whistling from his mouth.

I attacked again and again until his head was pulp. With each blow, I raised my hand higher, conducting the channelled malevolence of the universe. I felt nothing. Heard nothing. Cared nothing. This victim was no more than an apparition. *All is echo and surface*, I said to myself. *Echo and surface.*

The station had been ransacked. Three Force Publique officers lay dead. Each bore multiple wounds to their chests and faces. The insides of shelters had been turned inside out. Munitions, documents, medical supplies, maps and trinkets of empire spilled out onto the ground like the splitting open of a great-bellied sea beast stranded on a beach.

"Over here, Long Tooth," cried a voice from the river. "Over here."

Hidden behind an embankment was a small rowing boat, clinging to dry land. Inside squirmed the empty faces of the captain, Hercule and Antoine. Men rendered as two-dimensional as playing cards, without ground or grip.

"Let's go," screeched the captain. "Before they return and finish us off."

We pushed off from the side and took it in turns to row back down river. During breaks, we lay flat on our backs and shared a bottle of Napoleon brandy. After my third shift I fell asleep, curled up like a new-born baby. Stalking my dreams was the last native I murdered. The left eyelid half closed, the right eye slanted. A scratching sound followed him, like the most deranged of creatures was digging psychotically to the earth's core. I found myself locked in a cage full of severed hands that came alive. Grabbing, pulling, pinching, grasping, twisting.

I woke to see the captain, Hercule and Antoine pointing their rifles at me, grinning. They'd tied me to the end of the boat with rope wrapped around my waist. My hands and legs were left free.

"All talk Long Tooth," the captain sneered. "All talk. You've been in a play all along. A trick."

I tried to speak but emitted only sheepish groans.

"You cheated us at cards. Nobody cheats us. We let the jungle teach you a lesson. We hope you might return and tell us where the inner station was. We certainly don't. None of us know. But you fucked that too. Firing blanks, Long Tooth. You won blanks at the card game. You've been firing blanks all this time. You won nothing. You have nothing. You are nothing."

He fired his gun into my face three times. Three empty spasms of hot air.

"Blanks," he cackled. "Nothing but a fucking blank."

"We're surprised you made it back," said Hercule. "We even took bets. Maybe we should have left you. But you could be a good shield from the spear chuckers. Who knows, we may even eat your fat guts to stay alive. We're animals out here, you see. Always will be."

I screamed in anguish. I would butcher them all, then hack down every single tree, every single living thing, rip out everything of value and hoard them like the greediest of pigs. No black, no white, just red. Bloody, flowing, red, from the source to the mouth of this vile, godforsaken river.

"These hands are not capable of cheating," I pleaded. "Not these hands. It was the savages. It was the jungle. It was the earth on which they stand. The sound. That dreadful sound."

"Hungry boys?" said the captain, spreading out a deck of cards on the floor of the boat. My captors had the excitable look of young boys who'd killed a wild beast and were deciding which part to eat first.

"If you win, Long Tooth, I will untie you and drop you off on the bank," he said. "But every time you lose, you have to forfeit something."

Each hand dealt me was rigged. There were no tricks left to play. My first defeat stripped me of my clothes. The second shorn me of my hair, Hercule hacking it away with a knife to festoon the boat's floor with curls of gold. After my third defeat, I offered my finger. The captain shook his head and passed me his machete. The things a man can endure when he is no longer in possession of his mind. With terror and spite, I brought the blade down on my broken wrist. Three strikes, each one descending me to ever deeper pits of indescribable pain.

"This is not your hand," said the captain, holding up that former part of me before throwing it over the side of the boat. "We want something else."

I continued to hack away into nothingness.

"This is not your foot."

Whether I'm hostage to dream or reality, I cannot discern. Natives resurge on either side of the river, felling my tormentors with spears. Hercule through the chest. Antoine in the back. The captain as he swims across the river under some deluded notion he can escape. The beautiful majesty of the

Congo is shaking off its parasites, like a proud lion irritated by fleas.

The natives do not aim for me. They take pity on an imprisoned man. I consider using my machete to cut the ropes, break free and throw myself on their mercy, begging them to restore me to wholeness. But there is nothing to restore and never has been. I continue to chop away at the unvanquished itch that's plagued me for as long as I can remember.

"This is not your calf," I say.

I relish the punishment, like I the relish the splashings of red on my feeble, pallid skin. I can turn my hand to anything, after all. If I have the strength, I will hack myself into eighty-eight pieces. One for each piano key. If I have the vision, I will discover the still indiscernible melody that is the tune of Loki. But for now, I will settle for the scratching of blade on bone, a tawdry equivalent to the stripping of rubber from precious plants rooted in the ground.

"This is not your thigh."

My mother plays piano with me. The Montparnasse businessmen sit across the riverbank, gawping through looking-glasses like fat hogs spying dancers at the Moulin Rouge. The oaf in Brussels asks me how far I would like to go.

As far as possible, I whisper. *As far as possible*.

I wonder what will happen to these pieces of me. Maybe they will be scattered across Europe, trinkets presented to indifferent ladies of leisure as they pass complacent hands over piano keys or roll a billiard ball across green baize. I have gone to the darkness for them. Become a carcass for my own ravenous appetite, spiralling to hell with a gabble of hungry white goblins intent on making exhibitions of ourselves.

Africans line the banks in unison. A hundred pairs of eyes, solemn and serene. A hundred harmonious voices, lowered in lamentation. Hands join in solidarity and pity. They read me too well. I fancy one of them is my beautiful boy. His superior face is a perfect picture of wisdom, issuing divine command.

"This is not your land."

In my dying mind's eye, I stand tall on the stage in my coat tails and white tie. The lights of the opera house sparkle in my blond hair. Another sleight of hand. Another trick. Another sham performance. A superficial silence before an applause that never comes, like the crackle of distortion one hears on a gramophone deprived of any succeeding tune.

I listen closely, longing to hear the closing bars of my movement. Beneath the glittering emptiness, a dull scratching sound speaks solely to me.

Bravo Loki, it says. *Bravo!*

Angelo

Hovering by the third-floor fire exit, Sergeant Mitch Travers tinkled the miniature Liberty Bell and invited Detective Dwight Huckerby to begin. Rising from behind his desk, the master of ceremonies raised his paper cup of Miller and addressed the horn-shaped huddle of cops.

"On this December night in the Year of Our Lord Nineteen Hundred and Sixty-Eight, we pay tribute to one of our most beloved shepherds," boomed Dwight's voice from under his grey handlebar moustache. "Today our noble brother, Saint Angelo Dorovoce of Los Angeles, leaves us after five thousand years of service to dangle his rod wherever he pleases."

Laughter fell awkwardly in the hushed office. All phones were off the hook. On the night before Christmas Eve, absentees were either beavering elsewhere in the Parker Center, patrolling the streets or tucked away at home.

"Recreation is long overdue," continued Dwight. "In his time at the LAPD, Angelo never fired a gun in anger. His gun. My gun. Or anyone else's gun for that matter. Unless one of the busboys in Chameleon says otherwise.

"Dispatches show as a young wop on D-Day, Angelo was the best courier in Normandy. Messages back and forth. Lightning speed. Insiders say he was just struggling to find the bathroom. As the allies advanced to Berlin, he was the first guy to correct the road signs the Nazis knocked out of shape. Bet you he logged the co-ordinates of every piss along the way."

Setting down his Miller on the nearest desk, Dwight picked up a yellow memorandum stained with coffee.

"He's proved a master of paperwork. But in honour of our favourite Catholic cop, I have a confession. In triplicate. FUCK. THAT. SHIT."

To strained chuckles, Dwight tore the paper in tune with his last three words and threw it like confetti over his head.

"There is one thing Angelo was better at than ticking boxes," said Dwight. "Talking. He doesn't do much of it, but when he does, it matters. Angelo chatted three people out of suicide jumps. Solved two hostage situations. Kept the peace here after God knows how many Super Bowls. And I've lost count of the eulogies to fallen brothers. So many brothers."

Mitch pinched the flesh between his left thumb and index finger to stifle the tears. Outside the window, under the bruised San Fernando sky, slow bullets of light fired down the freeway taking lonely wanderers home. Tomorrow, they would have one less gentleman to protect them.

"Now it's time to honour him, as he retires from the force at the grand old age of one hundred and thirty-two," continued Dwight. "The most mild-mannered cop on the Western seaboard. One hundred percent focused on his job. One hundred percent focused on the city he loves. The city we all love.

"We've seen some terrible shit on the streets. We hope it doesn't affect us. At least not too much. With Angelo, that shit never laid a glove on this man's soul. This man. *This man*. This man represents the most decent of us. The soul of our city. He will now spend his twilight years fishing by his beloved lake. Least the catch will be less slippery than internal affairs."

A few gritted smiles. Dwight fixed his eyes on a figure among the crowd.

"Now Angelo, you stop being a town guy and become a country guy. Not a cop. A citizen, whatever the fuck one of those is. No longer a man with a gun but a man with a big heart. Whatever the fuck one of those is too."

Dwight sunk the rest of his Miller, crumpled the cup in his fist and tossed it in the trash can. Through a wall of woops and cheers, he invited the guest of honour forwards with a cock of his head.

"For a man who loves peace so much, we wish you all the peace in the world. Merry Christmas and goodwill. And thank you Detective Dorovoce. For your service. Your friendship. Your talking. From the bottom of our hearts."

Stepping into the spotlight was a man with wispy blond hair, a flat nose and pencil moustache. He wore a navy-blue tie and a sky-blue suit over a starched white shirt. Angelo was a thin sketch of a man, still waiting for life to colour him in. The Californian sun always seemed to pass right through his pasty skin.

"We have a gift for you, you soft son of a bitch," Dwight continued. "For the most patient man alive. To the Clark Kent of the force, who never transformed into Superman."

From behind the water cooler, Dwight raised a white and red megaphone with a pink gift bow tied round the handle. A message was printed on the outside. DON'T BE A HERO ANGIE. Dwight raised it to his mouth and tilted his head, like a ring announcer at a wrestling match.

"We hope your voice gets a little bit louder in your old age," he bellowed. "Enjoy your new beginning, my good friend. Let your guard down for once. Try a donut. You'll be doing jack shit by the lake, except hiding from wildlife."

"Then he'll finally be a real cop," crowed a voice to generous guffaws.

"We love you, Angie," said Dwight. "The city will miss you. The department will miss you. The glass house will miss you. We will miss you."

Whistles, claps and the slapping of backs. Mitch thought Huck's eulogy nice but nowhere near enough. The guys didn't know Angie as well as Mitch did. Like the way he stared into the Pacific's beautiful stillness, as if waiting for a ship to appear on the horizon. His knack for seeing how things would turn out. How he called it on Vietnam. The Panthers. Even the goddam World Series every year.

"Thanks Huck, that means the world to me," said Angelo. "Thanks all of you. For your kindness and good wishes. I feel bad bowing out after such a tough year. Tet. Nam. Seventeen thousand Americans dead. Dr King gone. Bobby too. In our city as well."

The mood tightened. A tense-faced recruit was fidgeting with his zipper lighter, watching the flame rise and fall as he struck the flint wheel.

"Riots in Chicago. The students at Garfield. Lots of bad feeling."

"Don't go all Black Panther on us now," shouted Dwight. "You ain't Tommie Smith, Angie."

"No, I'm not. Wish I could move that fast."

"Yeah, that's what your hookers say."

Near-universal laughter this time.

"I guess what I'm trying to say is that part of me doesn't want to go," said Angelo. "There's a lot to do. This Nixon guy is bad news."

A suck of discomfort. Many looked at the grey carpet in disappointment. A few nodded.

"Too many guns, too much anger," continued Angelo. "A sign of the times. Everyone will be looking at us to see how we handle it. That's why you're all the heartbeat of this city. Nobody can tell you more than me what violence can do. One day they'll start to shoot children in classrooms. Kids buying guns. Killing other kids. If we're not careful everything's gonna go up in flames. You can't keep burying pain. It always catches light in the end."

Mitch pictured Angelo's wife Gabriella, a peace advocate of boundless enthusiasm, confined to a wheelchair by a burglar's bullet. Then his own two boys, playing Cowboys and Indians on the lawn, asking for toy guns and firecrackers for Christmas.

"It's up to us to show the way," Angelo continued. "Listen to these longhairs coming up. They're expressing themselves. That's gotta be good. Our city is divided. We need to bring it together. The youth will help us do that.

"I saw a few up on Laurel Canyon the other day, dancing on the sidewalk outside a drugstore. So free, so beautiful. It's our job to help them. It's our job to ask more of ourselves. So we all reach the promised land. So we –"

"Shut the fuck up!" shouted Dwight, to riotous giggles.

"I will soon," said Angelo. "Father Giovanni taught me that listening is the way through division. That's why I love fishing. It's like listening. You wait and wait and if you're patient, something comes along. Don't be afraid to connect. To be the difference. You're a bunch of fine cops. Damn fine people. I love my country. I love this force. I love all of you."

Angelo made the sign of the cross to polite applause and gave way.

"Now, Mayor Yorty couldn't make it," swaggered Dwight. "Neither could Chief Reddin. He's too busy starring in Dragnet. But we do have a very special guest. Bill, turn the fuckin' music up baby. Let's see if Angie has any signs of life down there."

Through a record player behind a desk somewhere, Marvin Gaye crooned *I Heard It Through the Grapevine*. A blond-haired young lady in a long black raincoat parted the crowd. Mitch thought she looked like Nico from the Velvet

Underground. She strolled up to Angelo, loosened the belt of her coat and let it fall. Hoots of delight greeted her bare flesh, bra and panties.

"This is where we find out if you wear ladies' underwear," whispered Dwight, clutching Angelo's cheeks with his palms. "Merry Christmas you beautiful motherfucker."

Twenty minutes later, the party left LAPD headquarters, piled into cars and headed to the Chameleon bar. All except Angie, who liked to walk. Mitch drove to the bar alone. The back pain from his football years was raging, so getting in and out of his Chevrolet took a while.

While stopped at the lights, Mitch saw Angelo leave the Parker Center. He was holding his megaphone in his left hand, beige Mackintosh draped over his right forearm. Angelo would have paused at the large bronze sculpture in the foyer called *The American Family*, which depicted two parents holding the hands of a child, then said a final goodbye to the clerical staff. To Susie, the wiry blond who manned the telephones. A lonely soul, tightly wound. Came to the coast because she wanted to be a movie star. Threw herself at Mitch after the gala dinner, then look confused when he gestured to his wedding ring, whispered a few words of kindness and politely asked her to dress.

At Chameleon, the cops sunk Buds, bourbon and tequilas. They talked baseball tactics, reminisced over cases and shared their contempt for those nasty pieces of shit fouling the streets. Soon after Larry the owner turned the sign on the door from 'open' to 'closed', they bitched about LAPD leadership, then bitched about each other. Randy and Buck exchanged abuse from separate booths; Angelo got steaming drunk for the first time in a long time. His evening ended with Mitch lifting his face out of a pool of Jack Daniel's. Some cops scurried home, others stayed. Dwight went looking for adventure in forbidden places, muttering bullshit about a top-secret case.

Grimacing, Mitch carried Angelo to a taxi. He would let him sleep it off on the couch at Chez Travers in Lincoln Heights. Angelo shouldn't be alone. Proper police have a look about them. Angelo never had that. Mitch had learned to spot a brave face with too much going on behind the eyes.

The next morning Mitch set a black coffee and eggs benedict in front of Angelo at the breakfast bar. The winter Californian sun burned orange through the blinds. TV newscasters talked excitedly about Apollo 8 orbiting the moon. Cathy had left early for last-minute Christmas shopping. The boys were re-enacting the Battle of the Little Bighorn in the lounge.

"Fuck, the war did come home last night," Mitch said. "We were dropping JDs like bombs on Dresden. Need a ride home, Angie?"

"No thanks MT. I'm good to walk. Fancy a stroll in the city. I won't be seeing it for much longer."

"When you heading to the lake?"

"Day after tomorrow. Maybe."

"You can always spend Christmas here. Cathy would love to see you. They're showing *It's a Wonderful Life*."

"That's kind of you MT. Still have a lot of packing to do."

And unpacking too. Mitch was surprised Angie made it to Christmas. In January's Tet offensive, some gook scumbag had blown the head off Anthony, his only son. At the Fourth of July fireworks, his crippled wife Gabriella died from a heart attack. Now came retirement from the only life Angelo knew.

The ex-cop finished his eggs and slurped the last of his coffee. Rising from his chair and stretching his back, Angelo picked up his Mackintosh and laid it across his hooked right arm. All he needed was a hat, a horse and a petticoated southern belle on whose delicate hand he could plant a gentlemanly farewell kiss.

"Thanks for looking after me, MT. Damn fine coffee and eggs too."

"Damn fine of you to say so," said Mitch. "Listen, don't be a stranger. Invite me to the lake. We can sit round a fire and talk about all those pranks we could have pulled. And don't forget this either."

He passed Angelo the megaphone, which had laid upturned on the coffee table next to the Sears catalogue. DON'T BE A HERO ANGIE.

"I won't," Angelo said. "She never wanted to be seen cryin', you know."

"Who?"

"Gaby."

Through the window, Mitch watched his friend walk down the street. He wanted him to go out in a blaze of glory, switching on some secret light that would burn like an Olympic flame or shine like the bat sign in Gotham. All Angelo did was disappear calmly round the corner. Another lonely man in a city of millions.

***

Sun splashed the sidewalk as Angelo trudged down North Broadway. He was fuzzy-headed, bleary-eyed and without uniform, shield or gun. Near the State Historic Park, he wandered into a coffee shop. When all goes to shit in Dick Nixon's America, there would still be the bean. Mitch had served something, but it certainly wasn't caffeine. These junior guys.

A waitress named Joy attended him. She was middle-aged yet very well turned-out: lipstick, mascara and blusher all impeccable, accentuating green eyes flooded with warmth. Angelo considered inviting her for Christmas dinner, when they would light a fire, talk for hours, smoke Egyptian cigarettes and fall in love with each other's dreams. She even smiled at his megaphone.

DON'T BE A HERO ANGIE.

Jesus, those guys could blather on. Their heart was in the right place. Even Huck's. But they were all action and no thought. Dangerous. The force was a tinder box, like in that song by that black kid who set his guitar on fire. *Too much confusion, I can't get no release.* The sounds these fellas come up with. That stripper too. Someone's daughter.

Angelo stared out the window onto the sidewalk. A few yards down, a homeless redskin in a grey duffel coat and Dodgers baseball cap sat cross-legged and perfectly still. Propped against his knees was an open shoebox and a cardboard sign with CHANGE PLEASE written in magic marker. Glass, money and one hundred years of pain divided the two men.

They sure got burned by the white man. The buffalo too. Majestic animals. Stalked and skinned, like those sweet girls who come out here to be famous.

Same with the negroes. No longer his problem on paper, yet it always would be. *Cut me open Gaby, I've got LAPD running through me.* Deep within the redskin's eyes, Angelo imagined a pole of flames rising to the clouds from the desert sand. Around it danced the spirits of the redskin's ancestors. Dressed in white and chanting. Calling out to those forgotten souls long since passed.

Crack. Crack. Crack. Gunshot. Dallas. Memphis. The Ambassador Hotel.

Crack. Crack. Crack. Outside the coffee shop, a pickup truck backfired. The redskin hadn't even flinched.

Crack. Crack. Crack. If Angelo had been on duty that night Bobby was shot, he could have made a difference. RFK would have been on his way to the White House. Now all we have is Dick Nixon. Guns will be the end of this place. The end of us all. Young people angry. The city bleeding. His city. Two kids killed in Benicia. Just… senseless. The fire in some people's eyes.

Angelo finished his coffee, shuffled to the restroom and splashed his face with cold water. He wished Joy a merry Christmas then began his sobering walk northwards on Sunset Boulevard. Angelo preferred to move on foot. New cops thought every day was a car chase day, like in that new Steve McQueen movie. But he never liked cop flicks and hated that Hollywood sign on the hills. One look behind it and you could see there isn't much propping it up.

Maybe he should keep walking. All the way to LAX so he could fly to JFK. Over the ocean to Rome. See how the Carabinieri did things. Journey down. See a distant cousin in Palermo. Angelo had only been to the old country once as a teenager, when his nonna mistook him for a lady on account of his soft face and slender frame. Back when he had long blond hair, so rare among his heritage. The only son of Rudolpho and Claudia Dorovoce who made their way from Ellis Island to Pasadena. The WASPs always let them know they were outsiders. But he wasn't a European. He was an American. Like the redskin on the sidewalk.

That Christmas Eve night at his two-bedroom home in Elysian Heights, Angelo sat in his armchair doodling on a notepad. He'd started sketching the day after they got the news about Anthony. *Dead. Near the Perfume River.* If the US won the war, Angelo would travel to Vietnam and learn where his son fell. But the Stars and Stripes wouldn't win. One of the first things a cop learns is how to read a situation.

CHANGE PLEASE.

Crack. Crack. Crack. The truck from outside the coffee shop backfired again. Angelo remembered what he'd daydreamed at that moment. The ghost dance. When the Lakota dressed in white, formed a circle around a pole and reunited the spirits of the living with the spirits of the dead. He had a book about it somewhere. The Lakota could see something ahead and believed it was beautiful. True Americans, then.

On the notepad, an upturned Jesus fish had emerged in blue ink. From what part of Angelo's brain it had come, he could not say. He liked it though. When he returned from the war, he wanted to be a Disney cartoonist. He loved those movies. They reminded him of his elder sister Maria. Another one gone too early.

"Poppa called you Angelo because you're a messenger," she said one evening over puttanesca. "You have something to say."

At school, the kids teased Angelo because of his name and blond hair, asking what he'd done with his halo and wings. Back then, everyone seemed to think angels should look like Carole Lombard. Tinseltown had a lot to answer for. Soon everyone here will be a star. Nobody will have a real job. Computers will do everything. Everything was performance. Dwight's speech. The stripper. Mitch. Joy. The new president. Shifty guy that one. Too much to prove. Someone should shine a light on him. One day an immigrant movie star would move into Sacramento. A TV star will be president and they'll run auditions on the networks. Governor Ronnie would be perfect. Sign of the times. The way of the world. The gift of the... Gab.

Angelo set his sketch aside and fetched his book about the Lakota from the shelf. The ghost dance. *If every Sioux danced the new dance, all evil in the world would be swept away.* 1963. Camelot blown to smithereens. That Buddhist monk who set himself on fire. Gaby. Anthony.

Whatever time he had left. All his possessions dissolving into smoke and drifting over the Pacific.

After a dinner of spaghetti and meatballs, Angelo turned on the television to watch the Apollo 8 mission. All this dough on space travel while black families were starving to death. Just to swing dicks with the Soviets. The whole space programme would run out of steam by the mid-seventies. A lot of people could get killed, just like those poor guys who fried in Apollo 1. Yet for now, this was the best of America. The spirit of those brave men cut down on Omaha. Four score and ten. How the west was won.

"And God called the dry land Earth; and the gathering together of the waters called the seas; and God saw that it was good," said Frank Borman, reading from the Book of Genesis as he floated around the moon with Bill Anders and Jim Lovell.

"And from the crew of Apollo 8, we close with good night, good luck, a merry Christmas and God bless all of you. All of you on the good Earth."

We choose to go to the moon. Not because it is easy, but because it is hard. Because Americans see something ahead and they know it's going to be beautiful.

CHANGE PLEASE.

Tomorrow. Christmas Day. The first one in forty years without his wife. When the spirits of the living would reunite with the spirits of the dead to bring peace to all their kind. Yes, tomorrow.

Angelo woke at five o'clock. He showered, switched on his Christmas tree lights and imagined dancing around it with Gaby and the Lakota. After prayers, he made coffee, ate toast and watched the dawn rise over the San Fernando Valley. They were seeing the same sun right now in Bethlehem. Today and two thousand years ago. Long before that too. All the ancient civilisations. The first people. The first flowers. The first plants. The sun. Quite a thing. His life, Gaby's life,

Anthony's life, the whole of human history, barely registering an existence compared to that light in the sky. It'll burn our planet away eventually. Unless we overheat it ourselves first. All these cars, planes and factories. Can't be healthy.

Angelo turned on the radio and listened to Dean Martin sing *O Come All Ye Faithful*. He went to the bedroom and undressed. Opening the wardrobe, he took out the department store box that arrived by mail under Gaby's name. Soothing warmth flowed from his heart to his guts as he lifted the lid and ran his fingers through the platinum blond beehive wig. Not quite the same colour as Gaby's on their wedding day. In fact, it was closer to Angelo's when he was eight years old. *The blondest boy I've ever seen*, the lady said on the Staten Island ferry.

Next, he unfolded the bra, panties, white ballgown, lipstick, mascara and eye liner, laying them out on the bed. Angelo pictured all those negroes picking the cotton in the deep south. The seamstresses toiling away. The blue-collar delivery guys handing the ballgown to the department store guys. The smiling young ladies who sold them in the stores. Sweet girls, like that waitress Joy.

Sitting at Gaby's dressing table, Angelo put the clothes on. As a choir boy he'd seen Father Giovanni dress for mass. Slowly, with dignity and grace. He'd watched Gaby do her make up enough times as well. As a cop he'd learned to observe a process. He fetched some tissue from the bathroom and shoved it in his bra cups. *Steady, Angie, you don't want to look like Jayne Mansfield.*

As a final flourish, Angelo picked up the red lipstick and drew an upturned Jesus fish on the front of his dress, above the navel. Carrying his megaphone, he headed out the backdoor, down the side alley and onto the street. Nobody saw him come or go. Especially not at quarter past six on Christmas morning.

Angelo walked and walked. Gaby spent the final years of her life paralysed, but she walked far in her mind. Writing letters to fellow mothers of the disappeared. Campaigning for the end of American involvement in Vietnam. For all guns to be destroyed.

I shall keep walking with her.

Riverside Drive. Hollywood Hills. Laurel Canyon. Studio City. People emerged onto the streets with him. Never in groups, always alone. Preoccupied men, dreamy women, meandering vagrants. None were who they appeared to be. A community of actors, earning top billing in their own dramas.

On Ventura Boulevard, Angelo saw an abandoned Budweiser beer crate in a parking lot. He picked it up, placed it on the sidewalk and raised his megaphone.

"Who are we?" he declared. "Where do we belong? When will we confront who we are? I am nobody. Just a conduit for a bigger message. I'm here to… listen. To you. To everyone. If every American dances a new dance, all evil in the world will be swept away."

Passersby ignored him. Some glanced uncomfortably, then moved on. Finally, a vagrant swigging a bottle of Southern Comfort sat down to listen. By the time the sun set on another Christmas, a few more drifters had settled.

"I predict a day where there won't be any difference between men or women, black or white. We will all be one. What we need is transformation. Love. Dialogue. Compassion. A ban on all guns. Soon our schools won't be safe. Our politicians will deal in deceit. TV stars will be the new gods and goddesses. Soon you won't be able to tell what is real and what is fake. You need to look behind the fake signs. Discover the real ones for yourselves."

When the audience woke in the early hours, Angelo was gone. They formed a protective circle around the beer crate. At ten o'clock the next morning, Angelo returned wearing the same white dress and carrying his megaphone. He ascended his beer crate and continued his sermon to the congregation.

New Year came and went. For four to six hours every day Angelo was a fixed presence on Ventura Boulevard. Elsewhere in the city, rival black nationalists shot two Black Panthers, Bunchy Carter and John Huggins, at UCLA's Campbell Hall. Chief Thomas Reddin left the LAPD to become a television news commentator. Mayor Sam Yorty was re-elected, denouncing rival and ex-LAPD officer Tom Bradley as a communist and black power stooge. On the east coast Nixon was inaugurated and Eisenhower died.

At night in Elysian Heights, Angelo became fixated with Earthrise, the photograph taken by Bill Anders from Apollo 8 of earth's blue marble emerging from black space. Talk only went so far; images and symbols travelled so much further. He imagined the stars constellating into a ghost dance. Gaby and Anthony danced with them, flames in their eyes. With them were the low-life criminal and the Vietcong soldier who'd gunned them down.

"There are no individuals," Angelo proclaimed to his followers. "There is only one life force running through everything. There is no 'them and us'. We must dissolve all division. Look behind the signs, that's what you need to do."

A nickname was coined: the Angel of Ventura. Once some bored teenagers tried to follow Angelo home but got lost. Most people held back, unwilling to spoil the magic. Summer rolled out; young men and women wore less and less under blazing blue skies. Sirhan Sirhan confessed. James Earl Ray pleaded guilty. Troops started to withdraw from Vietnam. Ted Kennedy drove off a bridge, but the poor girl with him drowned. Man made it the moon. *One giant leap for mankind.* Angelo much preferred Genesis.

August brought the Manson murders in Benedict Canyon. A pregnant actress, butchered in her own home. 'Death to pigs' written in blood on the walls. *The Wild Bunch* and *Easy Rider* arrived at picture houses in the fall, while Nixon secretly bombed Cambodia. At year's end, a new kind of police force called Special Weapons and Tactics targeted the Black Panthers' headquarters. The two sides exchanged five thousand rounds of ammunition. No one was killed. Plenty were entertained. The Hell's Angels killed someone in front of The Rolling Stones at the Altamont Speedway, bringing the curtain down on the sixties.

"Violence is in our nation's bloodstream," said Angelo two days before Christmas, three hundred and sixty-three sunrises after first stepping onto his beer crate. "Look at the Old West. The massacre of native Americans. Every empire is built on blood. The violence we export around the world. Look behind the signs. Dissolve all division. Dissolve it all."

By then, everyone had drifted away. The Angel of Ventura was another lonely voice. Nobody offered their point of view or asked any questions. They were all looking forward to the seventies, where they could see something ahead and knew it was beautiful.

***

On Christmas Eve night, Mitch Travers paced Ventura Boulevard for last-minute gifts. He'd been overworked since his transfer, neglecting Cathy's hints about what she and the boys might like from Santa Claus.

"Look behind the signs. Behind the signs."

A familiar voice. Steady and soft. Mitch flicked his eyes up the street. A lady with unreal blond hair was standing on a Budweiser crate. Her white dress wafted like net curtains. She waited patiently, like a fisherman on a riverbank.

"This is a sick society," said the preacher. "We must cure it. Soon one day they'll start to shoot children in classrooms. Kids killing other kids. If we're not careful everything's gonna go up in flames. You can't keep burying pain. It always catches light in the end."

Mitch sidled along the shopfronts towards her. Barefooted. Hairy ankles. A slight paunch. The Adam's apple and neck wrinkles. A man well past his prime. The nose gave it away, flat at the tip. And the megaphone.

"This city is more than a disconnected sprawl of humanity. It is a heavenly realm for uniting people. The stars, the streetlights, the car lights, the neon signs and camera flashes. Our billboards and our buildings. They connect us on a surface level. Yet underneath there is so much more."

Mitch walked quickly past. Propped up on the crate was a sign. CHANGE PLEASE (Don't worry, you can keep your money). On the dress was an upturned Jesus fish, drawn in red.

"Cathy, I'm going to be late," Mitch blurted into the payphone receiver.

"Jesus, Mitch, really? It's Christmas Eve."

"Yes, really," he said. "It's a missing person's case."

Christmas lights illuminated Angelo's path as he walked home. Mitch stayed about fifty paces behind. When the ghostly figure in white disappeared inside Angelo's house on Avalon Street, leaving the door ajar, his ex-colleague sat on the kerbside to rest his back. As a cop, Mitch thought he'd learned to read the signs. The road signs, the traffic signs, the warning signs, the body language signs. Stop. Go. Danger. Trouble ahead. The signs of life. The signs of the Lord. The signs of Satan. Sign of the times.

Mitch pushed the door back and soft-footed along the hallway's reddish-orange carpet. He followed the smell of tobacco into the lounge. The last time he sat there was Gabriella's wake. Angelo was clothed in black that day. Now his old friend was throned in white, sitting in his favourite armchair and smoking a cigarette. There was a playfulness in Angelo's eyes which resembled that hippy pop star who sat in bed telling the world to give peace a chance.

"Merry Christmas, MT."

"Merry Christmas, Angie."

"I saw you while I was preaching. Knew you'd recognise me. Knew you were following me too. Once a cop, always a cop."

"What's going on, pal?"

"Exactly what you see."

"I see a lot."

"You bet, as Sitting Bull would have said."

Mitch sat on the couch, palms placed gently on his knees.

"I see a few empty spaces too, Angie. Fancy colouring them in?"

"What do you want to know?"

"Who are you now?"

"A messenger. From the future."

"Let me help you, Angie. Looks like you could do with some."

"You don't seriously believe that MT. It's the city that needs our help."

"You're too gentle, Angie. The more you talk, the more you'll get –"

"What? Assassinated? All the good ones do. And what's wrong with talking, anyway. You sound like an asshole."

Mitch scanned the lounge. In the house, it was business as usual. Pictures of Gaby, Anthony, the Pope, that matinee whoremaster who used to be President. The map of LA, gifted to Angelo on his fiftieth birthday.

"None of these possessions matter to me anymore MT. They may as well drift into the sky like smoke."

"Is this really who you are now?"

"Well, it looks like me. Sounds like me. Smokes the Marlboro I like. Sits in my house too."

"What are you seeing, Angie?"

"Manson defending himself on trial. Words justifying evil. Hunger. Real and fake. I see the Buddhist monk in Saigon on fire. You remember that picture, back in 63? That guy knew there was no difference between life and death. Nothing to cling to. Creation and destruction are the same. He crossed over, just like that. Everything is ashes. Eventually I will leave this body and change into something else."

"What are you trying to tell me, Angie?"

"I've not retired MT. I've only just started work."

"Work?"

"You heard it all last Christmas. You heard it today. What's it going to take for you people to listen? To really listen."

"Is this who you are?"

"That's the third time you've asked me that."

"This is a lot to deal with. What's with the fish?"

"It came through me and onto my notepad."

Angelo took a drag from his cigarette. He switched his gaze from Mitch to the window and Avalon Street beyond.

"I'll keep walking and talking, MT. For her. For Anthony. For me. For you. For the guys on the force. For everyone in this city."

"What you're dressing like, ain't…"

"Natural?"

"No Angie, it ain't."

"It's the most natural thing in the world. I don't want to be in my body. I want to be in hers. The dead are with us, MT. We absorb their spirits, you know. Not just family, loved ones. Everybody. The native Americans too."

"The redskins. What they got to do with anything?"

"We wronged them, MT. Exiled them from their own lands. Christian, Jew, Muslim, Buddhist, Sikh, Navajo, Hippy. We're all of them and they're all of us. We're all wanderers. Exiles. And what for? A neat little house and a neat little pension full of neat little things that mean nothing."

Angelo stubbed out his cigarette in his Murano glass ashtray and looked Mitch firmly in the eye.

"I look across this land and see all those who've died and all those to live," he said. "I imagine them dancing. Arms linked. Around the city. Around the world. A ghost dance. That's what we need. A ghost dance for everybody. For all those we've loved and lost. To unburden of ourselves of all this shit we've accumulated. To take the pain away. To set ourselves free."

Slowly Mitch crossed the divide from spectator to actor, inhaling Angelo's homily like it was blessed smoke from a peace pipe.

"How can I help, buddy? How can I make the pain go away?"

"Now, there's a question," said Angelo, offering his visitor a cigarette and light. "Come on, MT. Look around. You're in Hollywood. To be genuine you've got to put on a show. Just make sure it's better than anyone else's. Fancy helping me go out in a blaze of glory? Like I said, pain always catches light in the end."

Just after midnight, Mitch returned home without any presents. Mitch Junior was asleep on the couch next to the Christmas tree. He'd tried to stay awake for the big man from the North Pole. Mitch picked him up and carried him to bed, then went to the kitchen and poured himself a Jack Daniel's. He wrote letters to all his family, apologising for not getting any gifts. Then he quietly made a Christmas cake, with icing in the shape of an upturned fish. Before he fell asleep in his armchair, he concluded Los Angeles was the greatest city in the world.

The next day Mitch filmed the kids opening whatever presents they had on a Canon Cine Zoom camera Cathy bought him. Exhausted, he made a mess of carving the turkey. Then he brought out the Christmas cake, lit with four candles. Cathy cried. That afternoon, Mitch fell asleep in the armchair, thinking about his missing person case. It was already turning into something else. Not an ending. A beginning. A performance. A Christmas story.

***

"I always liked that part of town," Mitch told the captain. "Took a wrong turn on the empty streets. Guess I was busy in my head."

New Year's Eve 1969. Sergeant Travers was off duty that evening and happened to wander into Elysian Heights. In his statement, he recalled two young men whispering on the corner of Avalon Street and Echo Park Avenue.

"This was about ten o'clock. No sir, I couldn't tell the colour of their skin."

Minutes later, slivers of smoke rose against the purple sky and pumpkin orange glowed from one of Avalon Street's houses.

"It was too far gone to rescue whoever was inside," said Mitch. "I evacuated the neighbouring premises either side. Thank God it was detached. Lucky the fire department arrived so damn quick. That beast could have spread. Only when I saw the mailbox with the pattern of the angel wings did I realise it was Angie's place. Goddam coincidence or what? I called the lake using the number Angie left me. Nobody picked up. So I tracked down the retired couple in the nearest cabin. Angie hadn't been there in eighteen months."

Fire fighters quelled the blaze. All doors of the house were locked from the inside. No corpse was found. The next day detectives interviewed the neighbours.

"We used to hear him chanting inside. Always making funny noises. The guy could never shut up."

"He used to dress up as a woman too, but we didn't pay it any mind. You know what California's like these days. He can do what the hell he likes in his golden years."

"Angelo was still in there, I'm sure of it. Heard him talking to someone. Around ten o'clock, just before the blaze. Such a nice guy. Just a little… strange."

Investigators concluded arson. A Molotov cocktail thrown through the kitchen window. A vengeful hit. Two dirty punks. Panthers possibly, cowardly targeting an ex-cop. Or someone with a beef about transvestites. They rounded up all those people still living and out on the street who Angelo put away.

"Nice guy. Just doing his job."

"Too good to be LAPD scum."

"Who'd want to burn a guy like that?"

Two clues intrigued. One neighbour, looking down from a second storey windows on Angelo's rear garden, claimed to see an elderly man dance around the blaze, raising his knees and chopping the air with his hands. In the charred house's sidewalk mailbox, cops found an envelope with handwriting that matched those meticulous incident reports Angelo used to write. Three words only. *Dissolve all division.* Inside was a newspaper cutting from June 1963 showing a Buddhist monk on fire at a road junction in Saigon.

Mitch, knowing better, chose to know nothing.

The cops gathered in the Chameleon bar. As the colleagues talked, Mitch sat quietly a couple of empty stools away, nursing a smoke and a Budweiser.

"A woman," said Dwight. "He dressed up as *a woman*."

"Always the quiet ones."

"A real showman after all."

"Complete fuckin' disintegration."

"A cry for help. We should have seen it coming."

"Some people go through life trying to be cops. Some ain't real police."

"The gig was just too tough for Angie."

"I always suspected he was a fag."

"Gaby *was* always a bit uptight."

"They'll fish him out the river. Guaranteed."

"We don't know that's what happened. No body. No death."

"You think he's still alive?"

"Maybe he's changed again. You know. He went from Angelo. To a transvestite. Maybe he's turned into something else now."

"I guess we never really knew him at all."

"Well, whatever happened, happened," said Dwight. "Death is death and it is what it is. We do know one thing. He was one of ours. Let's remember the Angie of old. One of ours has gone."

The bar fell silent to *A Whiter Shade of Pale*.

"Mitch you're pretty quiet," continued Dwight. "His oldest friend. And you just happened to be at the scene. Anything to say?"

All the cops eyeballed him.

"Nothing much," said Mitch. "We've talked more about Angie now than we ever did when he was alive. He was a great soul who passed over. He went out in a blaze of glory. Like I knew he would. The city can believe what it wants to believe. Sometimes the surface is enough."

Mitch finished his cigarette, stepped onto an upturned crate in his mind and raised a glass to everyone in the bar.

"To a great soul who passed over. We love you, Angie."

Wiser cops sensed something was amiss. But in the LAPD, it was sometimes better to keep your head down. A couple of journalists delved into Angelo's background. An ordinary man from the old country. Paid his taxes, raised a family, served the public. Honoured by his colleagues. Loved by his wife and son. All three defeated by Vietnam. Grief-stricken. Frightened of retirement. A lonely man inspired by the hippy movement who dreamed a new version of himself. A quiet voice fading into the marginal folklore of this make-believe city.

Soon the upturned fish appeared all over Los Angeles. Walls, fences, posts, signs, pavements. Some said it represented God's work. Others that it symbolised two arms reaching to the sky in love. A few saw hands held over a head in surrender. One view was the arching lines originated from the same point, spread apart then came back together. Overcoming the divide. No matter how much people talked, they never agreed. Authorities painted over the signs, so the gatherings moved inside. Lost souls crossed fences, lawns and thresholds to search for meaning in each other's spaces.

Tribute acts appeared across the city. Misfits dressed in white robes proclaimed second sight. A drifting and disconnected community of angels. A few said they were there in late 68 when the mystical Messiah of movieland possessed the body of a mild-mannered ex-cop.

"I was the first to hear him, you know. The first to really hear him."

"There are no individuals, he would say."

"There is only one life force running through everything."

"This body is disposable. There is no 'them and us'."

"Look behind the signs."

"Dissolve all division."

"Dissolve it all."

Three people spotted Angelo soaring up to heaven above the Hollywood Hills. One sighted him walking on water off Venice Beach. A couple even visited their local LAPD station and claimed to be him. Soon his legend drifted away like stardust. The sixties faded too, that halcyon decade when things seemed like they were about to change. When everyone could live as one on the good Earth.

On the fourth of July 1970, the second anniversary of Gabriella's death, Mitch left the Parker Center early, pausing in front of *The American Family*. That afternoon he paid his respects at the Forest Lawn Memorial Park. Someone had laid fresh flowers on the grave, together with a polaroid of Gaby, Angelo and Anthony, spruced and polished in his military uniform.

In his lonelier moments that summer, Mitch looked at the letters on his badge. Sergeant. Los Angeles Police. Tucked underneath was a Christmas gift tag with a symbol of an upturned fish on it. He'd drawn it himself, to keep in touch with the old friend who was here, there and everywhere. Where Angelo resided now since his make-believe death, Mitch could not say. His friend had either gone further into the past or into the future. Sicily. Vietnam. The moon. Or maybe he was somewhere on the golden coast, staring into the Pacific and imagining the promised land.

My eyes have seen the glory of the coming of the Lord.

"Hurry dad," came a voice one evening. "The show is about to start."

His boys. Too young for Vietnam. Not for the next war. Mitch grabbed his bottle of Budweiser and entered the lounge.

"Kids, I need you to listen to me."

The crunch of popcorn.

"Will you listen?"

The cocking of make-believe guns.

"Kids?"

The theme for *Hawaii Five-O* surged into the room.

"Angels walk among us, you know kids," Mitch declared. "Angels."

"Pops," said Mitch Junior, training his fake pistol on screen. "Are you ok?"

That Christmas Eve, a postcard arrived at the Travers house. Under the title *Greetings from LA*, the card showed a view of the city from the hills at sunrise. A fake, flashy and fiery town, full of traffic, chatter, soaring egos and never-ending streams of pop music and DJ patter from cars, shops and homes. The wail of police sirens, ambulances and fire engines. The fevered talk of preachers and sandwich board salesmen. A place where pain always catches light in the end.

In the picture, the San Fernando Valley sparkled under the sun. A spherical blaze of glory from space, blessing everyone in LA. Everyone in America. Everyone on the good Earth. Everyone's true selves. Everyone living and everyone dead. Everyone joining hands in a forgotten ghost dance.

On the back of the card was a message, written in blue ink by a hand that cared. By a man who loved to deliver them. What little words there were ran over the dividing line.

To MT, Cathy and the boys. I can see something ahead for you all and I know it's going to be beautiful. Merry Christmas. I'll always be watching over you. Love, Angie.

Mundi

Friday evening was drawing in as Rebecca finished her seventh loop of Hereford. More youngsters than usual hogged the bright green City Zipper. Down the aisle they'd shuffled: a trickle of forgettable faces, companionless except for the phones in their hands and the chips on their shoulders.

Shrunk in the back row, Rebecca scrutinised the sandwich of turned heads. Necks stooped, noses in screens, visions blurred. As the bus turned onto Edgar Street towards the railway station where Rebecca boarded three hours earlier, she reimagined each passenger's portrait in her mind. A rogues' gallery of the lonely, all searching for their special places on this disorientating earth.

June, her annoyingly upbeat neighbour at the Compass retirement community, said kids could track each other's locations anywhere in the world. Wanderers all, despite knowing where to find the nearest McDonald's and what their chums were eating on holiday. Rebecca had seen enough lost souls in her eighty years to know.

Springtime air spirited people onto the streets for weekend drinking. A pastoral poet, or anyone with a vaguely lyrical disposition, might have likened them to cows awakening in verdant meadow. Rebecca did not. *Like livestock at those rip-off country shows*. She poked each docile partygoer with a mental cattle prod and imagined them jerking with electrified life.

The station came into view. She pushed the red bell button on the yellow pole, heard the ping and waited for the bus to slow. Deceleration was declared by a beep, beep, beeping that reminded her of auntie Ruth's life-support machine. Rebecca rose to her feet, clutching the pole and screwing the floor with her walking stick. Pain ripped up her spine, spat out through jets of strained air between gritted teeth. Her breath was shortening by the day.

World, put me out of my misery. An absent-minded stroll into rush hour traffic would do.

Impatient eyes crawled over her. En route to the promised land of the kerb, Rebecca noticed the driver. Her eyes passed over him when she first boarded. New fellow. Full head of hair. Smooth in complexion. Middle Eastern. Nice smile too, with a strong jaw and decent teeth. Must be in his mid-sixties. Still slim. White company shirt buttoned to the top under a lime green tie. Yes, she'd known a wanderer like this once. In the summer of love, when a few days' bliss cast shadows over the long years that followed.

"Oy, brown eyes," she said, tapping the plexiglass with her walking stick. "Do I know you?"

"No, ma'am," he said. "No, I don't think so at all."

"You take the corners quicker than the last fella. Slow down, Abdul. Some of us are fragile. This isn't camel racing in the desert."

"Yes, ma'am," he said, chuckling.

A sense of humour. Not one of those uptight folks who takes offence at the slightest. *Woke* was the word, June told her.

"Do you mind?" snapped someone a few rows behind. "Some people have homes to go to."

"Good for you," growled Rebecca.

"Bye then, handsome," she continued, wincing slowly onto the pavement. "I'll expect a smoother ride tomorrow. Room up front for two?"

"Behave yourself, m'lady."

"You're no fun. Don't I get a pass at my age?"

"Of course, ma'am," the driver said. "If my timetable allows it."

Exiles Incorporated

The doors closed, the electrics whirred, and the City Zipper lurched away. Blankets of warm air floated in its wake, settling around Rebecca's head and lifting the muscles either side of her mouth. Her lips curled with them.

"We never did say goodbye, did we?" she said to the twilight car park.

The bus, one of three City Zippers, was called the Green Horse. Another was named Pilot. Maybe on Monday she would get to ride their brother, Handsome Norman. Chance would be a fine thing.

After switching to the 476 bus at the railway station, Rebecca's journey ended on Ledbury Road, outside the lunatic asylum where her two children had left her to die. The Compass retirement community housed her one-bedroom ground floor flat and backed onto her birthplace, Hereford County Hospital. She'd spent twenty years there as a cleaner, bleaching floors and listening to patronising matrons prattle on amid the churning cycle of birth and death.

Compass was her third home in Hereford, after the semi-detached on White Horse Street where she lived with Simon for more than fifty years. Before that was the terraced home at the north of Widemarsh Street where she grew up. In all her time as a Herefordian, she'd never met a real SAS man. Except those who told you they were. In the pubs they got so close she could feel the spit on her cheeks. Words. Cheaper than air. A thousand times heavier.

Another day, another no-cost afternoon of circulation on the City Zipper. A welcome respite from the inane clapping in the hobby room, where the neediest of Compass residents dressed in loud colours and pretended to like each other. A bunch of bloody chimpanzees, wasting precious time in convoluted faff. A few were antisemites, Rebecca damn well knew it. She'd fallen out with a couple over the war in Gaza already.

"Don't worry mum," said David. "There'll be plenty for you to do."

Yes, my wayward son, an embarrassment of riches. Conservatory. Restaurant. Café. Salon. Jacuzzi. Pub. Library. Too much going on in too small a space. The way of the world. Just look at those kids' phones.

Inside her room, the bedside lamp bulb had gone again. The curtains were always drawn, so the sole illumination came from the phone, flashing pale green light onto the picture of her and Simon on their wedding day. David called last month, so it wouldn't be him. Her daughter Judith perhaps, boasting about her and Doug's latest holiday. Torremolinos, this time. Tacky couple.

She pressed the button. A voice chirruped through the darkness. Her great-niece, Tabitha. The poppet with the brunette bob and white stockings at Simon's funeral. Jamie's little girl. Her idiot nephew, a self-absorbed sponger, was forever delegating familial obligations. Even got blind drunk at Simon's wake.

"Are you free on Monday?"

Something about the map at the cathedral. Tea and cake. A number to call, starting with 07. Rebecca considered summoning Jake, the community's handyman, to fix the bulb, but couldn't wait. The phone's buttons were visible from outer space, anyway. She listened again, memorised the number and dialled. When the automated voice began, she sank the receiver in annoyance.

Rebecca didn't have much appetite, so skipped communal lasagne and chips in the restaurant. Crawling into bed with her aches and pains, she watched *The One Show* and conjured swashbuckling matinee vistas of Abdul, dressed like Omar Sharif in *Dr Zhivago*. If my timetable allows it. *What a mensch.*

At daybreak after heavy sleep, she buzzed the keeper of light and screwdrivers. Jake was in his early twenties, communicated in grunts and hid a third of his face behind straggly unwashed brown hair.

"Why don't you enlist and help those Ukrainians?" Rebecca once said. "These Ruskies don't like it up 'em. Short back and sides while you're at it."

The phone rang while he was tinkering with the bulb. Jake remained oblivious, courtesy of those little pieces of white plastic lodged in his waxy ears.

"Yes, I'm, free on Monday," said Rebecca to Tabitha. "As free as any eighty-year-old. Monday. That would be good. I'm at Compass on Ledbury Road. I'll let them know you're coming."

"Actually, could you meet me in town?" said her great-niece. "Near the cathedral. That'll save time."

"The cathedral? You do realise we're Jewish? This whole Christianity business is just an upstart cult."

"Jewish," giggled Tabitha. "That must be awesome."

Typical. Her deadbeat dad hadn't bothered raising her in the faith.

"Matter of opinion. Well, I suppose I could venture out. Be warned though, I attract attention. Suitors can't keep their hands off me."

"There's a café on St Peter's Street called Eden House. We could meet there at eleven. I've seen it on Google. Looks nice."

"Yes, I know it. Opposite the Black and White House. Eden it is. I'm an Old Testament kind of girl, after all."

"Ace. Can't wait to see Hereford. It'll mean the world to me. Bye bye."

One of Jamie's. Chip off the old block, probably. Always ready to plead poverty. Later that morning on a lonely table in a corner of the Compass restaurant, Rebecca ground through her scrambled eggs and tried to put a face to her great-niece's voice. Not so easy, these days. Tabitha may not even be a girl. She could be a boy thinking he was a girl. Or a girl thinking she was a boy but with a girl's name. If conversation proved tedious, Rebecca would feign deafness.

Saturday crawled by. Rebecca stayed in her room, plodding through the *Daily Mail* crossword and knitting a small wall hanging. The fabric depicted the Israelites' exodus from Egypt to the promised land. A clump of tiny wanderers curled across a desert landscape into a valley between two mountains, heading towards a sun shaped as the Star of David. Underneath, woven in Hebrew, was the legend *The Land of Milk and Honey*.

Jewish. That must be awesome. Rebecca set down her needle and yarn. Like a spider surveying its web, she checked everything was in its right place. Little Miss Chuckle may want to visit the throne room to see if there were any coins hidden down the side of the sofa. Phone, painkillers, remote control and fly swatter, all in easy reach. Her wedding ring, in the tray on the mantelpiece. The Tanakh and Siddur in the newspaper rack. The universe is like a retirement village, she thought. Full of floating, disembodied stuff waiting to perish.

Tonight was the ending of Shabbat. Rebecca was too exhausted the previous night to perform her weekly commencement ritual, so travelled back in time pretending it was Friday again. Two candles, a glass of Vimto and two Warburton buns, covered in a napkin. Every Thursday she asked the grocery man if he had challah. The sarcastic little shit always made a point of not knowing. Last week he asked if it was the new Iraqi left back who'd signed for the Villa.

One candle to remember, the other candle to keep the faith. Both lit by the woman of the house. The pretend wine glowed almost like the real thing. Rebecca waved her hand over the flames, covered her eyes and remembered the tips of her mum's auburn hair splayed on her pillow during bedtime stories.

Rebecca whispered the blessing. Spoken too loudly and it would carry through the walls. June would prattle on about it for days. There weren't any practising Jews in Compass, although she suspected a lapsed one in the corpulent git who sat in the pub reading *The Sun*. Always wore that moth-ridden blue cardigan with missing buttons. His snoring was one of the few things to unite residents in laughter.

On Sunday morning, Rebecca ventured to the library looking for a trashy book. A holiday romance set in Petra. Forbidden kisses in caves with a mysterious camel racer. She used to love poring over atlases when she was a child. One time she and Simon talked about visiting the Holy Lands. But her long-dead husband was a dreamer, never a doer.

Today Rebecca couldn't find her place, in the library or any of its books. In the TV room, the Fourth Reich were watching repeats of *Strictly Come Dancing*. Rebecca shuffled in and sat at the back, so she didn't have to converse with June or the rest of the Gestapo. One of the Strictly dancers looked like a younger version of Abdul. She imagined the bus driver in a purple sequined shirt, flared black trousers tight around the bum with a rose between his teeth. *Allow me, ma'am.*

Sunday evening. Back in bed. BBC News. A handsome black chap in a red studio speaking about Gaza. An ancient people and a land cut to pieces. Beautiful young people mowed down at a music festival. Poor Palestinian children, dying. After experiencing so little of life, they now knew its greatest mystery.

The face of the man from the summer of love returned.1967. Her last lover before Simon. She couldn't bear repeat his name. A porter at the hospital. Gentle, funny, clever. Knew how to kiss. Driven apart from each other by the Six

Day War. *All religions believe the same thing*, he said. *They just tell different stories.*

She didn't know what was good for her back then. Unlike Little Miss Chuckle, who certainly did know a good thing. Calling her out the blue because she wanted to see the cathedral. The map. The excitable young pup was *absolutely in love* with the Middle Ages. When Rebecca last saw her, Tabitha was a shy slip of a girl, not even pubescent. A lot can happen to a girl in twelve years. Even more during eighty.

"I want a dream lover," Rebecca sang across the bedroom to the ghost of Bobby Darin. "So I don't have to dream alone."

Outside, more traffic than usual trundled down Ledbury Road. A road closed. Another diversion. Pointless digging. Too many cars. Boxed in, shut down. Inside, her breath dragged itself out of her body, before dragging itself back in. Going round in circles. Every day, going round in circles. *Maybe I should just keep going. My home is not here. My home is not out there. My home is…*

Monday morning. Rebecca woke not knowing where she was, intrigued by the prospect she might finally be dead. Her watch said seven o'clock. Getting out of bed took about thirty minutes. Another ten to get to the bathroom. *Yes, I'm free on Monday alright, you tricksy little minx. I'm just a free and easy song and dance girl with nothing but time on my hands.* Rebecca washed, brushed her teeth, combed her hair and dressed. It was nine thirty by the time her limbs loosened. She looked at herself in the flat's circular mirror. *Pucker up, buttercup.* Missing breakfast, she trundled to the bus stop on Ledbury Road, lungs wheezy and stomach grumbling. Perhaps she could squeeze a scone out of Tabitha.

Sitting at the back of the 476, she half-watched Hereford scroll past. Rebecca had rarely left the town except for a few trips to the seaside. She refused to go to the continent after what happened in the war. *It's no better anywhere else*, said those supposedly informed. *Women, know your place.* Like the eight schoolgirls killed in the fire at the Garrick while performing for soldiers during the Great War. Or those at the Rotherwas Munitions Factory, where women made the bombs and bullets for the men to drop and fire. Rebecca was born a few weeks before D-Day. So many killed by then. Frogmarched onto trains, bullied through the gates, herded to the gas chambers. Innocent lungs poisoned in concrete tombs.

In the Eden House of Coffee, a squeaky-voiced singer shrieked through the speakers. *And it's always you and me, always and forever.* Amid old timber and unadorned girders, pictures of old Hereford lined the walls, accompanied by pop art prints, decorative books and bric-a-brac. To Rebecca, every café looked the same these days. Resting places for wanderers uncomfortable in their own skins, seeking refuge in beans from Nicaragua or some other place she'd never visit.

A family of four huddled near the window not really listening to each other. A silver fox in cycling shorts read the *Daily Mail*. A young couple grinned at their phones. *Blimey, Sonny Jim has landed on his feet with her.* A woman wrote in a notebook muttering to herself. *Don't these people have jobs?* The beep, beep, beep of pagers announcing drinks ready for collection.

Rebecca scanned the menu board, recalling June's advice about how cafés put anything in the drinks to save a few bob. *Beep, beep, beep.* She should have said no. *Beep, beep, beep.* She should have stood her ground and not let herself be bossed about by a stranger. *Beep, beep, beep.* Uppity little brat. *Beep, beep, beep.* I don't have much time. *Beep, beep, beep.* But she has all the time in the –

From the café's midst rose a young lady about Rebecca's height. She had a lovely figure. The stonewashed denim jeans seemed sprayed onto her hips. A stripy green sleeveless vest revealed smooth pearlescent arms decorated with soaring patterns of butterfly tattoos. Her pale face was crowned with luscious brunette hair tied in a bun. The yellow light suspended above her table accentuated her fairground smile. She floated from the chair, arms outstretched. *My goodness, she looks like Audrey Hepburn.* Rabbi Jonathan was right. No matter how rotten the rest of the basket, life can still yield a peach.

"Thank you for coming," said Tabitha, voice rising in search of approval as she guided Rebecca to her table. "I knew it would be a good idea to get you out of the house."

"No bother at all, dearie. Really no bother at all."

"Dad tells me you like Earl Grey."

"Yes I do. Good old Earl. So smooth they named a drink after him."

Tabitha laughed, bounced to the counter, ordered and paid. Rebecca swooned a second time. Her great-niece was like a nightingale about to break into song, before fluttering to an island paradise where locals would sculpt porcelain effigies in her honour. Fragile, floaty, light to the touch. Open to new things. A spirited young woman searching for her place in the world. A place that must surely be everywhere.

Beep, beep, beep.

"Gosh it's very busy, isn't it?" Tabitha said, returning with the drinks. "Maybe we should have gone to La Madeline. But that'll remind me of Proust. Still, we are going back in time."

Rebecca was too engrossed in Tabitha's dark eyes to reply. *So much life. So much desire. Any man in their right mind would wilt.* As she spoke Tabitha bloomed like a rose, petals of personality lacing the table. Herbal tea. *The Great British Bake Off.* Art galleries. Travel. People who played sport. Any kind, but rugby was best. She liked a good set of muscles. On both men and women. About to graduate. Ready to travel the world. Heading to Australia. Only twenty-one.

Her great-niece sipped her drink, eyes flicking towards the window to see if the sun would emerge from behind the clouds. Presumably she would chirrup when rays of light streamed into her space. Tabitha might even turn her used green tea bag into a coach and horses so Rebecca could go to the ball. Abdul taking her arm. That sequined shirt. Two unbuttoned. Peachy bum. Might scrub up well. Smile like Tabitha's. Kindly eyes under the glitterball as he moved in for a kiss, stealing her breath as he did so.

"Do you ever slow down?" Rebecca said.

"Gosh, I don't have time for that."

"What's in Australia, anyway?"

"This," she said, raising both hands in excitement and grabbing her phone. Tap. Tap. Tap. Swipe. Swipe. Swipe. A red mountain in the middle of a desert. Ayer's Rock. Rebecca recognised it from that travel show she watched with that posh gentleman who had the silly side parting.

"Uluru. Some things are so old they have a certain mystery."

"I know that feeling."

"I'll be flying all the way around the world. Going via Dubai. Then Los Angeles on the way back."

"Maybe you'll become a movie star. Don't trust strange men."

"I'm not sure whether I prefer boys or girls yet. I've tried both. My orientation is fluid."

Fluid. To travel. Make choices. Take opportunities. *Beep, beep, beep.*

"Wouldn't you like to be a mother?" Rebecca ventured.

"The world doesn't revolve around men. Or the next generation."

"Yes. Men. Sometimes I wish I'd stuck with our half."

"Uluru changes colour depending on the time of day. Taller than the Eiffel Tower. Imagine. I want to walk all the way round it. But first, the map!"

"Ah yes, the map."

"Sounds amazing."

"Never seen it."

Tabitha's jaw fell. She placed her phone on the table and pushed it away, like she was readying herself for juicy gossip.

"But it's right on your doorstep?"

"I was sick on the day of the school trip. And I don't like churches. I'm more of a synagogue girl."

"That's ok, I enjoy nightclubs as well," said Tabitha with a smirk.

"Well, that makes two of us," said Rebecca. "Do you watch *Strictly*?"

"Gosh how I love it," replied Tabitha, bouncing in her seat. "So much fun. Not many men can dance like that."

"I know someone who can."

"Who?"

Rebecca sipped her Earl Grey and lowered her voice, like a spy revealing some secret code.

"Local man," she said, arching her eyebrows. "Drives a bus. Pretty much a pensioner. Still in good nick. Hotter than this tea, anyway."

"Sounds amazing. A bus driver. Must be very rewarding. You get to help and meet so many people. Everyone is a traveller, after all."

"Yep, that's what this world is. A real community of wanderers."

"Who else is in your circle?"

"My circle?"

"Yes, everyone has a circle."

"No thanks. My mind goes round and round enough."

"My circle is my four school friends. We've been together for ten years. We're totally on each other's wavelength."

"Sounds totally amazing," said Rebecca, the sarcasm flying over Tabitha's head out the door onto St Peter's Street.

"When I come back, we can cook a dish for every country I've visited."

"Kangaroo, then?"

Tabitha laughed nervously.

"Not sure that would go down well here, anyway," continued Rebecca. "What with all the customs changes. Brexit and the like."

"Not every custom changes in a country. Some rituals go back to the dawn of time. My ex-girlfriend's family is from Africa. She knows all about it."

The conversation covered every continent in the space of ten minutes. Rebecca was worn out by the time they reached emperor penguins.

"Come on then, Little Miss History. Let's see the scribbles on this piece of calf skin. Hereford's one hit wonder."

"So you do know *something* about the map then?"

"I'm Hereford, born and bred. People talk. Sometimes I listen."

As they left Eden House, Tabitha hooked her arm under Rebecca's elbow, lifting her chin with poise rather than pretension. Moving effortlessly through life. Country to country, past to present. One of Jamie's. Didn't know the old soak had it in him. Together they turned left at Hotel Chocolat and walked down Cathedral Close, window shopping under red, blue and yellow bunting.

Looming ahead was the Hereford skyline's dark stone centrepiece. Tabitha stopped, placed her hand on Rebecca's shoulder and guided her to look back.

"Let's take a selfie."

Tabitha raised her phone and leaned in. Soft, perfumed cheeks. The warmth of flesh on flesh. The sweetest of her scented breath filling Rebecca's lungs and absorbing into her bloodstream. *Please don't rush this dearie, there's really no need.* When Tabitha revealed the picture, Rebecca took the phone and moved it out the sun's glare. Two wanderers, breaking out of frame towards freedom.

"Can I call you nanna?"

Rebecca's mum. Shabbat. Hair illuminated by candlelight. Friday evening. When food, family and love were everywhere. Magic embroidered deep within, never to be unravelled.

"Yes, sweetie. I'll be your nanna."

They made their way to the annexe, past the main cathedral entrance and the organ's drone. Memorial plaques lined the route, including one dedicated to the girls who perished in the Garrick fire. A chamber of death commemorated by tablets of stone. Rebecca pictured her ancestors wandering across the desert to a land of milk and honey. Pogroms. Russia. Ukraine. Poland. Kristallnacht. The Shoah. Religion, the chief source of all the world's troubles. People trying to capture their position in the world. Why they are here and what it all means. Glorified selfies.

They pottered through the cathedral café to the exhibition. Tabitha bought two tickets and led Rebecca down the narrow hall through a slalom of information panels, copies and display cases. At the end was a facsimile of the Magna Carta. Rebecca heard the screechy voice of her old schoolteacher Mrs Wilks.

History's most important document. No free man shall be arrested, imprisoned, dispossessed, outlawed, exiled or in any way victimised, or attacked except by the lawful judgement of his peers or by the law of the land.

Exiled. Sometimes you can do that to yourself and not even notice.

"History," said Tabitha. "One long struggle of people trying to be free."

"Do you feel free, Tabby?"

"Sometimes, nanna. But we all end up in the same place. It's a shame how our family lost each other, isn't it?"

She knew about the fights, then. The wills. The cruelty. The grasping for worthless heirlooms. Disembodied things, waiting to perish.

"The world has lost itself," said Rebecca, as the automatic doors swung open into the map room. "People go their own way. Old age teaches you that."

The Mappa Mundi was a single sheet of calf skin behind glass, shrouded in dim light. Superimposed on to the continents were pictures about human history and the marvels of the natural world. Jerusalem at the centre, orbited by Babylon, Rome and Troy and a circumference of ocean. Biblical events, plants, animals, birds and strange creatures. Crete and the Minotaur's labyrinth. An Indian elephant carried a tower on its back, while a rhinoceros stood head-to-head with a unicorn. Africans had eyes and mouths in their bellies. Four-eyed sailors stared into space. Paradise with its river and tree. An island set apart. The forbidden fruit and the expulsion of Adam and Eve. A pathway through the Red Sea. Israelites fleeing slavery in Egypt towards the promised land. A place of milk and honey where they served better Earl Grey. Around the map was the word MORS. *Death*. A figure on horseback, journeying into another life. Christ at the summit, transcending all.

"It's remarkable it's still here," whispered a visitor to the silver-haired supervisor, standing sentry-like beside the map.

Rebecca listened in. Apparently, the calf skin had been stretched, scraped, soaked in piss and hung out to dry. *Like those fine folks at Compass.* The red, green, blue and gold colour was faded. Everything was in the wrong place. The cartographers had twisted and concentrated time and geography. More and more stories squeezed into a smaller and smaller space known as the past. The only thing missing was the future. A work of orientation out of date as soon as the final stroke was made.

Rebecca and Tabitha were reflected in its glass. This moment. This young lady. This time. The whole world in a single object. *Jerusalem.* That could be anywhere at all. Her old lover could be anywhere at all. Even in this room. She remembered their final kiss fifty-seven years ago. Two lonely particles, once part of each other, reunited to say goodbye in a cruel circular dance.

"I will see you in another place," said Rebecca.

"Pardon, nanna?"

"Sorry. I didn't realise it could be so beautiful."

"Yes, as maps go."

"No, not the map."

In the gift shop Rebecca bought a postcard of the Mappa Mundi. They stopped in the cathedral café and ordered quiche. Surrounding them on the walls were more memorial plaques. Local people who lived and died hundreds of years ago, their names carved into stone above cake, crumbs and crisp packets.

"Outside," said Rebecca when the food arrived.

"Sorry, nanna?"

"Outside please. Away from all this death."

Exiles Incorporated

In the Chapter House Garden, they found a table. Plaques in the ground. Memorial benches. Kids crawling over rocks. A family speaking a foreign language. A worn-out young lady pushing a pram. An ambulance whirring.

"Freedom," Rebecca said.

"Freedom?"

"From work, marriage, the mistakes of youth. Free to get a bus pass. To get into buildings for free. To say what I like and offend people. Free to let my mind wander."

Tabitha watched like a wary child surrendering to the weirdest of lullabies sung by a kindly witch.

"Do you know what I used to love about this city?" said Rebecca. "The river. The Wye. At one point it was given a Latin name, *Vaga*. Means 'wandering', you know. Now it's dying. Turns a horrible, ugly green every time it gets sunny. Awful smell. Flooded terribly just before Covid. Had to open the churches and leisure centres. I shall miss it when I'm gone. Soon."

"No nanna, you're still fighting fit."

"Everything's happening quickly. It'll be over anytime. I can feel it."

"Don't say that," rushed Tabitha, placing her hand on Rebecca's knee.

"Oh yes. I will say that. Death. Sometimes I'm terrified. Sometimes I look forward to it. The undiscovered country, from where no traveller returns."

"Ah you like *Hamlet*?"

"Nah, I haven't smoked in years."

Tabitha cloaked her bafflement in a giggle.

"A TV advert," said Rebecca. "Before you were born. One selling cigars. And happiness."

"I will visit again," Tabitha blurted. "I promise."

"I would like that. I want to know you, Tabby. Everything about you."

"Like what, nanna?"

"Have you ever been in love?"

"Yes, yes... I think so."

"How do you know?"

"When you're the only two people in the world. When you feel..."

"... breathless."

Rebecca thought of the astronauts on the International Space Station, gazing on earth like she'd gazed at the Mappa Mundi. Life was forever curving back on itself. The people in the Holy Lands. Both sides fighting for their lives. Waiting for their God to reach a healing hand through the insanity. *Jerusalem*. Far away but right here.

I don't want to die. Give me another year and a day. I want to fall in love again while there's still time. When it was so close that summer. When it was right there but I walked away. All because of what was happening in some faraway land. A Six Day War. A lifetime of regret. Everything in between a dream.

"I wish I'd seen more of the world," Rebecca said.

"But the world is here, in us two. I love you, nanna."

"I love you too. You're my guardian angel. My fairy godmother. The centre of my world."

"What a thing to say."

"Write me, Tabby. From Australia. With a picture that shows the rock. I want your handwriting to fly across the world and reach me. And when you get there, I want you to say to yourself 'as long as this rock stands, and the air and earth and fire and water around it, so will this day'. Our day. This moment at the cathedral. Before the map. When time stood still. Everything was where we wanted it to be. That would mean the world to me."

"I will. I promise."

"Because that would make sense, then, wouldn't it? There would be some kind of... pattern."

"A pattern. Known only to me and you."

And it's always you and me, always and forever.

The couple ambled to the bus stop on Broad Street, drifting islands of tranquillity in a sea storm of scurrying footfall. Rebecca sensed lightness in her heels. Pride in her spine. Tears in her heart. When the City Zipper arrived, they hugged each other tight, imprinting their shared memories upon each other.

"There should be a map about our day, Tabby," she said. "So thousand years from now fellow wanderers could look back and realise that long ago, for two people at least, everything was in the right place. Happy wandering, dearie."

"Happy wandering, nanna."

"I'll see you in another place."

"Yes. Let's see each other in our dreams."

Rebecca stepped on board. Abdul wasn't on duty. As the vehicle took off, she turned to glimpse Tabitha. Her great-niece had vanished across land and sea to some place nanna would never visit.

The bus circled. New people came on. A familiar face or two. Springtime rain, light and fresh. Birth pains. Time of the month. Time of the year. Time of life. Tomorrow Rebecca might not wake. If she did go now, her one wish was to be reborn as a flower plucked by Tabby on the other side of the world. Near Uluru. Her great-niece would pin it above her breast that would soon feed an unborn child. Rebecca would feel the small person's heartbeat. They say a butterfly beating its wings can cause a tornado thousands of miles away.

She tapped the bus seat in front of her. If she kept doing it, a person on this bus might be distracted. Snap out of the past or future. Into the here and now. Call some distant relative. Organise a reunion. Rediscover what was lost. Make new friendships. Watch strangers take each other's breath away. A happy couple who would create a new life that may change someone's world.

Outside, spaces opened everywhere. Each trying to orientate itself; each travelling to the same finite point. Pictures of the ancient Mediterranean. Exotic birds from Peru. Relics of the dark ages. Indian spices. Coffee from Brazil. A Muslim girl twirling. *This isn't a bus.* Piano music. The Golden Fleece pub. Adverts to follow the Bull Trail. *This is a time machine.* A peace protestor in the street. Earl Grey tea. The history of the world condensed into a jewel of purity. Eden House. Paradise, for a blissful twenty minutes on a single April day.

"I should have got out the house a bit more," Rebecca exclaimed to her fellow passengers. Nobody replied.

When Rebecca returned to Compass at about four o'clock, she turned off the lights and lay on the bed. From that darkened enclosure three parallel strands of memory and fantasy spun into space. One for her, one for Tabby, one for...

Are you free on Mundi, nanna?

Every Monday lunchtime at half past twelve, Rebecca returned to the map room. *Remarkable it was still around.* Her Jerusalem. The still point of her dizzying world. After a few weeks, the guide set out a chair for her arrival.

"Let me stay a little longer," she said to the guide every visit. "It would mean the world to me."

As spring turned to summer, Rebecca began a new hanging. She borrowed the fabric from a stash June acquired during multiple visits to Hobbycraft. The hanging would be a map of Hereford on which she would impose her own stories. Some from her life, some from make-believe. Every evening, she folded up her work-in-progress, tucked it under her pillow and dreamed of it expanding by osmosis, wrapping her in its chrysalis to the crooning of Bobby Darin.

I want a dream lover, so I don't have to dream alone.

Before dawn each day she was already at work, fingers flitting. The history of the world flowed into her flat. The mug on the table became a prized trophy of a Persian princess found on a battlefield by a handsome archaeologist. The circular mirror on the wall a portal to the future, guarded by a Celtic sorceress. Simon's wedding ring. Slip it on, say the magic words and go round and round in a never-ending first dance. Greek heroes, Indian princes, doomed lovers in the jungle. Gallant soldiers, fearsome mothers of the earth. A medieval romance, a Victorian novel, an Elizabethan tragedy.

This isn't a map. This is a time machine.

When Jake came by to fix the light again, Rebecca tugged him by the t-shirt and asked him what he was listening to. Drill music. The next day she visited the EE shop on Gomond Street and bought a phone and earbuds, while the bubbly black chappie talked her through Spotify.

"Becky dear," came June's voice two days later, followed by a tepid knock at the door. "Come to the activity room. We're playing bridge. That lovely decorator with the nice hair is coming to sing Frank Sinatra."

"Go away."

More insipid noises the next day.

"We haven't seen you for a bit. What are you up to in there?"

"I'm being visited by lots of strange men."

"Is it the new window cleaners?"

"Close. They're certainly giving me a good going over."

The next day, Rebecca didn't realise the phone's Bluetooth hadn't synced with her buds. Big Shaq's sound swaggered down the corridor, drawing perplexed faces to Rebecca's closed door.

"What's that awful racket, Becky dear?"

"*Man's Not Hot.*"

"Oh dear. Do you need us to change the thermostat?"

"Smoke trees, bitch."

Two days passed. Room service all the way. More music recommendations from the keeper of the light and screwdriver. *My goodness, the lad was a genius.*

"Rumours are starting, Becky. We're worried you're not well."

"They're all true. The devil has possessed me. Or after eighty years I'm finally in love."

The next day, the final feeble intrusion.

"Have you had a fall, Becky?"

"We all have. Now bugger off."

The letter came eventually, postmarked Australia. A handwritten note on A5 paper. Folded within was a photograph of Tabby, alone before Uluru. To Rebecca, the rock may as well have punched through the earth and emerged in the hospital grounds.

Australia is a very beautiful place, nanna, the letter read. *The world is a very beautiful place. But not as beautiful as our coffee at the cathedral. Still can't decide whether I like boys or girls. I miss you, nanna. Sometimes, I can feel you right there in my dreams, just like I said at the bus stop. I will carry our map wherever I go. See you soon for something other than kangaroo. Love you, Tabby.*

Rebecca held the picture for a long time, losing herself in her niece's dark, innocent eyes. All the pleasure and pain those pupils had yet to witness. All the time still to come. All those accumulated memories to be stitched and sewn.

Soon Tabby faded from view. Nanna moved to another place. The city at the centre of her world. The place where she could say farewell. Not to Simon. To the one before. The only one. Her dark prince from the other side of violence whose name she could never bear to say. The fellow outsider she kissed during the summer of love. That magic four-letter word. So close back then. A matter of hours. Minutes even. A phone call. A letter. A leap of faith. A line from her place on the map to his.

"I'll finally say goodbye to you if it kills me."

Through the weavings of Rebecca's thread under lamplight, the Arabian prince emerged in the hanging. A lone figure near the cathedral. She knitted the word Jerusalem underneath. Space above and below to represent all the places they could explore together. *Life. Life. Life.* Death will either be an absolute nothing or a magnificent something. Maybe she would be free. Maybe she would find him. Fold into his arms and drop into his lap. Maybe, maybe, maybe...

YOU ARE HERE read the bus stop sign outside Compass. Dusk on August bank holiday Monday. What Rebecca was waiting for, she did not know. The 376 didn't run on public holidays. The City Zipper never came this way. The summer had been turbulent, but no riots took place on Ledbury Road. Labour won the election. Jesse Norman clung onto his parliamentary seat. Taylor Swift hadn't visited. Not many of the boat people either. A shame, thought Rebecca. Someone had to bring colour to this place.

"Are you free on mundi, nanna?"

"Yes, dearie. But for how long?"

Months. Weeks. Days. Hours. Minutes. Seconds. Her body was broken, her memory shot. She could not feel parts of herself, often waking from daydreams and wondering where she was. Faces from her school days reappeared on hurtling passersby, like she was riding some sentimental ghost train. Light retreating behind the clouds transported her to childhood picnics. Father calling, from where she could not see. Her fingers sliding down the plastic between her and the bus route. Tiny hands turning the pages of the new atlas gifted for Christmas. The world fresh, open and within reach under twinkling lights. The flashing red of a toy fire engine. Mother's hair on the pillow. Candelight blessings. A dance somewhere in an empty playground with only the stars for company. Gone. Forever gone. The infinite sleep was upon her. But then, but then, but then...

...the City Zipper came down the hill. The Handsome Norman. Her beautiful boy behind the wheel. A dark man from the desert, whisking her to a foreign land. Neither here nor there. Neither real nor make believe. Monday. Monday. Mundi. *I'm not ready to go. I will make this count. I will make every moment count.* Rebecca mounted, imagining herself as Mae West, or every worldly-wise lady who's discovered how helpless men really are.

"Drive on, handsome," she said from the front row of the bus.

"Where we goin' so late in the day, m'lady?"

"Late? I've just woken up."

"I need an ambulance. Ledbury Road."

In the quiet of each other's company, they completed the loop many times. Nobody else boarded. Midnight approached. Rebecca imagined the City Zipper turning into a pumpkin followed by a night of ballroom dancing. The next morning, Abdul would scour every retirement home in Herefordshire carrying her abandoned Hush Puppy.

"We're back to where we started," he said. "Are you feelin' ok?"

"Yes. I'm feelin'... young."

"Good for you. Especially now you've done your final loop."

"An elderly lady. She's fallen."

"Wasn't bad, was it? But I would really like to go round again. You know, like the dancers on telly. Returning to where they began. As happier people."

"I'd love to help. But there's no overtime this job."

"I was over time long ago."

"Don't you have a home to go to?"

"My home is with you."

"No, she's all alone. By the bus stop."

The driver relaxed his hands on the wheel.

"We can work this out, can't we?" she said. "Even if the rest can't."

With softening brown eyes, he looked through the windscreen into the deserted road. His mind was travelling with Rebecca's to the Holy Lands. To a torn world of hurt and healing. Where together they could pour soothing balm into the valley of every psychic tear and into the grave of every lost innocent.

"Quick, into the old people's home. They may know."

"Ok, m'lady. I'm keeping my eye on you."

"Likewise, Abdul. You'll do as well as any."

"I'll tell the boss it was my fairy godmother. And my name's not Abdul."

"Yes Faizad, I can see that on your dashboard. For this one night, let's call each other whatever we like."

"Don't worry lady, we're getting help. You just lie still."

While Hereford slept, they did another few loops in silence. Rebecca's spirits rose and fell with the suspension of the bus. From the confines of her metal tube, she projected the earth's wonders onto the empty tapestry outside. The bus pulled up at Compass for the last time.

YOU ARE HERE.

"No, no signs. No breath at all."

"End of the road now, Cinderella."

"No it's not. I want to go round again. It would mean the world to me."

"We can't just keep going round in circles."

"Then let's not. Let's go off course. See the world."

"Ok, name a place. Bermuda, Barcelona, Beijing."

"Jerusalem."

"Ah, the holy city. Where Muhammad, peace be upon him, was taken in his night journey and ascended briefly to heaven. Where Abraham spoke to God. The cradle of Christianity."

"That'd be the one. Lively part of town."

"But I don't know the way."

"This may help."

Rebecca drew the hanging from her bag, recalling the warmth of Tabby's cheek when they posed for the selfie.

"Here you go, stick that on your fridge. Think of me every time you reach for the milk and honey. And all those everyday moments when it seems like nothing happens. Until time sews their magic into your soul."

"Step away please. I said step away."

Faizad unfolded the hanging. It was about the size of the bus's steering wheel, crammed with people, places and pictures, like a super-elaborate jigsaw puzzle nobody was meant to solve. At the centre was a golden dome under which rested the word 'Jerusalem'. Next to it, floating in empty space, was a dark-skinned man standing next to a bus wearing a white shirt and green tie.

"We're taking her to County right now."

"It's not the Turin Shroud, sonny."
"What does it mean?"
"It means I want a dream lover, so I don't have to dream alone."
"I don't under –"
"This place isn't my home anymore. Never has been. I was born to wander. We were both born to wander. Will you wander with me?"

Faizad gazed down at the landscape and up into Rebecca's eyes. Then out onto the open road, all routes rearranging across his mental map.

"One, two, three. Lift."

"Been a scary time, lately," Faizad said. "You think Britain is your home. Until you're told it isn't."
"I know. Not just here. Everywhere. Where's your home?"
"I wish I knew. With you, I suppose. Just for tonight."
"We'll find it. If we have time."
"How long do we have? The bus only has so much power."

"Is she going to make it? Tell me she'll make it."

Rebecca pushed the red bell button twice.
"Come on, live a little. Let's take each other's breath away."

"But you don't know me."

"I know enough. You're every man I've ever met."

"How many's that?"

"Not enough."

"This bus only goes so fast and so far."

"Don't we all. Just don't get any ideas. You're still a little young for me."

"Ok, until we both run out. Of whatever we have left. Jerusalem it is."

"Jerusalem it shall be. I shall not cease my mental fight until it's built. In England's green and pleasant land."

"Ah, you're into rugby too. My kind of woman. Six Nations fan?"

"More an All Nations fan. A world in union."

"Try again. One more time."

Faizad hooked the hanging onto his rear-view mirror, turned the wheel and floored it. Rebecca imagined Tabby waving a magic wand. Granting wishes to everyone she met. Living life through everything. Floating to the ground amid an aisle of palm trees to be greeted by her dream lover so she didn't have to dream alone. Some musclebound Australian surfer with tousled blond hair and a billowing white linen shirt. A mother in the making. Near a rock called Uluru. On a tiny blue marble called planet Earth. Open with her heart. Fluid in her orientation. Finding her everywhere place on the map.

Beep, beep, beep, beep.

"What's my boss going to say?" said Faizad, shaking his head.

"Say you were abducted at gunpoint by some crazed tapestry-making witch. I fancy spinning a yarn or two to the coppers."

"Ok that's enough, I'm calling it."

The bus trundled along to Rebecca's tapping feet. Some men always moved too slowly.

"We don't have much time," she said, breath tightening.

"Gone as soon as she hit the ground."

The City Zipper jerked onto the A4103 and out of Hereford. Into the thick, black undulating fields. Heading East. Night sky cloaked a humdrum reality bursting with ghosts from the past. Joining them was everyone from the hanging. Everyone at Compass. Everyone who'd paddled the Wye. Everyone who'd beheld the Mappa Mundi. Everyone from any place once called home.

"No ID. Just this in her bag. Must have been some kind of artist."

Time weaved its spell. Quicker now, unfurling and threading in defiance of the chasing fire. Above, billions of stars sewed light into infinite space. Some photons were ancient history by the time they graced human eyes, their energies absorbed back into the creator's divine fabric, only to be resurrected on earth by the tender power of people's sight.

"She must have some relatives. Somewhere."

Descending from the universe came the music of wanderers. Rockets firing, engines purring, wheels turning, hooves galloping, footsteps running, breath pounding, lovers dancing. Tip tapping gently through disorientating darkness, like rain cooling restless desert sand. Always the dance. Only the dance. Forever the dance. Releasing signals to the other side of a lonely world, where lost children woke among loved ones to see the sun rise over Uluru.

Where everyone was free on Mundi.

"Nanna? Nanna? Are you in trouble?"

"Will we make it?" Faizad said.
"Yep, I promise. Jerusalem here we come."
"No, I mean will we *all* make it?"
"Yes. Both our sides. We just need to live –"
"No. Not just our sides. Every side."
"What choice do we have?" said Rebecca. "Let's just keep going until the wheels comes off or creation implodes."

"Nanna? Where are you? I can feel you in my dreams, nanna. Something's wrong. Talk to me nanna."

The City Zipper sped into the countryside, away from heavy rooftops sheltering thousands of turbulent night thoughts. The couple could not see far in front. Rebecca wished that in the summer of love, she'd looked further. Just a few minutes, that's all it would have taken. One moment to observe the full picture. To notice the whole map. Everything was behind and not much ahead, except the urge to gaze back into a fading horizon domed with crepuscular gold.

"Nanna? Nanna? Please don't leave me nanna. I love you. Don't leave me. Don't leave me. Don't leave –"

Soon all that remained was air, earth, fire, water and whatever the two of them decided was God. In this undiscovered country, there was no map, so they followed the only route they knew. The wheezing of a tiring battery, the remorseless ticking of a clock and the nervous holding of frail hands. The clinging of their empty lungs and the silent thunder in their hearts.

Together they wandered to their final freedoms in harmony, dancing through this impenetrable cosmos in the quickest of times. Never to rest, never to say a prayer and never to whisper a word, for their breaths had bid farewell to their bodies a long time ago.

Wychbold, Worcestershire
June 2023 – May 2025

Acknowledgments

Thank you to Chicago, a sanctuary city for immigrants where these twelve tales of lonely outsiders came to life.

I've only seen a fraction of this beautiful world, so thank you to the poets and storytellers who inspired me to travel places distant in time, space and mind: Homer, Rumi, Geoffrey Chaucer, Anton Chekov, Joseph Conrad, James Joyce, Franz Kafka and Gabriel Garcia Marquez.

My sincere appreciation to Ian Feeney for saving lives (again) with his excellent artwork, my mother Jackie for being the book's first reader, and to the many historians whose passion for the past made *Exiles Incorporated* such a pleasure to create.

Every book I write is an exploration bringing me closer to where I belong. My everlasting gratitude goes to the two people whose kindness and patience make the long nights and lone wanderings worthwhile.

To my daughter Sofia, whose travels have only just begun, and to my wife Hollie, for turning every place we encounter into home.

We journey on together.

L'amore e l'arte sono le più grandi avventure

Printed in Dunstable, United Kingdom